T
MARLOW MURDERS

An absolutely gripping crime mystery with a massive twist

BIBA PEARCE

Detective Rob Miller Mysteries Book 7

JOFFE BOOKS

Joffe Books, London
www.joffebooks.com

First published in Great Britain in 2023

Cover art by Nebojša Zorić

ISBN: 978-1-83526-187-3

CHAPTER 1

The early morning haze hung over the river like theatrical stage fog. Barry, who'd trod a few boards in his time, reflected on it as he walked his elderly greyhound through Higginson Park. The trees were stark and bare, but above them, the sky, a muted grey, cast a soft diffused light over the riverfront. It was a beautiful morning, despite the chill.

His boots crunched over frozen grass, while Halley lifted her paws like a show dog and glanced forlornly up at him. "Come on, girl," he crooned, increasing his pace. "We'll be back before you know it."

Barry walked three miles every morning and had for the last thirty years, with a few exceptions, like the time he contracted pneumonia, and last year, when he had his knee operated on. That's what happened when you got old; things began to give out.

Still, he loved his refreshing morning walks and figured they were one of the reasons why he was still in such good shape, even though he was in his mid-seventies. That and bowls, which he still played every week down at Marlow Bowls Club, even though it wasn't the same without his late wife, Winnie. He sighed, and wondered if she was up there looking down on him and Halley. "Morning, darlin'," he muttered, as he turned on to the river towpath.

The polished barges floated quietly in front of him, tethered to the mooring. A hardy woman with windswept hair and an enormous puffer jacket sat on one of the decks, smoking a cigarette. He nodded to her, as he always did. She raised her free hand in response.

His route seldom varied. They walked through the park to the river, then towards the bridge, and up the high street in a big loop, back to his house. It was almost exactly three miles. The pale stone arches and white steel railings of the nineteenth-century suspension bridge beckoned from afar, but Halley hung back, sniffing around a wooden bench.

Barry waited, used to Halley's ways. She was a curious girl, always on the hunt, although she was getting old now, like him. At twelve, she didn't venture quite as far as she used to. She was still surprisingly quick, though, when she picked up a scent. He'd seen her course along the towpath after a field mouse or cat, faster than most breeds half her age.

"Halley, this way." Crikey, that breeze was icy. Barry pulled his coat more firmly around his frame. The greyhound didn't budge. He turned and squinted at the frosty ground. What had she found? There was something green lying on the grass, like a towel or some sort of garment. Halley looked up and whined, as if to say, *Come and look*.

Sighing, he retraced his steps back to the bench. Underneath it lay the green thing.

"What is it, girl?" He bent forward to take a closer look, grimacing as his knee complained. It still gave him trouble when he put pressure on it. Reaching down, he picked up the item. It appeared to be an elf or pixie hat, the type worn by children to dress-up parties, except this one was rather large. Maybe part of an adult Christmas costume. It was a bright emerald green, with a red bobble on the top.

Halley stood panting proudly. He patted her on the head and placed the hat down on the bench. Someone might come looking for it. He pictured a drunken Christmas party, a group of raucous youths stumbling home through the park. One of them took off their hat and laid it on the bench, forgetting it, and it had blown off overnight.

"Good girl. Now, come on. Let's go." He made to walk away when something else caught his eye. In the white-tipped grass lay a mobile phone. Rose gold, the back covered by a transparent protector case.

How strange.

He picked it up and studied it, turning it over in his hands. The movement prompted the screen to light up. A photograph of a young woman in her late twenties appeared. She had fine blonde hair, laughing blue eyes and a plump, cherubic face. In her arms were two identical little boys. Must be twins. Both had their mother's eyes.

Barry gnawed at his lower lip. This was odd. First the hat, now the phone. As if someone had left them here last night, then walked off and forgotten about them. He looked around, but couldn't see any more discarded items.

The hat he could leave on the bench, but the phone would get stolen, then the young mother would never find it. Perhaps he'd better hand it in at the police station. Barry hesitated — what to do? Halley grew bored with her find and trotted off along the towpath towards the bridge. She knew the way.

Making a decision, Barry picked up the hat and the phone, then turned to follow her.

* * *

The next evening, Barry had just sat down in front of the six o'clock news with a cup of tea, when a photograph of a young woman appeared on the screen. He gasped as he recognised it, tea sloshing into his lap. Pale blonde hair, laughing blue eyes. It was the woman on the phone! With shaking hands, he put his cup down and turned up the volume.

'Debby Morris, a mother of twin boys, was last seen leaving a charity Christmas party in Marlow, Buckinghamshire around midnight

on the thirteenth of November. According to her husband, Ian Morris, she never made it home."

What?

He leaned so far forward he almost tumbled out of his chair.

She was missing.

Stunned, he gawked at the image on the screen. When he'd handed the phone and the hat to the duty sergeant at Marlow Police Station, the young officer hadn't known who they belonged to. He'd patiently taken delivery, saying he'd hold on to them in case anyone claimed them, but without the passcode, he couldn't access the phone to see who the owner was.

By now, the battery could have died. They wouldn't know it belonged to Debby Morris, the missing woman. The police officer hadn't even taken his name, just smiled benignly at him and muttered a thank you.

This was different.

This woman was missing, and he'd found her phone and part of her costume in Higginson Park. Was that where . . . ? A chill shot down his spine.

A charity Christmas party, the newsreader had said. That's why the hat had been lying beneath the bench. She'd gone as an elf. He blinked at the television screen. She would have made a pretty elf with that softly spun golden hair and big cherubic eyes.

"If anyone has any information on Debby's whereabouts, please can they contact Marlow Constabulary on . . ."

Barry jumped up, grabbed a notepad and pen and scribbled down the number that appeared on screen. Then, with his heart racing, he went to the phone.

CHAPTER 2

DCI Rob Miller also saw the news broadcast.

"That's not good," he muttered.

"What's not good?" His longtime girlfriend, Jo Maguire, came into the room.

Rob nodded to the television screen mounted on the wall. "Debby Morris. She's been missing for forty-eight hours. Didn't make it home after a party."

Jo grimaced. She knew the significance of that as well as he did. "Where is that?"

"Marlow."

"Wow." Marlow was a fashionable riverside town in the Thames Valley, surrounded by meadows and woodlands. It was not a criminal hotspot. "I hope they find her."

He gave a grim nod. "So do I."

She perched on the sofa beside him to watch the rest of the news segment. The presenter was saying how Debby had two little boys and a worried husband at home.

Jo gave a heartfelt sigh. "Poor kids. It must be hell for them."

Rob reached for her hand. Jo had lost her older sister when she was a teenager, so she knew first-hand what the family were going through.

There was a general appeal for information. Anyone with any information should contact Sergeant Weatherby at Thames Valley Police on . . .

Jo cleared her throat, then rubbed the front of her neck.

"You okay?" Rob eyed the raised white scar across her throat. It had been six months since the incident, and she was only just beginning to get full sensation back.

"Yeah, it just tingles sometimes."

Rob would never forgive himself for that. It was right here, in their home, that a psychopathic killer had held Jo hostage, before slitting her throat. He shivered just thinking about it. Jesus, she'd been lucky. The knife had missed her windpipe by mere millimetres, but had caused a lot of other damage. Her voice box had been mangled, which had resulted in a deeper, huskier tone, and she'd spent over a month in hospital, but at least she was alive.

She squeezed his hand and shot him a weak smile. "I'm okay. Honestly."

Amazingly, she didn't blame him. As a detective herself, and a former police officer, Jo knew the dangers their work entailed. She'd stared down the barrel of a gun, metaphorically speaking, many times over the years, but she'd never come that close to death.

The reality, however, was that it was *his* friend who'd attempted to kill her. *His* consultant who'd fooled and manipulated him. And he should have seen it. He was a bloody detective, for Christ's sake.

The biggest fallout had been at the Met Police headquarters. The nationally renowned serial-offender branch of the Major Investigation Team, the same crew who'd apprehended the Surrey Stalker and the Shepherd, was shown to be weak and fallible. They'd invited a criminal mastermind into their midst, shared sensitive information with him and let him dictate the course of the whole bloody investigation. It was unconscionable.

The punishment? Rob had been suspended pending an investigation by the Independent Office for Police Conduct.

At the time, he couldn't have cared less. He was in no position to go back to work anyway. Jo was hanging on to life in hospital and he had a ten-month-old baby to look after, not to mention his own mental health.

The IOPC had looked into the contact he'd had with Tony Sanderson, focusing on the actions and decisions Rob had made during the course of the investigation, and whether they were in accordance with police policy, guidance and training.

"DCI Rob Miller and his team are a law unto themselves," the Mayor, Raza Ashraf, had said to the IOPC officers. Yet, after a careful review and analysis of all the evidence, they couldn't find anything other than misplaced trust to hold against him. Tony Sanderson had fooled everybody, including the university where he worked, the FBI, who'd taught him everything he knew about criminal profiling, and his family, who knew nothing about his secret vendetta. Besides, Rob had nearly lost his partner in the process, and his team had apprehended the serial offender before he could kill again. Rob received a rap on the knuckles and management advice to prevent the same thing happening again.

The rest of the team weren't immune to the fallout either. They were removed from operational duties until the investigation was over. No contact with the public, assigned admin tasks, but at least they were working. No point in paying a police officer to stay at home.

The Deputy Commissioner, who played golf with Raza Ashraf, had questioned their Superintendent's role in allowing DCI Miller such free rein, and it was only because Felicity Mayhew was the Police Commissioner's golden girl that she'd survived.

After the investigation, Rob had decided to take a further two months of compassionate leave. Jo and the baby needed his help, and emotionally, he wasn't ready to go back into the fray. The outcome of the case had affected him badly. He'd had reporters camping outside his house for weeks afterwards, angling for an interview. Tanya, his nanny and cleaner, had been harassed on her way to work. Trigger was the only member of the household not to mind the frenzy of attention.

The golden Labrador had made the front page of the *Mail*, but to be fair, his tongue-lolling grin probably sold more newspapers than Rob's dour mug ever would. That didn't stop them documenting every aspect of his fall from grace, however, and Rob had become a virtual prisoner, only leaving the house to visit Jo in hospital.

He took a deep breath. Those dark days were over, thank God. The reporters had gone, and the news cycle had dried up. The cost-of-living crisis and the war in Ukraine took centre stage. Most important, Jo was almost back to her normal self, aside from the subconscious way her fingers traced the scar whenever it tingled, or how she cleared her throat every now and then.

"Do you miss it?" She nodded at the television. The newsreader had moved on to another topic now. A locational shot with a dark-haired child standing on the side of a dirt road, dried tears streaking her grubby cheeks as a tank rolled past in the background.

Rob looked away from the screen. "No."

"Liar," Jo said softly, then got to her feet. Jack was thumping on his tray in the kitchen. Tanya, who was now working for them full-time, could be heard clearing up. The Polish nanny had started working for them over a year ago, when her previous employer had been murdered. Rob, who'd worked the case, had offered her a job, and she'd gratefully accepted. Turned out to be the best decision he'd ever made. After Jo had been attacked, Tanya had moved to Twickenham, which was only a short train ride from Richmond, so she could be more hands-on. Jack adored her, as did Trigger, who followed her around incessantly from room to room.

"I hope it's not too late." Jo nodded to the television as she left the room. It took Rob a moment to realise she was talking about Debby Morris, the missing woman. They were rehashing the headlines, the photograph of Debby back on the screen.

He grunted. Thames Valley Police better get a move on, or it would be too late. Every second counted in a missing person case.

Right now, the police would be retracing Debby's steps on the night she went missing to try to figure out what had happened. Had she vanished of her own free will, or had something happened to her? Was there any DNA left at the scene? Any signs of a struggle?

Her spouse would be questioned, as would the people at the party. Who was the last person to see her alive? What was her mental state? Had she been acting strangely? The husband's alibi would be scrutinised, his behaviour analysed. It wouldn't be an easy time for the family.

Forty-eight hours had passed already. Witnesses grew less cognisant with every day — no, every hour — that went by, memories faded, details were forgotten. It was imperative that the detectives assigned the case work around the clock to gather as much evidence as possible in order to find Debby Morris.

Rob leaned back and rested his head against the couch. Except it wasn't his case. Thames Valley Police were conducting this investigation. It had nothing to do with him or the Met's Major Investigation Team. Stifling a yawn, he turned off the television set and went to join Jo in the kitchen.

CHAPTER 3

Three weeks later

PC Victor Trent had just finished his morning cup of tea when he got the call. A hysterical woman screaming that there was a dead elf floating in the Thames.

"Sorry, did you say an elf?" But the woman was talking to someone else in the background and didn't hear him.

"Excuse me, ma'am, can I take your name?" Trent had been an officer at Thames Valley Police for a little over a year now and enjoyed his job. Normally, Marlow was a quiet town. Not many crimes were committed here, other than the occasional bike theft or, even rarer, a break-in. Obviously, this woman was a few sandwiches short of a picnic.

"Meredith. Meredith Williamson. Oh, please. You must come quickly. She looks terrible. So pale."

Maybe she wasn't as mad as she sounded. "She? I thought you said it was an elf?"

"She's wearing an elf's costume," the woman shrieked. "For God's sake. I wasn't talking about a real elf."

Trent flushed, despite there not being anyone around to see him. "Of course not, ma'am. What is your location?"

He took down the details. It was an isolated spot about midway between Marlow and Cookham. "I'm on my way."

Rushing out of the office, he told Michelle, the administrative assistant at the Dean Street station, that he was responding to a 999 call. She glanced up in surprise. "Shouldn't you notify Phil?"

His supervisor, Sergeant Philip Weatherby, was in Bisham meeting with the vicar whose vestry had been vandalised for the third time that month. PC Shelly Andrews was on annual leave and PC Amun Kassem was on a course on interrogation techniques, which he hoped would lead to a transfer to the larger, busier Maidenhead branch. That left him.

"I'll call in my location. Can you update him when he gets back?" She nodded as he raced out to the patrol car. A thrill ran through him as he activated the siren. There wasn't much call for sirens in Marlow, and he'd never used it. But this was different. This was a potential dead body.

Trent sped out of the little car park, down the high street and across the suspension bridge towards Cookham. Mrs Williamson had given her location as the river towpath in Cock Marsh, along from the Bounty pub. The body was supposedly floating in the river, caught by the reeds.

While at a set of traffic lights, he programmed his sat nav with the destination, or as close as he could get to it, then put his foot down. He pulled into the opposite lane and overtook several cars dawdling along at the new 20 mph speed limit.

He sped up Winter Hill, past the golf course, and on to Terry's Lane, where the terrain changed. Instead of asphalt, it was now a dirt road, still wide enough for his vehicle, but filled with bumps and potholes. On one side was the golf course, which oozed into Cock Marsh, and on the other were meadows and farmland belonging to smallholdings. He saw several dog walkers on the track, as well as two young riders on horseback who glared at him. Reluctantly, he turned off the siren.

In the summer, this was a popular part of the county, particularly during the nearby Henley Royal Regatta when the well-heeled, champagne-swilling rowing crowd descended in droves, leaving chaos in their wake. It was always a hectic time of year for the constabulary, who had to deal with drunk university students, lost handbags and phones, and the occasional alcohol-related injury.

He much preferred winter, when the roads were quiet, the residents were mostly indoors in front of their wood-burning fires and it was too cold to commit any serious offences. His vehicle danced and jiggled along the dirt road towards the river. As he got closer, the lane got narrower. Soon, it became a dirt track with brush and trees on either side. He debated driving down it, but the branches would scratch the side of his patrol car and he'd get it in the neck from Sergeant Weatherby.

Sighing, he pulled over and got out. He'd have to do this last part on foot. Luckily, he had long legs, and broke into a quick stride. The icy, moist air prickled his face. It was colder than usual for this time of year, but nothing compared to up north, where he'd grown up. Once, when he was a kid, it had got so cold he and his friends had got stuck to the playground equipment and had to be thawed off. He glanced up at the slate-grey sky. Maybe they'd get some early snow.

His phone rang halfway down the track. It was Michelle. "I've had your caller, Mrs Williamson, on the phone again. She says to hurry. I've dispatched an ambulance, just in case, but I'm not sure if it will be able to get down there. Anyway, if it turns out to be nothing, at least they can calm her down."

"Thanks, Mich. I'm almost there." His breath turned to mist as he panted the last few yards to the river. She'd said to the left of the towpath.

Trent heard Mrs Williamson before he saw her. A buxom lady in Wellington boots and a thick parka, with a muddy cocker spaniel in tow. At least she'd had the sense to put it on a lead. Trent didn't like dogs. Not since one had taken a bite out of his calf when he was a boy. She was talking loudly, telling everyone who walked past what she'd found. A small crowd of shocked dog walkers and joggers had assembled on the grassy bank, their murmurs blending with the squawks of woodland birds and the occasional bark of a dog.

"Stand back, please," he ordered, in his most authoritative voice.

The crowd parted and Trent stepped forward towards the edge of the bank and peered down into the water. "Oh Lord," he muttered, feeling the colour drain from his face.

"See, this is what I've been telling you." Mrs Williamson poked him in the arm. He barely felt her.

"Come away, Meredith," a slender woman with shaggy, dark hair said, taking Mrs Williamson by the arm and tugging her backwards.

Trent couldn't stop staring at the body in the river. Eyes shut, she looked like she was sleeping, except she was so pale, her skin an unearthly mottled white against the dark bottle-green of the water. Her hair, like golden silk, spread out around her, riddled with weeds and small twigs. She looked like some sort of river nymph. She was young, he guessed mid-twenties, and was wearing a bright green elf outfit cinched at the waist by a thick, red belt.

Her face was bloated, and there were multiple scrapes and bruises on her body, probably from river debris. The elf costume left little to the imagination, and Trent shocked himself by thinking that, alive, she would have been very pretty.

"Are you going to get her out of there?" Mrs Williamson demanded, her voice carrying over the murmur of onlookers. Trent took a steadying breath, then turned around and threw up.

"Good Lord, man," said an elderly gentleman, waving a walking stick. "Get a hold of yourself." The crowd had moved back, out of splashing distance.

Trent nodded, feeling the nausea subside somewhat. He wiped his mouth, then turned back to the body.

Think.

What did the police handbook say about finding a dead body? He couldn't remember. His mind was completely blank. Instead, he reverted to Plan B and called Michelle.

"It is a dead body," he blurted out, remembering she'd already called an ambulance. "Call off the paramedics. They can't get down here anyway."

And there was no point. The poor girl had been in the water for some time, judging by the state of her. Decomposition hadn't fully set in, but her skin was blotchy and covered in purple striations over the grey. He gulped down another surge of nausea.

"Is it bad?" Michelle asked, in a breathy voice.

"Yeah, it's bad. Mich, I think it's that girl who disappeared a few weeks back. Debby Morris." Her photograph had been stuck on the pinboard in the office ever since she went missing. He'd been involved in the initial investigation, along with Sergeant Weatherby, interviewing her friends and family, and the last people to see her the night she vanished. When nothing had come to light, they'd assumed she'd run off, deserting her family. He felt bad about that now.

Unable to help himself, he stole another glance at the corpse. She was unrecognisable from that pink-cheeked, smiling lass on the wall. He hadn't realised how much death changed a person's appearance. It did suck the soul out of you.

"Debby Morris? Oh my God, Vic. Are you sure?"

"It's her, yes. At least it looks like her." *Sort of.*

"Holy crap. This is huge."

He gulped down muddy river air and only just stopped himself retching. "I know." Now he was calmer, his brain kicked into gear. "Here's what we're going to do. Call Weatherby, tell him to get down here pronto."

"I'll try. His phone is off."

His heart sank. "Really?"

"There's no signal at the vicarage."

Conveniently. The vicar's wife made a stand-out full English breakfast — he knew because he'd experienced it first-hand — so Weatherby was probably indulging and in no hurry to get back to the sleepy police station.

Trent thought fast. It was down to him, then. He hoped he wasn't going to get into trouble for this, but they couldn't leave her lying in the water. Even now, the crowd of onlookers was growing bigger and, overhead, storm clouds threatened.

"Okay, we're going to need the fire department to get her out of the water, but first we need a scene of crime officer, to make sure they do it right." The guidelines in the police handbook came back to him now. He could do this. "And, because of where she is, we're going to need an air ambulance to transport the body to the mortuary. Oh, and see if the pathologist wants to come down here or not."

"Basically, you want me to call everyone," Michelle said.

"Exactly."

Trent hung up and turned to the crowd. It was easier looking at them than *her*. "Get back, please. This area is off limits. Please move back." They shuffled backwards a few metres but didn't leave. Trent knew he should secure the area, but like an idiot, he'd left the police tape in his vehicle, which was a quarter of a mile back up the track.

He couldn't leave the victim with this lot; they'd decimate the embankment and destroy any forensic evidence that might be here. Unsure what to do, he tried to shield her body with his, standing in front of her and glaring at the onlookers. Some of them began to disperse, as the cold set in and hungry dogs began tugging on leads.

A thought struck him, and he turned to the woman who'd called it in. "Mrs Williamson, I'm going to need you and your friend to give a statement."

She pulled her pooch towards a log. "I'll be over here, officer." Her friend shot him a tentative smile and followed. Trent's feet began to go numb from the cold. He ushered the remaining few gawkers away, and then went over to the log.

Damn, he didn't have his notebook either. He'd been so anxious to see the body that he'd left everything in the vehicle. Then he had a brainwave. Taking out his phone, he went to his voice memo app. "Okay, Mrs Williamson, please explain to me, in your own words, how you discovered the body. I'm going to be recording this conversation, if you don't mind?"

She nodded, puffing out her already substantial chest.

"I was walking Gertie along the towpath, when I saw her floating in the water." Trent wasn't immediately sure whether Gertie was the dog or her friend. Both seemed equally submissive. "We stopped, didn't we, Jan?" The slender woman nodded.

Trent let her continue without interrupting. "I stopped and took a closer look — you know, just to be sure."

Trent nodded. "Did you touch the body?"

"Heavens, no." She looked quite alarmed at the thought. The friend also shook her head.

"Okay, good. Carry on."

"Then we called you. There's not much else to tell."

Trent glanced at the friend. "And your name is?"

The friend opened her mouth but didn't get a chance to answer. "Janice Gallagher," Mrs Williamson said, cutting her off.

Trent felt a tinge of irritation. "If you don't mind, ma'am, I'd like your friend to answer for herself."

Janice's hand fluttered to her face. "Yes, I'm sorry, officer. It's exactly like Meredith said. We were walking along when we saw her lying there in the bushes by the bank, looking like Ophelia."

He frowned. "Who's Ophelia?"

"You know, the painting?"

He didn't, but he nodded anyway. "Was there anyone else around?" They both shook their heads.

"It's her, isn't it?" Janice whispered. "It's Debby Morris."

"I can't be sure at this stage," he said curtly. Trent knew better than to tell a member of the public anything about a police investigation, and this one was going to be massive. He could picture it now. The press would go crazy. Debby Morris, the missing mother of two, found in the Thames three weeks after she disappeared, and he was the one who'd found her. Well, kind of. He was the first responder on the scene.

"Do you think she was murdered?" Mrs Williamson asked, licking her lips.

A cold dread snuck up Trent's neck. The last thing they needed were rumours of a murder spreading like wildfire around the community. "There is no evidence of that."

Mrs Williamson pointed to the body in the river. "That's evidence enough, I'd say."

He shook his head. People were so quick to jump to conclusions. There were several ways she could have ended up in the river, murder being just one of them.

"If you'll both give me your contact details." He nodded to include her friend. "Then you can go home. I'm sure you'd like a nice cup of tea." Mrs Williamson snorted, but Janice nodded eagerly.

Just when he'd got rid of them, more people arrived. Bad news travelled fast. A couple of cyclists stopped and began taking photographs with their phones. "No photos, guys. This area is out of bounds. Please move on."

They ignored him. More people arrived, with bigger cameras. Journalists. His heart sank. His crime scene, for lack of a better word, was getting out of control. He was losing his grip on the situation. They were trampling all over the bank, turning the soggy grass into a mud bath.

"Get back!" he yelled, but there was one of him and many of them. His pleas fell on deaf ears. Where the hell were the reinforcements?

"It's her," he heard someone say. "It's Debby Morris."

A shriek. "Oh my God."

"It's definitely her," said another voice.

A camera flashed. Trent held up his hand. "No photographs!" But he may as well have been speaking to a gaggle of two-year-olds. More reporters arrived.

The *whop-whop* of approaching rotor blades caused everybody to look up. The distinctive red-and-yellow underbelly of London's air ambulance flew into view. It hovered over them for a few minutes, then began descending. There was a meadow directly behind them, with another turnstile leading to the towpath. It was the most obvious place to land. More importantly, there were no people on it.

Everybody watched as the helicopter touched down on the grass, then shuddered to a stop. Two paramedics jumped out and ran towards the turnstile. The crowd finally moved aside to give them room. Trent breathed a sigh of relief. It was going to be okay.

CHAPTER 4

Rob hadn't been up long when his phone rang. Glancing down, he saw it was Superintendent Felicity Mayhew. What on earth did she want? Whatever it was, it couldn't be good. "Good morning, ma'am."

"Morning, DCI Miller. I trust you're well." She wasn't one for platitudes.

"Yes, thank you." After a rocky start, they'd managed to achieve first-name basis, but since the cock-up that was his last investigation, he'd gone back to being DCI Miller. No more Rob and Felicity.

He waited, letting the silence draw out. Nothing like an awkward moment to get people to fill the gap. Even her. She cleared her voice. "They found Debby Morris."

Debby Morris, the woman who'd gone missing last month in Marlow.

"Oh yeah? Where?" He didn't have to ask if she was alive. Mayhew wouldn't be calling him if she were.

"Four miles downriver from where she went missing. I believe it's near Cookham. A dog walker discovered her early this morning."

"Drowned?"

"Looks like it." Mayhew hesitated. "We need to ascertain whether it was an accidental drowning, suicide or intentional."

He scowled. "We? Isn't this Thames Valley's case?" Thames Valley Police had their own major investigation squad, entirely separate from the London Metropolitan Police. They should be the ones leading up the investigation.

"Yes, well it turns out Debby Morris is Chief Superintendent Wallace's goddaughter, and he wants a London team on this."

"Is he authorised to make that decision?"

"No, but his good friend the Police Commissioner is."

The new Commissioner had vowed to clean up the force. No more corruption, no more embarrassing scandals, and no more poor performance. Her main goal was to restore confidence in London's largest police force by issuing a series of reforms. It was too soon to know whether they were working or not, but there'd been a major shake-up in the last six months since he'd been away. "You'll be Senior Investigating Officer," she continued when he didn't reply. Nepotism never sat well with him.

"Why me? I've been off for six months. Surely Galbraith—"

"Galbraith's on annual leave. He's taken his family to Disney World." He heard her shudder. "You're due back next month, anyway. You may as well start now."

Great. Three weeks before Christmas and he had to go back to work. "I'm not sure I'm—"

"It's not negotiable, DCI Miller. You're the only SIO we have who's got the experience and is available. Besides, your team needs a case to sink their teeth into. They've been twiddling their thumbs long enough. A sergeant from Thames Valley is on the scene, but they've been informed of the change in jurisdiction, and they're waiting for you."

Rob bet they weren't too happy with that. The biggest case in recent years and it was being handed over to the Met's Major Investigation Team.

"And get a move on, before the scene is completely destroyed," she added. "Apparently, the press is all over the place. Bloody vultures."

Rob took a deep breath. This was happening. He was now officially back on the job. He dragged his brain out of the quagmire and into the present. "Is she still in the water?"

"As far as I know. SOCO are on their way, as are the fire department and the air ambulance. It's a tricky spot to get to. Somewhere called Cock Marsh; can you believe it? They'll take some time getting her out of the river." A couple of hours at least.

"I'm leaving now."

Rob hung up and stared at himself in the hallway mirror. Dishevelled hair, sleep in his eyes, rumpled T-shirt. Christ, he looked like he'd just fallen out of bed. Upstairs, he could hear Jo talking to Jack as she changed and dressed him. Trigger was slurping and crunching his way through his breakfast in the kitchen, and Tanya would be here soon. Another day in the Miller household had begun.

He went upstairs to tell Jo.

* * *

Rob parked in a small, muddy car park at the bottom of the horse track and got out to inspect the sides of his car. Bloody branches. He fingered a section where the paintwork had been scratched. He was claiming damage expenses on this one.

The car park was packed with several press vans and a multitude of motorcycles and bicycles. He'd seen the PC's patrol vehicle at the top of the track. That was probably a smart move. There was no room down here to turn around. He'd have to reverse all the way back up to the lane.

An icy wind buffeted his face, and Rob was glad of the thick, black coat that Jo had bought him last year. Why was the countryside always so much colder than London? Even though Marlow was only thirty miles west of the city, it had a distinctive village feel. Out here, along the towpath, halfway between Marlow and Cookham, was about as rural as it got.

Rob took a pair of Wellington boots and a duffel bag out of the boot. The path would be muddy this time of year, and he didn't fancy ruining his work shoes. He pulled them on, slung the rucksack over his shoulder and headed off along the path. On his right, the river ran wide, dark and green, but at least it was still. Out here, it wasn't tidal — not like in Putney, where it often burst its banks at high tide, submerging the towpath and catching unsuspecting walkers by surprise. That meant the body was not in danger of being swept away or compromised by the tide.

To his left, a low hedge flanked the river path, interspersed with bracken and nettles. Beyond that, grass-strewn meadows stretched back as far as the eye could see. Between breaks in the hedge, he saw the yellow-and-red flashes of the air ambulance waiting in the field. He increased his pace.

Rob pulled open a wooden turnstile gate, twisted through, and trudged along, wellies squelching, to where a large crowd had gathered on the bank. *For fuck's sake.* Thames Valley were supposed to have control over the scene. Where the hell were they?

He cringed at the churned-up grass and muddy patches. Any chance of recovering footprints or other forensic evidence, should they need it, had long since vanished.

"Who's in charge?" he boomed.

A couple of people glanced up, surprised. He wasn't in uniform, only jeans and a black fleece underneath his winter coat. Mistaken for another passer-by.

A young man with anxious eyes and flushed cheeks popped his face above the crowd. "I am. PC Trent, from Thames Valley."

"DCI Miller from the London Met's Major Investigation Team." He showed his ID. "Why haven't you cordoned off the site?"

"My car's at the top of the track, sir. Didn't want to leave her."

Fair enough.

Rob looked past the young constable to the body in the river and sucked in a breath. It still got to him, even though he'd seen more than a few corpses over the years. That was probably a good thing. The day he stopped reacting, he'd know it was time to quit.

Pallid, mottled skin. Bloated features. Tangled mass of hair floating around her face. Even in this state, he recognised her from the television appeal. A smiling blonde woman with her arms around two small boys.

Debby Morris.

Shit.

"There's no sign of life, sir," one of the air ambulance medics said, dripping Thames water over the muddy bank. Rob gave a stiff nod. It might seem obvious, but they still had to check. One of the many boxes they had to tick.

"Do you want us to get her out?" a burly firefighter asked. Beside him stood a woman from SOCO in blue coveralls. He turned to her.

"If you give the go-ahead, they can retrieve her body."

"We've taken multiple photographs," she told him. "I don't think we're going to get anything from the water. The police divers might have more luck."

"Okay, go for it," Rob told the firefighter.

The man beckoned to his team, and under the crime scene officer's supervision, they set about retrieving Debby Morris's body from the river.

While they were doing that, Rob unzipped his duffel bag and took out a wound-up length of police tape. Handing it to a hovering Trent, he said, "Cordon off the scene so we can get these bloody people out of here."

Trent rushed to do as he said.

Rob faced the crowd. "Show's over, folks. Clear off. This area is off limits. Anyone loitering will be arrested." Trent's eyes widened.

People began backing away, but not fast enough for his liking. Rob walked up to a journo and put his hand over the end of his camera lens. "Starting with you."

"Okay, okay. Take it easy. I'm out of here."

"I am taking it easy."

Reluctantly, the press packed up their equipment and trudged back to their vans. They probably had enough footage to feed off for the week, anyway. The other onlookers went back to their warm living rooms and log fires. They'd no doubt be in the pub later, regaling their friends with the story.

Trent was searching for something to wrap the tape around. He had the eager, slightly nervous expression of a rookie officer, fresh out of the police college at Hendon. "Where's your Chief Superintendent?" Rob would have thought the top brass at Thames Valley would have been down here as soon as they'd heard of the discovery.

"Chief Superintendent Mullins is on holiday, sir. Sergeant Weatherby is in charge of our local precinct, and he's currently engaged elsewhere."

"You call in the cavalry?" Rob nodded to the emergency personnel.

"Yes. I hope I did the right thing, sir."

"You did, Constable."

His face lit up.

"Use the turnstile—" Rob pointed to the tape still in the constable's hand — "then wrap it around those trees over there, and down to the willow at the water line." It would cordon off the entire river frontage, but he didn't care. People could go around or turn back. This area was now out of bounds.

The firefighters laid Debby Morris on the grass, near the hedge. By the level of decomp, he could tell she'd been in the water for at least a couple of weeks.

"Do you mind if I take a look?" he asked the scene of crime officer.

She shrugged. "Go for it; just don't touch. You know the rules."

Rob squatted down beside the body. Judging by the costume, it looked like she was supposed to be Santa's helper or a Christmas elf. Short and low-cut, with a wide red belt, the costume was probably from Amazon or some party store.

Hadn't the news reporter said she'd gone missing on the way home from a Christmas party?

She wore no jewellery, not even a wedding band. Strange, since he'd seen pictures of the distraught husband on television with their two young kids.

The dress had ridden up and exposed most of her thighs. Her legs were covered in scrapes and puncture wounds, but there was no bruising. Most probably post-mortem. She'd been in the river for some time, and with the foul weather they'd been having, she'd have been bashed around a fair bit.

There were no bruises around her throat or neck that would indicate strangulation. No stabbing or gunshot wounds, although admittedly the latter were rare in this country. At first glance, it appeared as if she'd simply drowned.

A clipped voice said, "What are you doing?"

Rob glanced up to see a slim, mousy-haired woman in a pathologist's outfit glaring at him.

"I'm the Senior Investigating Officer," he said, straightening up. "Who are you?"

Her eyes ran down his body. "You don't look like an SIO."

"What do SIOs normally look like?"

She huffed and pointed to the victim. "I'm Dr Carmichael, the pathologist on call. I was in the area, so I thought I'd come down and take a look at the body." Normally, in cases where the cause of death was uncertain, the pathologist wouldn't bother coming to the crime scene. The first time they'd have any contact with the victim was during the post-mortem.

Rob stepped out of the way. "Don't let me stop you."

He watched as she conducted a preliminary examination, touching Debby Morris's face with her gloved hand. A push here, a prod there. She peered into the victim's mouth, then ears and nose. Lifting up the hands, she inspected the front and the back, then checked underneath the fingernails. "Any forensic evidence would have long since washed away," Rob said.

Dr Carmichael didn't look up. "I wouldn't be doing my job if I didn't check."

She was right about that.

He watched while she studied the victim's arms and legs, pausing at the many cuts and scrapes.

"Those made after she died?" asked Rob.

"I'd say so." She gently lifted a clump of matted hair off Debby Morris's forehead, then inspected her head. Frowning, she ran her fingers along the scalp, feeling for bumps.

"Got something?" he asked.

"I'm not sure."

Rob leaned forward. "What do you mean?"

"There's a small gash on the back of her head. Probably also post-mortem, although it feels like there's some swelling. That wouldn't have happened if she'd already been dead. I'll have to get her back to the lab to look properly."

Experience had taught him to keep an open mind about these things. Could be something; could be nothing.

"Help me turn her over," Dr Carmichael said.

Surprised, Rob knelt down. In the corner of his vision, he could see Trent watching, eyes glued to the body. Together, they rolled Debby Morris on to her stomach. A long zip ran down the back of the green dress. Carefully, Dr Carmichael undid it, then peeled back the sodden material.

"More scratches and cuts." She shook her head. "I need to clean her up before I can say for sure how she died."

"What about the time of death?" He knew it was a long shot. Three weeks in the river would make it impossible to tell with any degree of certainty.

"I can't even hazard a guess at this stage."

Rob gave a reluctant nod. As eager as he was, Dr Carmichael was right not to jump to conclusions.

"Will you let me know when you do the post-mortem?" He reached into his pocket for his card and handed it to her. "I'd like to be there."

She took it, somewhat reluctantly. "I can do that."

"Thank you."

He stood back beside Trent, and the two of them watched as the paramedics carried the victim's body to the waiting helicopter.

CHAPTER 5

PC Trent was in awe of DCI Miller. When he spoke, people listened. Okay, he had a loud, booming voice, but he also had a natural authority that Trent found rather intimidating. There was nothing kind or friendly about the Senior Investigating Officer. He was brusque, curt and had a steely gaze that Trent was sure unnerved even the most hardened criminals.

"What can I do, sir?" The helicopter's blades began whirring.

"You can tell me who found the body."

"Oh, that would be Mrs Williamson and her friend. They were walking Gertie — um, Mrs Williamson's dog — when they found her."

Rob nodded, his gaze on the chopper. It lifted off the ground, rotors deafening, hovered menacingly over the river-bank, then banked to the east and headed in the direction of London. Trent waited for DCI Miller to reply, even though he got the impression his mind had already moved on to other things. "Got her details?"

"Yes."

"Text them to me. Here's my number." He handed Trent a card too. On the back was scribbled his mobile number.

DCI Rob Miller
Metropolitan Police
Major Investigation Team

Trent shivered, but it wasn't from the cold. The SIO had given him his personal number. "Of course, sir."

"Jingle Bells" pealed out over the cold morning air. Trent grimaced and flicked his phone to silent. His niece had installed the ringtone last weekend, and while it had seemed like a good idea at the time, he regretted it now. "Sorry," he mumbled, glancing at the screen. Sergeant Weatherby. His boss wanted an update on the situation.

"You going to get that?" Miller asked, as it continued to buzz.

Trent answered it with a breathless, "Sir?"

Weatherby gave him an earful about not notifying him sooner. When he'd finished ranting, Trent said, "We tried. Your phone went straight to voicemail, sir." Miller was watching him, probably wondering why on earth a police officer had a Christmas ringtone on his mobile phone. He swallowed nervously. So much for good impressions.

"DCI Miller from the Met's major crime team is here. They've got jurisdiction, sir." More ranting. "I'm not sure. That's what he told me."

The SIO held out his hand. "May I?"

Trent gulped and handed the phone over to the DCI.

"This is Detective Chief Inspector Miller from the Major Investigation Team. To whom am I speaking?"

Trent heard a pause, and then Weatherby said, "Sergeant Weatherby, Thames Valley Police."

"Sergeant Weatherby, the Met's major crime squad has been assigned the Debby Morris case. I am now the Senior Investigating Officer. The orders have come from the top. I'm sure your Chief Superintendent has been informed."

He listened for a moment, then said, "Thank you for sending your officer, PC Trent. He's been extremely helpful."

Trent felt like hugging DCI Miller. Weatherby had been giving him a hard time ever since he'd arrived two months ago. No matter how hard he tried, nothing was ever good enough.

He didn't hear what Weatherby said next, but the DCI grunted, then said, "If you have any questions about jurisdiction, speak to the Police Commissioner." He handed the phone back to Trent without saying goodbye. Trent put it to his ear, but the sergeant had gone.

"Were you around when Debby Morris went missing?" DCI Miller asked, his brain already on other things.

"You mean three weeks ago?"

Miller gave an impatient nod.

"Yes, I spoke to her husband when he came into the station to report her missing."

"What exactly did he say?" Miller's gaze was very unnerving.

Exactly? Hmm . . . Trent racked his brains. "Well, he came in on the afternoon of the fourteenth of November and said his wife hadn't arrived home after a party the night before."

"The Christmas party?" The DCI narrowed his eyes. Trent realised he was expected to be more specific. Details. Miller wanted details. He cleared his throat.

"It was a charity Christmas party. Takes place in November every year at Hollyhock Manor. That's the big house overlooking the river. It belongs to—"

"Which charity?" Miller cut in.

"The Lifegiving Foundation. It's run by Dame Constance Blanchard."

Miller gave him a blank stare.

"She lives in Marlow," Trent explained, realising the Met detective had absolutely no idea who she was. "She's a minor celebrity around these parts. Used to be an opera singer, but now she's a philanthropist. Does a lot of charity work."

A solemn nod. DCI Miller had a fantastic poker face, Trent decided. It was impossible to work out what he was thinking. The ash-grey eyes appeared stormy, as if there was a tempest raging inside, yet he gave nothing away.

"I want to go to the place where she was last seen," he said.

"Okay, if you come to the station tomorrow, I can arrange—"

"Now."

"You want to go to Hollyhock Manor now?"

"Was that where she was last seen?"

"That's where the party was held. An elderly resident found her phone and hat in Higginson Park three weeks ago. That must be where she went in the river." He'd put that together while waiting for the medics to arrive. Higginson Park was a recreational ground beside the river in Marlow. It made sense that if her belongings were found there, then that was probably where she drowned. It was a good theory, and he was proud of himself for thinking of it.

"This resident, do you have his, or her, details?"

Trent nodded. "His, and yes, sir. He called the station when he saw the appeal on the news."

"Good. Let's talk to him, and then we'll stop by the park where she vanished."

Trent felt a thrill of excitement. Miller wanted him along for the ride. "Yes, sir!"

* * *

Barry Wilson was a lean old guy in his seventies with thinning white hair and a trimmed beard to match. Sparkling blue eyes followed them as they walked into the living room and sat down, then Mr Wilson lowered himself into his armchair and patted the greyhound curled at his feet.

"Thanks for seeing us, Mr Wilson," Rob began. "I believe PC Trent told you we were coming."

"Yes, he did. Please, call me Barry."

Rob cleared his throat. "Barry, I'd like you to tell me what you found in the park the morning after Debby Morris went missing."

The old guy glanced at Trent, and then back at Rob. He'd obviously figured out Rob was Trent's superior, or someone of importance, and didn't complain about having to repeat the story. "I was walking Halley through the park. It's the same route we take every day, isn't it, girl?" He ruffled her ears. She lifted her head, raised a lazy eyebrow, then put her head down again. "Anyway, Halley stopped at a bench. I didn't see it at first. I was already down by the river, but when she wouldn't come, I walked back to see what she'd found. I spotted the hat first. It was one of those elf hats with the bobble on top, like you'd wear to a fancy dress party."

Rob nodded.

The sinewy hands continued to stroke the dog's head. "I was going to leave it on the bench in case the owner came back for it, when I saw the phone."

Rob turned to Trent. "You have the victim's mobile phone?"

"Yes, sir."

He frowned in frustration. "You didn't think to mention it?"

Trent cleared his throat. "Well, we analysed her call logs when she went missing, but there was nothing—"

Rob held up a hand, effectively cutting him off. "We'll discuss it later." Trent gave a meek nod. Back to Barry, he said, "What did you do next?"

"I took the phone and hat to the police station." Barry nodded at Trent. "I spoke to this young officer, told him what I'd found and handed over the items." He shrugged. "That's it."

"You didn't try to turn on the phone?"

"Only to see whose it was, but it was locked. The photograph on the front was of Debby Morris. I recognised her the next evening when I saw her picture on the news. That's when I called the number on the television."

"Who did you speak to?" Rob asked.

"A Sergeant Weatherby, I think?" He looked at Trent for confirmation.

The PC nodded. "Sergeant Weatherby is in charge of the missing person case."

"Was," DCI Miller snapped. "It's now the Major Investigation Team's case. We need to go over the details of the missing person investigation. Can you set up a meeting for this afternoon?"

Trent gave a hurried nod and pulled out his phone. "I'll be right back."

Rob waited until the young officer had left the room, then he turned back to the witness. "What did Weatherby say to you?"

"He was suspicious at first. Apparently several people had called in to say they'd seen her at some party, and he thought I was just another one of them."

Rob pursed his lips.

"When I said where I'd found the items, he got a lot more interested. He met me at the park bench, and I showed him exactly where they were."

Rob nodded. Good. That was standard procedure. Presumably, the Sergeant had then analysed the phone logs to identify the last people she'd had contact with, or if anyone had any idea of her whereabouts.

"I don't know what happened after that."

"Thank you." Rob got to his feet. "Appreciate your time."

Barry nodded. "I heard on the radio you'd found her. Is that right?" The greyhound looked soulfully up at him, as if awaiting the answer to his master's question.

The macabre discovery hadn't officially been released yet, not that it mattered. Everybody would know by the evening news.

"We've found a body that we think is Debby Morris, but it hasn't been confirmed yet."

A sad nod. Rob decided he liked Barry Wilson and his dog.

CHAPTER 6

Higginson Park had turned into a vast winter wonderland. The lawn sparkled with frost, broken only by the meandering concrete path that curved down to the river. The stark tree branches, devoid of leaves, glistened with an icy sheen, and the hedgerows were dusted with a snowy white powder. It was lunchtime, when harassed parents usually brought their children out to let off some steam, or office workers took a sandwich break, but today it was too cold for any of that.

Above, bulbous pewter clouds threatened rain, or snow, or something in between, and moisture hung heavily in the air. Rob shivered as the cold clung to his face, damp and cloying.

He turned to Trent, who'd pulled on a pair of thick ski gloves. "Show me this bench."

The young constable strode down the path until it veered to the left. Near a hedge of dark green holly stood a solitary bench. An inscription read: *For Clifford, who loved sitting here enjoying the view.* "This is where Barry Wilson found the hat and phone. They were on the grass underneath the bench."

What would Clifford think now?

Rob stared at the frosty ground, then looked up and turned in a slow circle. The river was less than ten metres away, the water a still but forbidding charcoal grey, the same colour as the unenthusiastic sky. Not a ripple marred its surface.

Flanking the towpath were several large, wooden barges, their polished hulls creaking against their moorings. A couple of smaller recreational craft were tied up alongside the barges, but they were covered by tarpaulin, abandoned until the springtime.

The Thames Path stretched into the distance on both sides, running parallel to the river. The start was in Gloucestershire — could you believe it? — and he had it on good authority that you could walk all the way to the Thames Barrier in Woolwich. A hundred and eighty miles or thereabouts. Not that he'd ever tried it. The only stretch he'd walked was between Putney and Richmond, and that had taken him and Trigger nearly two hours.

On the other side, the park extended to the beginning of the high street, and included a skate park, café, picnic area and playground. Everything but the café was shut, and even then, he could just make out one lone figure behind the closed glass doors wiping down tables. It was only the stalwarts like Barry and his dog who braved this type of weather.

He pictured Debby Morris in her skimpy elf costume crossing the park. He wondered at her state of mind. Was she depressed? Upset? Suicidal? Perhaps she'd drunk too much and was inebriated. Feeling reckless. Had she fallen into the river and drowned? Or gone in on purpose, determined to end it all?

Or had someone been lurking in the shadows, waiting for her?

It could have been an opportunistic attack, like a mugging. He dismissed that idea as soon as it occurred to him. First, she was unlikely to have had anything valuable on her person, other than her purse. Would someone risk killing her for a few credit cards and a mobile phone? Second, the phone had been left behind. Could she have dropped it in the struggle? Had the assailant not realised it was there? Rob frowned. Her attacker would have had plenty of time to go back and get it if that had been the case.

"May I ask what you're thinking, sir?" Trent gazed eagerly at him.

Rob turned, surprised. He'd been miles away. The young constable was eager to learn. He liked that. "I'm considering options. Either she was drunk and sat on the bench where she left her hat and phone, then stumbled down to the river where she fell in and drowned. Or she went in on purpose."

Trent's eyes widened.

"Alternatively, she could have been attacked, but I don't think it was random. If she was, whoever did it was lying in wait. They knew she'd be passing this way the night she vanished, which means this was a premeditated, planned attack."

Trent gulped. "You could tell all that by looking at the bench?"

"Not the bench. The phone was left behind, which tells me it wasn't a robbery. It didn't look like she'd been sexually assaulted, so it wasn't rape. That leaves one of three possibilities."

Trent finished his sentence. "It was an accident, she took her own life or she was murdered."

Rob smiled. "Correct."

* * *

Rob had to fight a barrage of reporters and news vans to get to the door. "Don't say anything," he yelled at Trent, who followed, close on his heels. After repeatedly refusing to comment, they finally made it inside the Marlow branch of the Thames Valley Police.

A man with a thick neck and protruding belly stood by the reception desk, behind which a young woman sat chewing gum. "I've never seen anything like it," he was saying.

They both looked up as Rob and Trent swept in, bringing with them a gust of frigid air.

"It's only going to get worse." Rob stuck out his hand. "DCI Miller."

"Sergeant Weatherby," the man said, shaking it while he blatantly sized him up.

The young woman had stopped chewing and was glaring at him like he'd done something wrong. Obviously the news that the Met had taken over the investigation had spread.

Rob nodded. "Can we have a word?"

"Follow me." Casting one last look at the reporters outside, Weatherby turned and walked down a short corridor to an office on the left. He waited for Rob to precede him inside, then followed, cutting Trent off.

"Go get yourself a cup of tea, Constable," he barked. "I'd like to speak to DCI Miller in private."

Trent's shoulders sank. "Yes, sir."

Weatherby's office was average-sized, with sash windows overlooking an overgrown back garden. Thames Valley Police resources didn't stretch to landscaping. The Sergeant's desk was cluttered with paperwork, and there were two empty mugs beside his computer. Rob could have killed for a cuppa himself, but no one was offering.

"Take a seat." Weatherby gestured to the vacant chair, fighting to retain some sense of control.

"I heard the Chief Superintendent is away." Rob eased his long frame into the chair.

"Yes, although he's on his way back. I spoke to him this morning."

Didn't want to miss out on the limelight.

"Chief Superintendent Mullins works out of the Maidenhead office," Weatherby said. "I run things around here."

Rob felt himself begin to thaw. The radiators emitted a cosy heat that made his eyelids heavy. It had been a long, cold day, mostly outdoors. The clock above Weatherby's head reminded him it was only 5 p.m.

"I must say," Weatherby began. "I'm a little confused as to why London Met has the case. I would have thought Thames Valley was—"

"I just follow orders," Rob interjected, with a vague shrug. He wasn't here to argue whose case it was. "What I really need to know is what has already been done."

"We conducted an extensive investigation when Debby Morris went missing," he began.

Rob expected no less. "Your team specifically?" A missing person case wouldn't have been handed over to the Thames Valley murder squad, not unless it was suspicious.

"We had several officers working the case," Weatherby replied. "We interviewed almost everybody at the party, we put out an appeal, and—"

"Could I have copies of the reports?"

"It's all on HOLMES," Weatherby said, referring to the system used by the police nationwide to manage complex investigations.

"Great, thanks." He could print out the various reports when he got back to the Putney office. Hopefully, it would give him some background into Debby Morris and the circumstances behind her disappearance.

"I heard Trent took you to where she disappeared?"

"Higginson Park." Maybe Weatherby would give him some local insight. "Where her hat and phone were found. It seems fairly isolated."

"Not really. In the summer, you have to fight for a picnic spot."

"Except this is the middle of winter," Rob pointed out. "And when she left the party, it would have been dark and deserted, yes?"

An irritated nod. Weatherby didn't like being contradicted. "The host, Roman Petrovic, thought she left around midnight, but he couldn't be sure."

"What was her general mood like?" Rob asked. He'd get back to the host and other guests in a bit.

"Everybody who spoke to her said she seemed fine."

Rob kept his gaze locked on Weatherby. "No mental health issues, no depression, or emotional problems? Nothing that might have had a bearing on her disappearance?"

The sergeant's eyes narrowed. "No, nothing like that. Are you saying she committed suicide?"

"I don't know. That's the point. We can't rule anything out at this stage."

"I suppose not." Weatherby scowled at him. Rob couldn't really blame him. He wouldn't like it if someone swept in and took over his investigation either. Especially when they had their own major crime squad at Maidenhead itching to get involved.

"I'm going to need a list of everybody who was at the party."

"You should talk to Chloe Brooke. She was the event planner."

He made a note. "What about Debby Morris's husband? Friends? Family?"

"Her husband, Ian, was away on a work trip the night she vanished. He was the one who reported her missing."

"Did you check his alibi?" Rob asked.

"His mother confirmed it, as she had the kids," Weatherby said, defensively.

Rob gave a shrug. "I still need his address and contact details."

Weatherby clenched his jowly jaw but nodded.

"Anyone else I should know about?" Rob asked.

"There's a friend, Monica White. She offered to help with the search. I remember because she was very concerned about Debby. Wouldn't stop calling the station. She kept insisting something terrible had happened to her."

Now that was interesting. "Same goes for her. What about Debby's family? Parents?"

"She didn't have any."

At Rob's surprised look, he elaborated. "Her parents died when she was a teenager. I don't know the circumstances, but her husband said she was an orphan when he met her at university."

"Okay, thanks." Were the dead parents significant? Maybe not, but he'd still have to look into it. He'd get a member of the team on to it.

The team.

It had been a long time since he'd seen any of them. They'd all been suspended pending the outcome of the IOPC investigation, but as far as he knew, they were back at work now. These last six months, he'd tried to put the job out of his mind and focus on Jo and Jack. He'd taken long walks with Trigger, done a lot of thinking. Before he'd met Jo and had a family, the job had meant everything to him. Now it had almost taken everything from him. Nothing was worth that. Nothing.

Mayhew's phone call had put an end to his existential crisis, but then, investigating a murder in a sleepy town was one thing; being back in the bullpen was quite another. The relentless schedule, the office politics, the superintendent breathing down his neck. Was he ready for it?

Too late, the voice in his head whispered. He was in it whether he liked it or not.

He waited until Weatherby got the information he needed, then thanked the podgy sergeant and left the station. Walking to his car, he heard hurried footsteps behind him.

"Sir?" called a voice.

Rob turned around to see the young constable running after him. "PC Trent, what's up?"

"I'd like to offer my assistance with the investigation, sir." The words tumbled out. Trent cast a nervous look back at the building. Rob guessed he hadn't cleared this with the sergeant. "Anything you need . . . just ask."

"That's very kind of you, Constable." Trent reminded Rob of a hopeful puppy, dancing around, desperate to be included. This was a big case, and he'd need a liaison with Thames Valley. Rob considered him thoughtfully. "Do you know the spouse, Ian Morris?"

"Yes. I mean, I spoke to him after his wife's disappearance."

"Okay, good. Hop in and you can brief me on the way."

"Where to, sir?"

"His house. We're going to talk to him about his dead wife."

CHAPTER 7

Ian Morris lived in a modest, red-brick terrace house in Marlow's Chapel Street. There was no parking on the road, so they had to ramp the pavement and leave the hazard lights on. The entrance to the house was through a low door, typical of houses built in the Victorian era. Rob ducked as he went in. Trent wasn't as tall, but even he bowed his head, just in case.

"Sorry." Ian ushered them through a smallish, period-style living room with a large fireplace and wooden beams, into a more modern kitchen. His voice sounded nasal, like he'd been crying. "Nineteenth-century property. We've been meaning to renovate, but hadn't got round to it when . . ." He faded out.

Rob gave a sympathetic nod. "I'm very sorry for your loss."

"Thank you. It's been a nightmare." Ian sniffed and stared at his hands. Then he seemed to shake himself awake. "Won't you sit down?"

Rob and Trent took a seat at the well-used four-seater kitchen table. It was covered with ring marks, scrapes and gouges. Rob watched as Ian traced one of the striations with a fingertip, lost to a memory.

"Did you know Debby was going to the Lifegiving Foundation party?" Rob eased into the questioning with an obvious one. Of course Ian would know, but Rob wanted to establish a baseline. A bit like a lie detector.

He gave a sad nod. "She went every year."

"How'd she get an invite? I heard it was at some fancy manor house near the river."

"Oh, didn't you know? Debby works—" he swallowed, and corrected himself — "worked for the Lifegiving Foundation. She was their group treasurer."

Rob glanced at Trent, who gave a quick nod. Something else he hadn't been aware of, but then he hadn't had time to read the file. "I see. How long had she been there?"

"Nearly five years. When she got pregnant, the charity allowed her to work part-time." His eyes glistened with tears that threatened to fall, but didn't.

"Who did she report to?"

"The founder is a woman called Dame Constance Blanchard. You might have heard of her?" He cocked his head to the side.

That was the woman Trent had mentioned. Rob gave a nod. "Local celebrity, isn't she?"

"That's right. Very glamorous, but slightly eccentric."

He arched an eyebrow. "Oh? In what way?"

Ian hesitated, then shrugged. "You'll see when you meet her."

Rob frowned, and was about to ask for an explanation, when Ian added, "But she's nothing compared to Roman Petrovic, the billionaire who owns Hollyhock Manor."

"That's the place where the party was held?"

A nod. "Serbian, I think. Shady geezer. No one quite knows where he made his money. I heard it was from gun-running in the old Soviet Republic." Another shrug.

Rob arched an eyebrow.

"He slinks into town, always in that big black coat like a vampire, but never talks to anyone." Ian rolled his eyes. "He sits alone, or sweeps in to get a takeaway, always on his phone. Doesn't even glance up."

Trent cleared his throat. Rob turned to him. "Every now and then I see Mr Petrovic dining at the Compleat Angler," the PC said hesitantly. "That's the Michelin-starred restaurant by the river. He's often there with very beautiful women."

"But never the same one," Ian sniffed, as if that were a crime in itself.

They were getting off track. "Let's talk about the night Debby went missing." Rob brought the conversation back to Ian and his relationship with his wife. They could investigate the weird and wonderful characters another time.

Ian glanced up. "What do you want to know?"

"Did you speak to her that day?"

"Um . . ." He closed his eyes. "I don't think so."

Trent butted in: "There was no record of Mr Morris having called his wife the day she disappeared."

Rob shot Trent a sharp look. He wanted Ian to respond in case he had anything to hide. It was the inconsistencies in a suspect's story that often caught them out. No good if PC Trent answered for him.

The young constable coloured. At least he understood. The kid was young, but he caught on quickly. Rob continued with the questioning. "I believe you were away on a work trip, is that right?"

"I was in Oxford, seeing a client."

"What do you do?"

"Architect. I work for a company called Dream Design. They're based in Bisham." He jerked his head backwards in the general direction.

"I take it this client will vouch for you?"

"Of course, although I stayed in a hotel while I was there. My meeting with the client was earlier that afternoon."

"I'm going to need the name and contact details of both the client and hotel," Rob said.

Ian swallowed. "Am I a suspect here?" He looked worriedly from Rob to Trent and back again. "I thought Debby drowned."

"It's standard procedure. Until we know what happened, we have to ask these types of questions."

Debby's husband gave a sulky nod.

"How was your wife before you left for Oxford? Was she her normal self?"

"You mean was she upset? Depressed?" He shook his head. "She wasn't suicidal, if that's what you're getting at. Debby loved her family. She'd do anything for the boys. There's no way she took her own life."

"Could she swim?" Trent asked.

Rob glanced at him. He preferred to do the interviewing, since he was sticking to a tried and tested format here, but it was a surprisingly insightful question. He looked at Ian. "Well?"

"Um, yes, she could swim."

Rob knew that it was incredibly difficult to drown yourself if you could swim, especially in freezing, waist-deep water, which was where she presumably went in. Natural instinct would kick in. The shock. . . a gasp as the icy water enveloped her. . . the desire to breathe, to struggle, to survive. Debby would have had to have drunk a lot of alcohol or consumed some sort of tranquiliser in order to do that. Or been concussed.

He thought back to the pathologist's remark about the gash on the victim's head. Had Debby been hit prior to drowning? It would be a lot easier to hold her down if she was groggy. No struggling then. Less risky for the perpetrator. Less chance of DNA being found under her fingernails.

"I'm sorry to have to ask," Rob began. This was always a sensitive subject and often not taken well. "But how was your relationship?"

Ian gave him a long, hard look. "We were happy, if that's what you mean. I don't know what you're insinuating, Detective, but I did not kill my wife. I loved her. She was the mother of my children. We were a family."

And family was everything.

"I'm not insinuating anything. It's my job to ask."

Ian looked away, out of the patio doors on to a stark back terrace. It was a paved area, weeds growing between the cracks, and then it ended abruptly where the grass began. Or rather, the grass encroached on the paving stones, slowly taking over.

"Where are the boys now?" Rob asked.

"With my mother. She lives in Henley-on-Thames, not far away. We thought, under the circumstances, it would be better if they didn't go to school. They don't know what's happened yet."

"Haven't they asked about their mother?" Rob asked.

"We've told them she's gone away on a trip." He shrugged helplessly. Tears welled again. This time they did fall, running silently down his stubbly cheeks. He hadn't shaved in days. "God knows what we're going to tell them."

"We?"

"My mother and me. She's widowed; my father died a few years back. She helps a lot with the boys. They can be a bit of a handful."

Rob didn't envy him. Raising twin boys couldn't be easy. One was hard enough, and now he had to do it without his wife.

"Was your mother babysitting the night Debby disappeared?"

"The boys were at her house, yes. Debby would have dropped them off that afternoon." Rob made a mental note to get one of this team to follow up with the mother. Weatherby said they'd checked, but he wouldn't take his word for it.

He paused, thinking through his line of questioning. Something was bugging him. "What happened to Debby's parents? I believe they passed away when she was a child."

Ian looked confused, as if he couldn't figure out why he was being asked that question, or what it had to do with anything. "Um . . . yes. They were tea importers. They died in Africa somewhere, I'm not sure where. They were on a trip when the hotel they were staying in was attacked by terrorists." He shook his head. "I don't think Debby ever got over it."

"How old was she?" asked Rob.

"Eighteen. It affected her badly."

Rob could imagine. He'd lost his mother when he was a youngster, and while he only had hazy memories of her, it had been tough at the time. He'd gone off the rails, acted out, got in with the wrong crowd. It was like the safety net had been pulled out from underneath him and he'd lost his anchor. Perhaps Debby had felt the same. "In what way?"

"I met her a couple of months after it happened. We were at uni in Bristol, but that first year was bumpy, you know? She had to repeat a couple of subjects."

"What did she study?"

"Accounting. She had a real head for numbers." He bit his lip. Rob thought he was about to cry again, so he pushed on.

"When did you first realise something was wrong?"

A haunted look flashed across Ian's face, like he didn't want to go back there. Rob couldn't blame him, but he had to take him back there anyway. Into the darkness. Into the nightmare. "When she didn't pick the kids up the next morning. My mother rang and said she couldn't get hold of her. It was strange. Debby wasn't usually late." He took a shuddering breath. "I called her several times, but she didn't answer. Eventually, I drove back and fetched the boys on the way. By then, I was getting worried."

Rob gave a slow nod. "Yet you didn't report her missing until . . ." He glanced at Trent.

"The following afternoon," the constable finished.

"I wish I had." Ian studied his hands again. Rob noticed his nails were bitten down and ragged. "I thought maybe she'd gone to Monica's and stayed overnight there."

"Monica? Oh yeah. The friend?"

"That's right. She lives behind the fitness centre."

"Did you call Monica?"

"Yes, but she didn't pick up either. That's why I thought they might be together. Eventually, Monica called me back and said she hadn't seen Debby. That's when I started to panic."

"And you went to the police station to report her missing?"

"Yes." He gnawed on his lower lip. "I had no idea anything untoward had happened to her. I swear."

Rob studied Ian Morris. The man appeared distraught. His hair was messy, his clothes wrinkled, and he had a tea stain on his jogging bottoms. If appearances were anything to go by, he was telling the truth.

CHAPTER 8

The sun had yet to claw its way above the metallic-grey horizon when Rob walked into the Major Investigation Team's Putney headquarters the next morning. The duty sergeant in the lobby gave an impersonal nod, not realising Rob hadn't set foot in the building for nearly six months. It felt strangely foreign, yet familiar at the same time, like when you got home after being on a long holiday.

He rode the lift to the third floor and emerged on to a darkened landing. The lights buzzed on as soon as his body movement activated the sensors. A pair of glass sliding doors wheezed open, admitting him to the squad room.

It was empty, the only sounds the faint hum of computers and the electric flicker of the fluorescent strip lights as they came on. He walked through the mangle of desks to his own, situated in the corner near the back, nestled between a right angle of windows.

Down below, Putney High Street was springing to life. Commuters clutching coffee cups like their lives depended on it crossed the road on their way to the tube station. A trail of impatient red taillights stretched all the way up the hill, and the high-street stores were beginning to open.

Rob sat down and took out his laptop. He connected to the network, logged on to HOLMES and began printing reports. Nearby, a printer spluttered to life.

Next, he opened his desk drawer to get his mug. It was one Jo had given him a couple of months after they'd met. At least they hadn't cleaned out his desk. Smiling, he walked back out of the sliding doors to the small waiting area on the landing. A few years back, his late boss, Chief Superintendent Lawrence, had installed a coffee machine there. It wasn't great coffee, but it was a damn sight better than the crap they served in the canteen.

He'd just returned to his desk when Sergeant Jenny Bird walked in. She grinned, dumped her backpack on her chair and rushed over. "Great to see you back, guv."

He grinned, giving her a hug. "Thanks. How are you?"

"I'm good."

"How are things around here?"

She shrugged. "You know. Mayhew's the same as always, runs a tight ship."

Rob gave a stiff nod. He'd heard that the Superintendent had cracked down on the department since their fall from grace in the summer. Over the years, they had developed something of a reputation for pushing the boundaries, but Rob's last case had taken it too far.

Putney MIT Need Policing was one of the many newspaper headlines he'd read before Rob and the rest of his murder squad had been suspended, pending the IOPC investigation.

They were willing to let it slide when you got results, he thought bitterly. But when it all went tits up, suddenly everything was under scrutiny. *More thorough vetting for police consultants* was one of the investigation's outcomes. *Increased measures to protect police information* was another, along with *strictly no access to police files.*

To be honest, Rob didn't disagree, although no amount of vetting would have revealed the esteemed criminal profiler and author Tony Sanderson as a psychopathic serial killer, for the simple reason that there was nothing there to find. On the surface, he'd been an upstanding citizen, a caring husband and father, a brilliant criminal psychologist. He'd even assisted them with cases in the past, and they owed several of their victories to his dazzling insights into the criminal mind.

Takes one to know one, Rob thought wryly.

Tony Sanderson, the man who'd caused all this consternation, had swanned into the MIT headquarters like he owned the place. He'd sat at their boardroom table, listened in on case briefings, and tried to manipulate the course of the investigation. The worst part was, they'd let him. Rob — and by default, his team — had trusted him, thinking he was on their side, when nothing could have been further from the truth.

"Has Mayhew briefed you on the Debby Morris investigation?" Rob asked.

"We got a preliminary briefing, although she was a bit sketchy on the details. Said you'd fill us in today. I believe you saw them pull her out of the water?"

"Yeah. I took a few pictures with my phone, which I'll show you later. We're working with a young officer from Thames Valley on this, PC Trent. They're pissed off we've taken the case, but he will help bridge the gap. Trent was involved in the original missing persons investigation, so he can provide us with some much-needed insight into the various players."

"Players?" Jenny raised a narrow eyebrow. "The word on the street is that she drowned." Today's newspapers were filled with the gruesome discovery. He'd even spotted himself and Trent in some of the shots.

"She did, but we don't know how yet. The victim was last seen at a Christmas party, the night before she disappeared."

Her eyes widened. "That explains the elf outfit. I did wonder."

They glanced up as the doors hissed open and Superintendent Felicity Mayhew slithered in. True to form, she stalked between the desks in her four-inch heels, skirt suit, and a smart navy coat that set off her flame-coloured hair. Rob swore the temperature in the office dropped several degrees.

"DCI Miller, it's good to have you back." The cool expression on her pale, freckled face didn't change. No crinkle at the corners of her eyes, no tilt of the lips. Typical Mayhew.

He forced a smile. "Good to be here, ma'am."

"I take it you'll bring us up to speed?"

"As soon as the rest of the team gets here," he replied. Her arctic-blue eyes sliced through him, then she gave a brief nod and continued to her office.

"Good morning to you too," Jenny murmured.

"What's that about?" Rob asked.

Jenny rolled her eyes. "I don't think she likes me."

"You're competition," Rob surmised, reading the vibe between them correctly.

Jenny snorted. "Lucky for her, I don't have designs on the top job." Rob was aware DS Bird had used the last six months to do additional training and was establishing herself as a stellar interrogator.

Rob chuckled. "Indeed."

DS Will Freemont arrived next, followed by DC Celeste Parker. Will, a tech whiz and valued member of the team, pumped his hand. "About time you got back."

Celeste smiled shyly. One of the youngest constables, she was the newest member of the team. She'd worked with him on several cases in the past, including the Tony Sanderson one, so he'd promoted her before they'd all been suspended. "Welcome back, guv."

"Thanks, guys." Only one member left to arrive, and that was DC Harry Malhotra, the charismatic constable with the movie-star good looks who'd recently come out as gay. Rob hadn't worked with him since his big reveal, but he didn't expect it to change anything. Harry was Harry, a great detective, and a good friend. His sexuality had nothing to do with it.

Rob sat down and pulled up his notes for the briefing. He was still reading through them when Harry sauntered in, laughing with another detective on Galbraith's team. DCI Galbraith was a burly, no-nonsense Scot who ran the other murder squad based at Putney MIT. Occasionally, they combined forces, so the members of each team knew each other and worked well together.

"Guv!" Like Will, Harry gave his hand a good shake and thumped him on the back.

Rob grinned. "Good to see you, Harry."

"Likewise. Things haven't been the same without you." Harry jiggled his eyebrows suggestively.

"Oh?" Was there something he'd missed?

Jenny, who sat closest to Rob, leaned over. "There've been some new faces around here lately, one of whom you'll remember." She nodded towards the door as, on cue, a stocky, salt-and-pepper-haired man in his mid-forties with a rugged, lined face walked in. He was familiar. Rob stared at him for a long moment, then clicked his fingers. "DCI Linden?"

"Yeah, Mayhew hired him after we got suspended. We came back to find him here, running a team of his own."

"Oh? I didn't think we had enough detectives for an extra squad."

"We didn't, but with our team assigned to desk duty until the verdict, they hired four more detectives. Mostly DCs, but still . . ."

"I don't think they wanted us back," Will whispered.

"Who? Mayhew?"

"No, surprisingly she fought our corner. It was Raza Ashraf who kicked up a fuss. I think he was hoping we'd be found lacking and given the sack."

Rob grimaced. The Mayor had had it in for them ever since he'd been a person of interest in an investigation early last year. He hadn't taken kindly to being interrogated, or his personal life being turned upside down and splashed across the papers.

Rob glanced toward Mayhew's office, where she was already on the phone, her back to them. He could tell by her stance that she was yelling at somebody. After a rocky start, she'd surprised him. He wouldn't go so far as to call her a friend, but she'd turned out to be a better Superintendent than he'd thought.

"Okay, now we're all here, let me brief you on what's going on."

"Debby Morris?" Will asked.

"In the incident room. You too, Celeste."

She jumped up as they followed him through the maze of desks and down a short corridor that ran beside Mayhew's office. Rob shut the door as Linden walked past. The new DCI nodded a greeting at Rob, who nodded back. They'd get a chance to catch up later. He remembered Linden being a decent fellow, and not a bad detective, although he hadn't had a chance to put that to the test.

Rob turned to face the team. It felt good to be back, even though they'd all had a tough time with the internal investigation, but he didn't want to dwell on that. They'd moved on, and now had a shiny new, high-profile case to get stuck into.

"Okay, let's get straight to it. Debby Morris's body was found in the Thames roughly five miles from Marlow yesterday morning by a dog walker.

"It's always a bloody dog walker," muttered Harry. Celeste grinned at him.

"Cause of death was drowning, but—" he held up a hand — "we're not sure if it was suspicious as yet."

"Was she drunk?" Harry asked.

"We won't know until the post-mortem, which should be today sometime, but she'd been at a Christmas party, so it's possible."

"Did she leave the party alone?" Will asked.

"As far as we can tell, yes. There was a small gash on her head, but it could have occurred post-mortem. We have no evidence that she was murdered at this stage."

"Then why are we here?" Jenny frowned.

It was a good question. "Because we need to prove it, either way. The Police Commissioner wanted us on this investigation.

Apparently the victim is the goddaughter of a friend of his, Chief Superintendent Wallace from Southwark."

"Don't know him." Harry shrugged.

Jenny raised her eyebrows. "Seriously? The Commissioner?"

"You know he loves Mayhew." Their Superintendent could do no wrong in his eyes.

"Thames Valley must be fuming," remarked Will.

"They're not happy," Rob confirmed with a snort.

"You mentioned a PC Trent?" Jenny raised an eyebrow.

"Yes, he was helpful yesterday. Took me to the park where Debby Morris's phone and hat were found."

"Under a bench, wasn't it?" Jenny recalled. The images had been replayed on television ad nauseam after she'd disappeared.

"Yeah, it's a dark spot, so she could have sat down to recover if she was feeling unwell. Then she could have been attacked and pulled from the bench to the river."

Celeste made a note on her iPad. Everybody was using a phone or tablet to take notes, other than Will, who was on his laptop. Rob felt very old school with his bound notepad lying open on the table. He passed his phone around. "I'll get these printed and blown up," he said, "but at least you can see what she looked like when she came out of the water."

They scrutinised the photographs of Debby Morris in turn — being lifted out of the river by the divers, blonde hair swept back off her face, cheeks mottled and grey. Celeste shuddered. "She looks awful."

"Amazing what three weeks in the river will do to you," Harry muttered.

"Are we sure she didn't commit suicide?" Jenny asked.

"Not entirely. However, Trent and I interviewed her husband, who swears she wasn't upset or depressed. She loved her twin boys, aged four, and wouldn't abandon them. Debby lost her own parents at eighteen and knows what it's like to be orphaned. I don't think she'd do that to her own children. Suicide feels wrong to me."

"Still, we have to officially rule it out," Jenny said.

Rob nodded. "Absolutely. Harry, get on to her GP surgery and see if she was taking any medication or having treatment for depression. Any mental health issues, et cetera." Harry nodded.

"Celeste," Rob went on. The newest member of the team fixed her eyes on him. "I want you to do a thorough background check on Debby Morris, including her parents. Apparently they were killed in Africa about a decade ago. I want to know the circumstances around their demise."

"Do you think that's got something to do with her death?" Celeste asked, her eyes widening.

"Probably not, but you never know. Both parents died, then ten years later, she is found dead under mysterious circumstances after going missing for three weeks. I have no idea if the two are connected or not, but I feel like we should consider it."

"Righto, guv."

Will sat up straight. "What about me?"

"Look into the husband, Ian Morris. He seemed genuinely upset by his wife's death, but it doesn't hurt to do a little digging into his background. Also, his mum helps with the kids. According to Ian, the boys were with her while Debby was at the party. He collected them the next day when she didn't come home. Might be worth checking that detail."

"Gotcha." Will turned back to his keyboard.

"What do you want me to do, guv?" Jenny asked.

"You and I are going to pay Debby Morris's friend Monica White a visit. Apparently, they were very close."

"Ah, the best friend."

"Her husband said Monica was protective of Debby, and often used to put ideas into her head." That's what Trent had told him, anyway.

"What kind of ideas?"

"I'm not sure. Anyway, the day after Debby went missing, Monica rang the station non-stop. She told PC Trent that she was convinced something had happened to her."

"Do you think she knows something?" Jenny mused.

Rob shrugged. "Let's go find out."

CHAPTER 9

Monica White lived in a functional two-bed flat behind the Chequers pub, not far from Higginson Park. A pointed archway in the high street led to a quaint courtyard aglow with coffee shops. The apartment block was down a cobbled pathway, adorned with trees.

"This is nice." Jenny tilted her head at the giant oaks whispering above them.

Rob thought it sounded like the dead brown leaves were keeping secrets, and the hairs on his neck stood up. "Which number is Monica?"

"Twenty-seven. Third floor."

There was no lift, so they climbed a draughty staircase to the third floor and strode along an open walkway. The icy wind buffeted them. Rob's eyes started watering.

Wiping them with the back of his hand, he pressed the silver buzzer, and heard it grate through the flat. Within seconds, the door swung open with excessive force, and both he and Jenny jumped back.

"Yes?" An angry-looking woman with bed hair and red-rimmed eyes stood glaring at them.

"Are you Monica White?"

The bloodshot eyes narrowed. Rob could feel a negative energy pulsating off her. Not animosity, but something else. Grief, perhaps? "Who wants to know?"

He held up his warrant card. "DCI Miller and DS Bird from the Met Major Investigation Team. We're looking into the death of Debby Morris. Do you mind if we ask you some questions? I believe you were friends."

At the mention of Debby, the staunch shoulders drooped, as the fight seeped out of her and sadness took its place. "Yes, she was my friend. I suppose you can come in."

Rob glanced at Jenny, who said, "Thank you."

They followed her into a neat but minimalist living room. A cream corner sofa took up most of the space, along with a television, a pine dining table set and a geometric-patterned rug. Monica didn't have much else in the way of furniture. There weren't many photographs or personal items scattered around. In fact, apart from the rowing prints on the walls, and one framed photograph of a group of teenage girls wearing medals and wide smiles, there was nothing that hinted at her personality.

"Sit down if you want." She gestured to the sofa. The lights weren't on in the flat, but wide balcony windows let in muted sunlight. Rob glanced out and saw that it overlooked a grassy park, and in the distance, an old churchyard.

"Thank you." Jenny was taking the lead on this one. She had a softer touch than he did, although he suspected Monica White would be a tough nut to crack.

Monica studied Jenny, intelligent eyes roaming over her face, her body, and even lingering on her shoes. She noticed things, which would make her a good interviewee — that was, if she had anything to tell them.

Jenny smiled, breaking the tension. "Were you and Debby close?"

A nod, and then to Rob's surprise, Monica's eyes glistened. She swiped at them angrily. "We were best friends."

"I'm sorry for your loss," Jenny said, and Rob could tell she really meant it. Not like most coppers, where the words just ran off their tongue like they were commenting on the weather. Even he was guilty of that sometimes.

Monica bowed her head. Rob could tell she was battling to control her emotions. He studied the rowing picture on the wall, and the one with the medals. All four women in the photograph had strong, robust figures and triumphant smiles. Monica wasn't used to feeling weak or vulnerable.

"How did you meet?" Jenny asked.

"Through the charity." She gave a short sniff. "Marlow Rowing Club held a fundraising regatta a couple of years back, and they were one of our causes. I dealt with Debby in the finance office. We hit it off."

"That would be the Lifegiving Charity founded by Dame . . . ?" Jenny glanced down at the notes on her phone.

"Constance Blanchard. Yes." A nod of her head, accompanied by another self-affirming sniff. She seemed more confident now.

"Right." Jenny paused, taking it slow. "Monica, what do you think happened to Debby?"

Rob pursed his lips. That wasn't the avenue he would have taken, but he let Jenny run with it. She had read the situation and knew what she was doing. Monica was obviously a very self-assured woman, and would have her own opinions about what happened. Jenny had clearly thought the direct approach would work best.

The shoulders went back, and Monica's jaw jutted out obstinately. "I don't know, but I bet it had something to do with that husband of hers."

"Who? Ian?" Jenny glanced at Rob.

Monica scrunched up her forehead. "Yes, he was very controlling. Expected her to be the perfect wife, the perfect mother, all while trying to hold down a job." It was clear Monica was not a fan of Ian Morris.

"In what way?" Jenny asked.

"She ran herself ragged looking after those boys. Taking them to school, going to work, dropping them at his mother's." She held up a finger. "Don't get me started on *her.*" Monica was working herself up to a rant.

Jenny let her go with it. "His mother?"

"She thought she knew what was best for those kids. Always telling Debby what to do. What food to buy, what to cook, how to discipline them. I said to Debs, it's none of her damn business how you raise those kids. They're your kids. Not hers." She shook her head. "But Debby was a people pleaser. She tried her best, but I think it got too much for her."

"You think she took her own life?" Jenny asked.

"God, no." Monica shook her head so hard her short locks bounced around. "That's not what I meant." She paused. "But I think she fought back."

Jenny shot a look at Rob, but he didn't know what to make of this. Was Monica saying she thought Ian had something to do with his wife's death?

"Sorry, Monica, could you be more specific? Are you saying her husband . . ."

She threw her hands in the air. "Oh, I don't know, maybe. When she went missing, I had this feeling . . . I told the police something bad had happened. It wasn't like her. She wouldn't run off and abandon her kids. No way, not Debs."

"Did you talk to Ian?"

"He refused to take my calls. I even went round to the house, but he said the police were handling it; there was nothing more he could do."

Rob nodded. To be fair, that was probably true.

"What did you want him to do?" Jenny asked.

"I thought we should organise a search party. I don't know. Something. Anything." She'd felt helpless. Rob got it. A lot of victims' families felt that way. Out of control. Powerless to change fate. To turn back the clock. Monica was a doer, not a thinker. A woman of action.

"I went looking for her. I searched half the bloody Buckinghamshire countryside, but I couldn't find her."

She clenched her jaw, causing the muscles to flex and pop. "When all the time she was in the bleedin' river." Her shoulders caved in. It was clear she was more than a little cut up over her friend's death.

"You blame Ian because he didn't go looking for her?" Jenny said.

"He didn't appear overly concerned, that's all I'm saying. I'm not accusing him of anything, although I wouldn't put it past him. I've seen him lose it before; he's got quite a temper."

Ian hadn't struck Rob as a man with a volatile temper but then he'd only met him once.

"Did he ever hurt Debby?" Jenny wanted to know.

"Not that I'm aware of. Not physically, at least." Her forehead remained furrowed.

"Emotionally, though?" Jenny's voice was soft, concerned. Two women having a confidential chat. Rob eased back in the armchair like he wasn't in the room anymore.

Monica's gaze rested solely on Jenny. "It was little things. Nothing anyone would notice, if you didn't know them. A suggestion. A look. A frown. The way he put his hand on her arm, like a warning rather than a loving gesture."

Rob had known she was observant. Monica had thought about this, noticed things over the years. "I said to her, he doesn't own you, Debs. You can do things your way. You know what's best for those boys. But she always ran to do his bidding. I tried to stand up for her, but Ian never listened to me." She hesitated. "We didn't get on."

No surprises there.

"Do you think he was capable of harming her?" Jenny asked.

For the first time, Monica hesitated. "I don't want to get Ian into trouble, but yes. I think he was. Did he push her into that river? I don't know. But I reckon he drove her to drink that night. That's why she was stumbling through the park on her way home. If she hadn't been drunk, she might have noticed someone following her . . ." Her voice wobbled, and she stopped. Clearing it, she took a shuddering breath. "I blame him for what happened."

Rob interjected. "You don't think she stumbled and fell into the river?"

"Hell, no. She was too good a swimmer for that. Even drunk, there's only three or four feet of water near the pontoon in Higginson Park. No way she would have accidentally drowned."

"So, you think someone pushed her in?"

A shrug, but her eyes were hard. "It's the only thing that makes sense."

"And you think her husband could have done it?"

"I'm not saying he did." Monica leaned forward, her voice a hoarse whisper. "But she was afraid of him. I know that much."

CHAPTER 10

Chief Superintendent Patrick Mullins stalked up and down the Marlow Police Station, hands on his hips. "Quite frankly, it's ridiculous," he huffed. "This is our investigation."

"It should have been, sir." Rob tried his best to be diplomatic. The man had kicked up a fuss, prompting a call to Mayhew, who asked Rob to smooth things over. Smoothing things over wasn't exactly his forte, but he said he'd do his best. "That's why I want to ask if PC Trent could be seconded to the Met's murder squad for the duration of the investigation."

The stocky man with prematurely white hair and a strong, chiselled face stopped pacing. "You want PC Trent on the investigation?"

"If that's all right with you."

A pause. Mullins studied Trent, who stood nervously behind Rob. Jenny shot him a bolstering smile. "No offence to PC Trent, but he's only just joined us. We have a large team of experienced officers that would be better placed to assist you with your inquiries."

Rob didn't doubt it. Thames Valley was the second largest police force in the country and looked after three counties and dozens of local policing areas. They had a serious and organised crime department, as well as their own major investigation team. But he didn't know them. He knew Trent.

"PC Trent was the first responder down by the river. He's familiar with the case, having worked on Debby Morris's disappearance, and he's already spoken to most of the witnesses. He's a valuable asset. Obviously, we'd be sharing resources, and both police forces would receive recognition for the outcome." Mayhew's idea.

The man is ambitious, she'd said. *This way, he gets some of the credit without doing any of the work.*

"I suppose we could spare him for the time being."

"It would just be until this investigation is wrapped up." Rob didn't know how long that was going to take. Could be weeks, could be months. "He'd still be based here, of course, but we'd like him to come to MIT headquarters for briefings and the like."

"Trent," Mullins said, "are you okay with this?"

"Yes, sir."

"Okay, then." Mullins nodded at Rob. "He's all yours, Detective Chief Inspector."

"Thank you, sir."

Mullins gave a curt nod, then strode off down a long corridor, presumably back to his office.

Rob turned to Trent. "Welcome to the Major Investigation Team, Constable."

Trent beamed. "Thank you, sir."

"Call him guv," Jenny said. "We all do."

He gave a happy nod. "What do you want me to do, guv?"

Rob masked a grin. Trent would fit in just fine. "First up, I need you to go to Oxford and check out Ian Morris's alibi."

"Alibi?" His smile faltered. "Are we treating Debby Morris's death as suspicious?"

"Not at this stage," Rob was quick to reassure him. "We're just covering the groundwork. If he's lying about where he was, it might put a different slant on things."

Trent's eyes widened in understanding. "I'll leave straight away."

"Call me when you're done. You've got my mobile number?" Rob had given him his business card.

"I do."

"Good. Oh, one more thing. Weatherby mentioned an event planner?"

"Chloe Brooke, yes."

"Could you give me her number?"

"Sure." He scrolled through his phone and pulled up her details. "Texting it to you now."

Rob was surprised. "You had her in your contacts?"

"Yeah. I had to chase her several times for the guest list, so I saved it on my phone."

Rob glanced at Jenny, who pursed her lips and shrugged.

"Okay, thanks."

"Shall I head off now, guv? To Oxford?"

"Yes, Constable. You'd better get on your way."

He gave a parting grin, then put on his hat and dashed out the door.

They were just leaving when Rob's phone beeped. It was Dr Carmichael, the pathologist.

PM at 3 p.m.

She was a woman of few words, but at least she'd kept her promise.

"Let's get back." Rob checked the time. "I've got an hour to get to the mortuary."

* * *

The Montgomery Centre in West London where the post-mortem was taking place was a fat, squat, concrete matchbox of a building, with a row of tinted windows. To add insult to injury, it overlooked a car park, and there wasn't so much as a shrub in sight.

Appearances, however, could be deceiving. No amount of money had been spared when the state-of-the-art lab had been equipped, much to the delight of the people who worked there. Rob hurried across a marble lobby and approached the desk, where a receptionist requested he sign in. He scrawled his name, then passed through a set of electric doors operated by the woman behind the desk. No unauthorised entry.

It was freezing inside, almost as cold as outdoors. Rob pulled his coat tighter around him as he strode down the carpeted corridor with its subtle, recessed lighting and abstract photographs on the walls. The labs were situated at the back of the building, but the door to number 2b, where Debby Morris's post-mortem was taking place, was locked. You needed a fob to get in.

Instead, Rob climbed an adjacent flight of stairs that took him up to the viewing gallery. Dr Carmichael was just getting started. Without interrupting, he took a seat.

Kitted out in scrubs, gloves and a face mask, Dr Carmichael began her inspection of the body. A lab assistant, also in scrubs, stood to one side awaiting instruction.

Debby Morris had been cleaned up and lay naked on the steel table. From where Rob was sitting, she looked almost purple, her body was so discoloured, scratched and battered. It was hard to believe that this was once a living, breathing young woman. A living, breathing young woman with her arms around two young boys. A cherubic face . . . pale blue eyes . . . Carmichael began at the head. Using a magnifying lamp, she carefully parted the victim's hair to inspect the bump, looking for evidence of trauma. Five minutes passed. Rob shifted in his seat. "Anything?"

She bent in, frowned, studied the scalp from a different angle. If this was how long she took on the head, it was going to be an excruciating afternoon.

"There's a laceration on her scalp," Carmichael said eventually, her voice tinny through the intercom system. "Caused by a sharp object."

"Like . . . ?" He left it hanging.

"A rock, a hard piece of metal, something with a point. Oedema at the wound site means the blood has flowed into the surrounding tissues. That could only happen ante-mortem."

"You mean before she died?" Rob blurted out, even though he knew what ante-mortem meant. He had to be absolutely clear on this.

Carmichael gave a little nod. "I would say so, yes. There's too much swelling for it not to be."

Rob's heart pumped harder. "Could it have happened when she fell into the river?"

"*If* she fell into the river, yes, although her blood–alcohol ratio was fairly low. She'd had one, maybe two drinks. Not enough for her to fall in of her own accord, I wouldn't have thought."

Rob tapped on the railing in front of him. "Any drugs or suppressants in her system?"

"Nope."

"Then someone must have hit her on the head."

Carmichael glanced up, her glasses catching the light. "That would be my assumption, yes."

He exhaled. The case had just got a whole lot more interesting. "What about the scratches?" Debby's body was patchworked with them.

"Haven't got there yet."

She went back to work. Rob had to wait until she'd recorded her observations on the head, face and neck, before she got to the torso. The woman was painstakingly thorough, almost more so than Liz Kramer, the pathologist he usually worked with, and would not be rushed.

"These marks were all made post-mortem," she confirmed, which was what Rob had expected. "Nothing here suggests she was manhandled or abused in any way prior to her death."

"Okay." He watched as she carefully inspected the hands and fingernails, then took scrapings.

"Mostly river debris." She placed the sample in a plastic tube and sealed it. "She was in the river for three weeks."

"Any idea of time of death?"

Carmichael shook her head without looking up. "Impossible to say from her body. Typical decomposition proceeds more slowly in water, primarily due to cooler temperatures and the anaerobic environment. Could be anything from the night she went missing, to a week later."

Rob gave a reluctant nod. That didn't help at all.

"Help me turn her over," she said to her assistant. Together, they moved Debby Morris on to her stomach. Immediately, Carmichael grabbed the magnifying lamp and brought it in close to the body. This time, she went straight for the back.

"What is it?" Rob could tell she was transfixed with something.

Ignoring him, she placed her hands on the victim's back and held them there. Then she abruptly looked up. "There's bruising on her back." Her voice was measured, as if she didn't want to say too much, too soon. "I didn't notice it before due to the river debris."

"Okay. What does that mean? Was she assaulted prior to her death?" The questions built in his mind.

"Given the shape and pattern of the bruising, I'd say these contusions were made by a large, male hand. They're in the centre of the back, as if she were held down." Carmichael met Rob's gaze. "Your victim was forcibly drowned. This, in addition to the blunt force trauma on her head, and you're looking at murder."

CHAPTER 11

PC Trent pushed open the heavy front door to the Musgrove Guest House in Oxford and nearly tripped over a pile of designer luggage lying in the doorway.

"Sorry." A harassed man in a wrinkled suit jumped up to move them, while his coiffed wife remained seated on a chaise longue.

"Thank you." Trent walked around him into the stylish reception room. The red-faced man tugged the heavy luggage into a corner and sank down beside his wife again.

The receptionist glanced apologetically at him, her eyes lingering on his uniform. "I'll be with you in one second." Beside her on the desk stood a standard inkjet printer and an ornate green-and-brass banker's lamp complete with pull-cord. Trent, who was a bit of a history buff, appreciated that it was probably an antique.

The nametag pinned to her blouse said *Emily*. After typing furiously for at least a full minute, she glanced up at the couple. "Your room is ready. Number seven, upstairs on the left." She came around the desk and handed them their key cards. "Enjoy your stay."

The wife swanned off, leaving her husband to carry the bags. Once they were out of the way, Emily turned back to Trent. "How can I help, officer?"

"I'm PC Trent with Thames Valley Police," he began. "I need to ask you some questions about one of your guests."

Her eyes narrowed. "I can't give out guest information."

"Oh, that's okay. I don't need his information. I already have it. What I need to clarify is when he stayed here."

Thrown, she mulled this over. He hoped she wasn't going to be difficult. He didn't want to disappoint DCI Miller. This woman was under no obligation to tell him anything without a warrant, but he wasn't about to tell her that.

"I suppose that's okay."

He gave a silent sigh of relief. "Thank you, Emily."

She smiled at the mention of her name. "What is the guest's name?"

"Ian Morris. I believe he stayed here about three weeks ago, on the thirteenth of November."

"Ian Morris . . ." She went back to the computer, not making the connection. "Is that I-A-N or the Scottish version?"

"I-A-N," he confirmed.

More typing. Eventually, she looked up. "I can confirm that Ian Morris was here on that date."

Trent smiled down at her. "I don't suppose you can tell me what time he checked in?"

She bit her lip. "I'm not sure I should be giving out this information. It goes against our GDPR standards."

"It's important," he told her. "This is a police inquiry. Ian Morris gave us your details so we could check out his alibi."

DCI Miller had texted him on the way here to tell him this was now a murder investigation, and that Ian Morris was a suspect. He didn't know how the DCI had obtained such information, only that he had. Maybe the post-mortem had been done, although it seemed too quick for that. Still, he didn't know how fast these things moved, especially when the Major Investigation Team was on the job. They probably had more clout than your average police department.

The penny dropped, and she gasped. "Oh God. You don't mean Debby Morris, do you?"

He nodded. "Ian Morris was her husband."

Emily's hand flew to her mouth. "I guess in that case—" she glanced back down at her computer screen — "he checked in at two forty-five on Saturday, the thirteenth of November, and out at eight forty-three on Sunday morning."

Trent felt vaguely disappointed. He was hoping to find something valuable to give the DCI, to contribute to the case in some way, yet it seemed Ian Morris had been telling the truth. He'd been here the whole time.

"You use key cards for the room doors, don't you?" He'd seen her hand them to that other couple.

"Yes."

"Could you tell me when he was in his room?"

She thought for a moment. "He didn't go up to his room when he first arrived. I remember because he asked if he could leave his overnight bag here at reception and went straight out again."

Trent recalled Ian saying he had met with a client at three o'clock. "What time did he get back?"

Emily pointed to the screen. "He entered his room at 18:17 and then again at 21:26."

"He went out in the evening?"

"The key card only records when they go in, not when they leave."

Trent nodded. Of course, because they didn't use the card to get out. "I see. So at some point he left the hotel, presumably to go for supper, then got back just before half past nine."

"That's right." She hesitated. "Actually, I saw him leave for dinner, because I was here, tidying up. It was around seven thirty."

"That's very helpful, thank you." Trent made a note. "He didn't go out again after that? Maybe later that night? After ten?"

"Not that I can see." Her eyes drifted back to the screen. "There's nothing else on the system."

Bugger. He'd have to go back to DCI Miller and tell him Ian Morris's alibi checked out. He couldn't have murdered his wife. Not unless he was a magician.

CHAPTER 12

"Everybody, this is PC Trent." Rob's team was waiting in the incident room when he walked in with the Thames Valley constable. "PC Trent, this is the murder squad." He introduced them one by one, but could tell by the glazed look on Trent's face that he wouldn't remember a single one of them. Not right away.

Trent flushed and said hello, then sat down next to Jenny, who was the only member other than Rob that he'd met before. Up front was the murder board, as it was known in the department. On it, Rob had pinned the blown-up photographs he'd taken of Debby Morris's body at the riverside, and some of the bench under which her phone and elf hat had been found.

Trent's eyes focused on the bloated, mottled face and he turned away. "You were there, weren't you?" Celeste asked, clocking his reaction. "When they got her out."

He gave a rueful nod.

"Must have been awful."

He tried to smile. "It wasn't great."

"I've never seen a dead body before," she whispered, then gave a self-conscious grin. "I'm new to the team too."

"Hardly," scoffed Harry.

She swatted at him, but looked at Trent. "I've worked with them before, though."

"Let's get down to business." Rob faced the table. "By now you've heard this is officially a murder inquiry. Dr Carmichael, the pathologist, has confirmed Debby Morris was hit on the head prior to being drowned. Also, there are bruises on her back, where you can clearly see a handprint." He pointed to a photograph from the post-mortem that he'd pinned to the board. There were a couple of grimaces.

"Looks big," Will pointed out.

"Yeah, we suspect it's a man's handprint," Rob confirmed. "Based on the size, a rather tall man, although as you know, that is not conclusive."

"Some small men have very large hands," Harry pointed out. "My uncle is only five four, but he's got enormous hands. Did you know, he can—"

"Let's save the stories for later." Rob shot Harry an apologetic look. He didn't want to get distracted, and if left to his own devices, Harry would have the whole team engrossed in seconds. Turning to Trent, he said, "Why don't you tell us about Ian's trip to Oxford?"

The Marlow constable cleared his throat. "Okay. Um . . . there's not much to tell. The receptionist, Emily, confirmed Ian Morris checked into the hotel on the thirteenth of November, and out again on the fourteenth."

"Then his alibi checks out," Jenny confirmed.

"He could have left and driven back to Marlow," Will pointed out.

Trent consulted the notes on his phone. "He did go out again, several times."

They all turned to him.

Head down, he said, "Ian Morris left the hotel at seven thirty or thereabouts, according to the receptionist who saw him go out, and he got back about half past nine."

"What time did Debby leave the party?" asked Jenny.

"Much later," Rob replied. "The pathologist can't give us an accurate time of death, but according to the host, she left the party around midnight. It stands to reason that she was attacked on her way home, when her belongings fell under the park bench. That's the theory we're going with, anyway."

"Well, it looks like Ian was safely tucked up in bed in Oxford at that time." Jenny sat back in her chair and folded her arms.

"I didn't find anything untoward either," added Will, who'd been doing a financial background check. "He's on an average salary and his expenses are steep, especially with the two boys, so there's not much to spare, but he's not in the red. He doesn't have any gambling debts or outstanding loans, other than the mortgage on their house. I can't see any red flags there."

"Did you speak with his mother?"

"Yes, Debby dropped the kids off earlier in the day. It was exactly as Ian said: she kept them overnight, and he collected them the following afternoon."

"Okay, then." Rob turned and drew a line through Ian's name. "It wasn't the husband."

Harry stuck up his hand like he was in class. Rob rolled his eyes, but said, "Yeah?"

"I know this is a moot point, now that we know she was murdered, but I spoke to Debby's GP. The last time she visited the surgery was ten months ago for a persistent cough. He prescribed a course of antibiotics, and she hadn't been back since."

"No history of mental illness, then? Or depression?"

"Nothing like that," Harry confirmed. "When I asked the doctor about it, he seemed surprised. She was a healthy young adult. His words."

"You're right. It's a moot point," Rob said, but he was glad they'd ticked that box. Debby's mental state wasn't in question.

"Celeste, did you run her name through the police database?"

"Yep," the young DC replied. "Debby didn't have any court judgements against her, no outstanding debt and no criminal history. Nothing that would give anyone a reason to want her dead."

"There must be something," muttered Trent. "Sorry," he said when they fell silent. "I just mean, well, obviously *someone* wanted her dead."

Rob gave a grim nod. "You're right. Someone had a motive to kill her. That's what we've got to find. Let's keep digging." He clicked his fingers. "What about that event planner?"

"Chloe Brooke?" Trent looked up.

"Yep, her. We need a list of the guests who were at the party that night. Any one of them could have followed Debby home. Then we need to go and talk to the host, Roman Petrovic."

"If he'll see you," Trent said. "He's notoriously private."

"Oh, he'll see me," Rob replied, eyes narrowing. "He won't have a choice."

* * *

True enough, it took Rob all of five minutes to gain entry to Roman Petrovic's house without a warrant. All he had to do was explain that if the billionaire did not comply, he would get said warrant and an entire army of police officers would descend on the place, mess up the carpeting, destroy the furniture and ransack the house from top to bottom, confiscating all and any computers and digital devices they found.

"I can give you twenty minutes," Petrovic said, in heavily accented English. Tall, dark-haired, with chiselled Slavic features, he exuded barely repressed tension. "Come with me."

They stepped into a vast entrance hall dominated by copies of Old Masters, or maybe they were the real thing, Rob wouldn't know. He felt their eyes on him as he walked into a dimly lit reception room. The windows were covered by heavy silk drapes in a deep burgundy. A soulless steel-and-chrome chandelier hung from the vaulted ceiling, and there were several vases of dark red, almost black, roses positioned around the room.

Petrovic didn't sit down, so neither did they.

"I know you." Petrovic looked past Rob at the young constable, who shuffled uncomfortably. "Have we met before?"

"Yes, sir." Trent stammered. "We spoke last month, after Debby Morris first went missing."

"Ah." Petrovic gave a stiff nod.

"We're now investigating her murder," Rob began. He was glad Petrovic had remembered Trent. It lessened the tension, although the billionaire was still coiled as tightly as a serpent, ready to strike.

"Murder?" he blurted. "I thought she drowned."

"She did, yes, but it wasn't accidental."

Petrovic's right eyebrow arched in surprise. "I did not know."

"It isn't common knowledge yet." But it would be. Soon. Tomorrow, the newspaper headlines would be filled with supposition, conjecture, and meagre bits of information the press had managed to garner from the public, their own unofficial police sources, and social media.

DEBBY MORRIS MURDERED. He could see it now. They'd flesh it out with snippets from her life, her marriage, her kids. Her husband would get the brunt of it. The spouse always did.

Petrovic's dark eyes settled on him. "What do you want to know?"

"Did you speak to Debby Morris at the party?"

"Of course. I spoke to all my guests." He scoffed. "It was my party."

Rob ignored the arrogant tone. "Actually, it was the Lifegiving Foundation's Christmas party, wasn't it?"

The Serb frowned. Rob didn't wait for a reply. "How did Debby Morris seem to you? Was anything bothering her?"

Petrovic shrugged. "How should I know?"

"Did you talk for long?"

"No. Casual chit-chat, that is all."

Rob studied him. His expression never changed. Guarded chocolate eyes, the hint of a furrow in his forehead, arms hanging loosely by his sides. On the surface, he seemed relaxed, but there was no mistaking his inner tension. Either Petrovic was lying, or he was uncomfortable around the police. Probably the latter, if the rumours about how he accumulated his wealth were true.

In the background, they heard a loud grunt, followed by an accompanying moan. Rob raised an eyebrow.

"Tennis," the Serb explained. "Djokovic is playing in Turin. He lost the first set. If we are done here, I'd like to get back to it."

"Almost," he said. Petrovic sighed.

"Did you see Debby talking to anybody else?"

"She spoke to a lot of people. It was a party." The mocking tone was back.

Rob glanced up at the ceiling. He'd seen some surveillance cameras outside on the way in. One at the gate, and another above the front door. He was betting there'd be more dotted around the property. "Do you have any surveillance footage?"

"I do, but before you ask, I'm not giving it to you. I respect the privacy of my guests."

Rob knew the warrant threat wouldn't work twice. Petrovic was well versed in his rights. He'd know they'd never get a warrant for the camera footage without a damn good reason, and there wasn't one. Petrovic had been accommodating, and hadn't given them any reason to doubt anything sinister was going on. Even if his house was creepy as hell.

"What time did Debby leave the party?" Rob tried a different approach.

Petrovic thought for a moment. "Around midnight." His eyes crawled to Trent. "You asked me this before."

"I was here with Weatherby," Trent muttered.

"The fat one." Petrovic uttered a scornful snort. "If we had policemen like that in Serbia, they would be shot."

Rob didn't think he was joking. "You're sure about the time?"

"No, I am not sure, but it was midnight when I noticed she was gone." Disdain dripped off his tongue. "She did not say goodbye." Petrovic wasn't used to being on this side of the table. Barking orders at others was more his style.

"Is that all?"

Applause erupted in the other room.

"That is the game," huffed the Serb.

Rob held up a hand. "That's all for now."

Petrovitch walked them into the hallway, where a young woman stood, her arms full of bright red poinsettia. She was young, early twenties, with long hair tied in a ponytail. She had a plain but friendly face. "Lily will see you out."

Petrovic pirouetted quicker than a ballroom dancer and disappeared back in the direction of the television noise. Lily gave an awkward smile. "Let me get rid of these." She set the pot plant down on a cabinet, then wiped her hands on her jeans. "Sorry about that."

"Is he always that congenial?" Rob grumbled.

She grinned. "He's not as bad as he seems. I'm Lily McIntyre."

Trent rushed forward to open the heavy door. "Let me get that." It was twice her height, and probably weight as well.

She flashed him a smile. "Thanks."

"Did you work the night of the party?" Trent asked, on a whim.

Rob pursed his lips. The young constable was intuitive and went with his instinct. He'd seen an opportunity to question the young woman and taken it.

"I did, yes."

"What was it like?"

"Oh, it was great. A stylish affair, not too big." She lowered her voice. "I was sorry to hear about that woman, though. You know, the one who died? I still can't believe she was attacked after she left here." She shivered.

"How do you know she was attacked?" Rob cut in.

"It's all over Twitter. Apparently, she was hit over the head then pushed into the river." Lily scrunched up her face. "I mean, who would do something like that?"

Rob groaned inwardly. It had begun.

"Did you speak to her?" Trent asked kindly.

"Only because she asked the way to the loo." Lily dropped her voice. "She seemed nice."

When Trent didn't continue with the line of questioning, Rob said, "Did she seem normal to you? Not upset or anything like that?"

Lily thought for a moment. "No, but I'm not sure I would have noticed if she was. I was run off my feet that night."

Fair enough. "Had you ever seen her at the manor house before?"

"You mean before the party?"

He nodded.

"No, never. Mr Petrovic doesn't have a lot of friends. He's a very private man, keeps to himself."

"So we've heard. What is he like to work for?"

"Different." She looked a little self-conscious. "At first he scared me — I mean, he's pretty intimidating — but once I started working here . . ." She shrugged.

"What?" Trent asked.

"As long as I do my job, he leaves me alone. He rarely asks me for anything and spends most of the time in his study or walking around the grounds."

The front of the house overlooked the river, but the back seemed to merge with the surrounding countryside. It was hard to know where his property ended and the meadows began.

"That's when he's not travelling," she added. "It's the easiest job I've ever had, and it pays well, too."

"What is it that you do for him?" Rob asked.

"Housekeeping duties, shopping, watering plants." She nodded towards the poinsettias. "Anything else he asks me to do."

"Cleaning?" Rob asked.

"No, he has a team of cleaners who come in once a week."

"What about the night of the party?"

"The party was organised by an event planner, Chloe Brooke. She's very glam. I met with her, and we arranged the whole thing." She sounded proud of herself. "It's the first party I've ever had a hand in organising, and I think it was a success. Well, apart from what happened afterwards . . . you know?"

Rob nodded. Chloe Brooke was next on his list of people to speak to. "Does your boss have a partner? Girlfriend? Boyfriend?"

She sniggered. "Oh, he's not gay, if that's what you're asking. Haven't you seen the women he dates? He went to a party with Kate Moss last week. I saw the pictures in *Hello*."

That's what Trent had said. Beautiful women. Supermodels, too. "No one in particular, then?"

"Nobody special, no." She lowered her voice. They both leaned in. "I heard his wife died and he's never found anyone to replace her. So romantic, don't you think?"

Trent smiled. Rob frowned. "How did she die?"

"I think it was something to do with her heart, but I'm not sure. It's just what people say."

"Is that why he supports the Lifegiving Foundation?" Trent enquired. Rob glanced at the constable. Another astute comment.

"Could be." Lily shrugged. Clearly her boss's charity work wasn't as interesting as the women he dated. "I'd better get back to work."

"Thanks for your time," Rob said.

She nodded, but her eyes were on Trent. "See you around."

He coloured. "Definitely."

CHAPTER 13

"Nice girl," Rob remarked, as they walked back to the car.

Trent's cheeks were still pink. "Yes, she is."

"Pity about her boss, though. What did you think of him?"

Trent raised his eyebrows, as if surprised Rob would be asking his opinion. "I don't know," he said slowly. "He's got secrets, but I'm not sure he had anything to do with Debby's murder."

That was what Rob had been thinking too. The Serb was as murky as a quagmire, but that didn't mean he was involved with Debby Morris's death. She appeared to be just another guest to him.

"What do you say we kill two birds with one stone and go see Chloe Brooke?"

Bisham, where she was based, was a ten-minute drive from Marlow. They didn't have an appointment, but he liked to surprise people. It kept them on their toes.

"Sure." Trent's grin told Rob he was chuffed at being included.

"Tell me what you know about her." Rob tapped his fingers on the steering wheel. They were waiting in the queue to cross the bridge. Marlow's suspension bridge only allowed one lane of traffic across at a time to prevent undue wear and tear on the structure, so the traffic backed up in both directions, sometimes creating a long tailback. Today, however, wasn't too bad.

"I met her for the first time when Debby went missing, but she didn't know much. Her statement is in one of the reports."

Rob had read it, along with all the other statements from various people with whom Trent had spoken, but it was always useful getting a first-hand account. The queue inched forward. "Did she know Debby?"

"Not well, but she did see her at the party. I don't think they spoke to each other." That was about all that was in the folder.

"What's Chloe like?"

"Efficient. Glamorous. Professional. She plans parties for most of the top businesses and wealthy individuals in the area."

Rob knew Marlow had a few of those. "Did you speak to everybody at the party?"

"Most of them. Chloe didn't get back to me on the guest list, despite several attempts to chase her, but those I did speak to were shocked about what had happened. The strangest thing was, for some reason, nobody remembered seeing her leave."

"Someone must have," Rob muttered, as the car rolled forward.

Trent nodded in agreement. "You'd think so."

It was their turn to cross. They inched through the tight gap and on to the bridge. Rob felt a gentle swaying motion as they eased slowly across. After that, it didn't take long to get to the offices of Frosted Lemons Events.

"Cute place," Trent remarked, as they walked up to the citrus-yellow front door. The quaint cottage Chloe Brooke used as her place of business was painted a fresh white with shutters to match the door. It was getting dark, even though it had just gone four o'clock, and a welcoming golden glow came from inside.

Rob rubbed his bare hands together. He kept forgetting his gloves. A gold plaque on the wall outside had the company name engraved on it, under which was Chloe Brooke's name. A bristly doormat said, *Welcome*. It was all very neat and efficient.

Rob pushed a button and they were buzzed in. A blonde assistant sat at a white table just inside the door, working at a white computer. The decor was clean and minimalist, and Rob was sure he picked up a faint scent of lemons. Was that deliberate, or his imagination? He wasn't sure.

A bright smile. "Can I help you?"

"Yes, we're looking for Chloe Brooke. Is she in?"

"Do you have an appointment?"

Rob held up his ID card. "I'm DCI Miller from the Major Investigation Team. This is Constable Trent from Thames Valley Police. We'd like to talk to her about Debby Morris." He got straight to the point.

The assistant's eyes widened, and she jumped up, nearly knocking the wastepaper basket over in the process. "I'll tell her you're here." Trent stifled a grin.

A short time later, she was back. "You can go in. It's the door at the end."

"Thank you."

Rob strode down the hall, followed by Trent. Opening the door to Chloe's office, he found her standing behind one of those electric desks that went up and down depending on whether you wanted to stand or sit. She was waiting for them.

"Chloe Brooke?"

She came around the desk, her arm extended. Slick, glamorous and meticulously made-up was his first impression. Everything from her hair and make-up to her matching skirt suit and court shoes screamed perfectionism. This was a woman who liked things just so. She paid attention to detail and wouldn't miss a trick.

"Yes, you've found me." Rob shook her outstretched hand, after which she turned to Trent. "Hello again, Constable."

He nodded. "Miss Brooke."

"Please, call me Chloe. Now, how can I help you gentlemen?" She had an easy way about her that put you at ease, no doubt honed through years of dealing with difficult clients. Event planning must come with its fair share of complications.

"We understand you threw a party for the Lifegiving Foundation last month, up at Hollyhock Manor."

She smiled at his choice of words. "Well, I planned it. It was hosted by Dame Constance, of course, and held at Roman Petrovic's place."

"I'm going to need to see a list of everyone who was invited, including the staff who worked the event."

Her gaze drifted from Rob to Trent. "Oh, yes. I remember you asking me for something like that before. I'm sorry, I don't think I ever got back to you." A self-deprecating smile. "It's been crazy around here these last few weeks. The lead-up to Christmas is manic."

The young constable was only slightly mollified.

Rob glanced around her office. It was warm, but not overly so. Just enough to take off the chill. The blinds had been pulled down over the sash windows, shutting out the darkness, and there was a half-drunk mug of something that looked like herbal tea on the desk.

"I'll put that list together and email it to you."

"We'll wait," Rob said. A flicker of annoyance crossed her face, but she hid it with a nod.

"Bear with me." Using the mouse, she clicked a few times, then started typing.

"Did you speak to Debby Morris at the party?" Rob asked, while they waited.

"Why, yes. Of course I knew Debby. Not well, mind you, but as someone to say hello to. She came every year."

"How many years have you been doing it?" Rob watched as she thought about this.

"Four." Her forehead furrowed. "Yep, that's right. It was four years ago that Roman walked into my office and asked for my help." A proud smile.

"He walked in. He didn't phone?"

"Yes. I mean, no." She shook an imaginary hair off her face. "He said I'd been recommended by a friend, and would I be interested in planning the Christmas party at the manor for the foundation. Obviously, I said yes. Roman Petrovic is not the kind of man you refuse."

"Quite," Rob mused. "I didn't know Roman Petrovic had friends."

Chloe smiled. "An acquaintance, then." Rob noted that she didn't dispute the fact.

"What is Roman Petrovic like?"

Chloe hit *Enter* and the printer whirred. "He's a pleasure to work with. I wish all my clients were more like him."

His eyebrows shot up. That was unexpected. "In what way?"

She tapped her finger gently on the keyboard. "He knows what he wants, gives me a brief, and lets me get on with it. There's no nit-picking over small details, no finicky last-minute requests, no complicated menu choices. It's all pretty standard, if expensive, cuisine. I always use the best caterers, the drink is top notch, and he never complains about the budget."

"Sounds like an ideal client."

She arched her brows. "He's a dream. Honestly, you don't know what some people are like. Absolute nightmares."

"I'm sure." He didn't envy her. Mind you, being a detective was no walk in the park either. "Let's get back to Debby," he said. "Did you see her leave the party?"

Chloe thought for a moment. "Actually, no. I can't say that I did. We talked a bit, just general chit-chat, and the last time I saw her, she was talking to that nice Tory MP."

"MP?" Rob frowned. Nobody had mentioned an MP.

"Yes, what's his name? The jolly one." She clicked her fingers. "Sir Ainsworth."

"Right." Rob rubbed his chin. "I didn't realise he was from these parts."

"Oh, yes. He's very popular in this district, especially with the older folk, of which we have a few." The printer spat out a sheet of paper. Chloe handed it to Rob. "There's your list."

He scanned the page, his eyebrows rising. "That's a hell of a guest list."

Chloe shrugged. "It's an important event."

"Staff?"

"I tagged them on the bottom. There were only two servers from the catering company, and a barman I hired separately."

"And Lily," Trent added.

"Oh, yes. But she wasn't affiliated to me. She belongs to Roman."

Belongs. Interesting choice of words.

"Okay, thanks for this." He flicked it with his thumb and forefinger. "We'll be in touch if we have any more questions."

As they walked through the reception area, Chloe's assistant said, "Terrible thing, what happened to Debby."

"Did you know her?" Rob paused at the desk.

"Yeah. Her boys are in my daughter's class at school. We chatted at the school gates sometimes. She was a nice person. I hope you catch whoever killed her."

"We're certainly going to try." Rob glanced down at the sheet in his hand. The guest list was a very good place to start.

CHAPTER 14

Felicity Mayhew studied the names on the whiteboard and gave a low whistle. She was meeting with Assistant Commissioner Matthew Gray this afternoon to bring him up to speed on the investigation, which was why she'd attended this morning's briefing.

DCI Miller's team had thrown themselves into the Debby Morris case, but then she'd expected nothing less. They were the best, even if the powers that be didn't think so. These guys closed cases, although she had to admit, their methods were slightly unorthodox.

When she'd first taken on the Acting Superintendent role, she'd found a team reeling from the loss of their old Superintendent, Sam Lawrence. The loyalty she'd seen then had made her realise the importance of her position, and she tried hard to win them over, but they were stubborn. She still felt like an outsider, eighteen months later.

Fitting in didn't come easy to her. She was ambitious, always had been, which made her come across as aggressive. As a woman, she'd had to work harder and be smarter and more efficient than her male counterparts. Not to get the job — that had become easier since the whole equal opportunity thing, and government institutions were bending over backwards to hire competent women. The hard part was earning their respect. She didn't want to be a token placement. A box the Met had to tick. She wanted to show that a police department with a woman at the helm could get results too.

These last six months fighting to save the department's reputation had been tough. Fighting for her job. Her career. The catastrophic error of judgement on Miller's part had come at the end of a string of complaints, mostly from politicians and wealthy or powerful individuals who didn't take kindly to being suspects in a murder case. But then, the team didn't compromise on their methods. Every suspect was treated the same, whether you were the London mayor or a member of the Secret Service. Felicity respected that.

On the other hand, if you wanted to get ahead, you had to network. It was who you knew. Treating your superiors as murder suspects wasn't going to do you any favours. DCI Miller hadn't learned that lesson yet, or he simply didn't care. She suspected it might be the latter.

She studied him across the table. Fine lines etched around his eyes, greying at the temples, a hardness that hadn't been there before. He'd taken a knock too, but she hoped six months off had given him time to get over it. She needed him. As much as she hated to admit it, her career was tied to his. He got the job done, and that made her look good. Apart from this last debacle, of course.

"You could potentially be stepping on a lot of very powerful toes here," she warned.

"I know." Rob fixed his gaze on her.

"We can't afford any more negative publicity. Please tread carefully." Felicity paused, prodding a name halfway down the list. "Especially with this one."

Sir Leland Ainsworth, MP.

His expression was sincere. "Yes, ma'am." At least he understood how close they'd come.

"Okay, what have you got?" She took a seat at the boardroom table along with the rest of the team, and a young PC from Thames Valley Police who looked about eighteen. He had yet to make eye contact with her.

"Let's start with the founder, Dame Constance Blanchard." Rob glanced down at his notebook. "Former opera singer turned philanthropist after a life-changing operation almost a decade ago."

"What happened?" Felicity asked.

"She had a kidney transplant," Rob said.

"Wow." Felicity raised her eyebrows. "Is that when she started the foundation?"

"It is, yes. The charity has been running for eight years now, and they've held their annual Christmas party — for their most important donors and friends — at Hollyhock Manor for the last four."

"What role did Debby Morris play?" This was one of the questions the Deputy Commissioner would ask her.

"I'll let PC Trent answer that one." Rob nodded at Trent.

The young constable cleared his throat. "Debby Morris was the foundation's treasurer. She dealt directly with the donors. According to her husband, they were both invited every year."

"Except Debby went alone this time," Celeste pointed out. "Because Ian Morris was away."

Rob gave a slow nod. "That's right."

Was there anything in that? Felicity wondered. The first suspect in these types of murders was always the spouse. "Have we looked closely enough at her husband?"

"His alibi checks out," Rob said. That was that. If she wanted more, she'd have to read the report.

"How well did Dame Constance know Debby?" Jenny brought them back to the founder.

"Not very," Trent replied.

Felicity was impressed by how much he contributed to the general discussion. She hated it when newbies sat in silence because they were too intimidated to say anything. The others were warming to him, which was unusual. This team was like a high school clique. They stuck together and didn't take to strangers. So much so that DCI Miller had promoted Celeste, a young DC and general office dogsbody, rather than hire somebody new. Hell, they barely tolerated *her*, and she was their bloody boss.

She studied Trent more closely. He was neatly dressed in the standard police constable uniform of black trousers, white shirt with epaulettes on his shoulders showing his warrant number, black tie, and police hat, which he'd placed on the table beside him. He was good-looking in a young, puppy-dog kind of way, with big brown eyes, long lashes and brown, curly hair cut short.

"The day-to-day running of the foundation was the responsibility of three trustees, along with Debby Morris," the newbie constable was saying. "Dame Constance only went into the office once a month to check things were running smoothly and sign thank-you cards."

"Let's put her on the back burner for now." Rob glanced at Felicity. "We're not dismissing her, but there are more likely suspects to follow up on."

Felicity dragged herself back to the discussion. "Agreed. Leave her till last."

"Okay, well, the first name on the list is Dmitri Krajicek." Jenny's gaze was on the whiteboard.

"Dmitri Krajicek is one of Ukraine's foremost composers," explained Trent.

"How do you know that?" asked Harry, whose eyelashes were almost as long as Trent's.

"I interviewed him after Debby Morris went missing three weeks ago, along with most of the others. Krajicek met Debby at the party. As far as I can tell, they didn't know each other prior to that."

"Krajicek has just purchased a riverside property in Maidenhead," Rob told them. "Two point five mil, if Zoopla is to be believed. He's also composing a piece for the London Philharmonic. They're playing it at the Southbank next week."

Felicity blinked, surprised. She hadn't thought DCI Miller the classical music type.

He caught her eye. "Google."

She masked a smile.

"All right for some," muttered Will.

"If he didn't know her, can we rule him out?" Jenny got up and walked towards the whiteboard.

"For now." Rob gave a curt nod. She crossed his name off the list. "What about his model girlfriend, Zara Rhodes? I presume she didn't know Debby Morris either?" She glanced at Trent, who nodded.

"What about Angelo Marcossi?" Jenny stabbed at his name with the marker. "Isn't he that Italian fashion designer? Does the long, floaty stuff."

Felicity rather liked his collection — in fact, she had one of his pieces at home, a flowy aquamarine caftan — but then she was interested in fashion, unlike DS Bird, who usually wore black trousers and a mannish shirt that did absolutely nothing for her figure. Even Jenny's shoes were flat and clunky. This was a woman who lived for the job. Felicity had never seen her with a boyfriend — or a girlfriend, for that matter. *None of my business,* she thought, and turned back to what Rob was saying.

"That's him," Rob confirmed. "And that's his boyfriend, Ansel. He's Dutch, and they got off a plane the morning of the party, so they didn't know Debby Morris. We can rule them out."

"Good," Felicity murmured as Jenny drew a line through their names, too. "What about Sir Ainsworth?" Political figures, MPs in particular, hated being involved in any form of scandal or police investigation and they could make life extremely difficult for you if you caught them on a bad day.

"The MP for Beaconsfield," Trent said. "He's based at Westminster, but goes back to his country estate in Marlow for the weekends."

Harry snorted. "Did he know Debby?"

"When I interviewed him, he told me that he'd spoken to her during the course of the evening," Trent said. "But didn't remember seeing her leave."

"I'm meeting with him this morning." Rob glanced across at her. "We can probably rule him out, but I want to make sure first."

"He stays on the list." Jenny stepped away from the board.

Pity, thought Felicity.

"Who are those people?" She squinted at the next three names, not recognising any of them.

Rob gestured for Trent to explain. The newbie turned towards Felicity, making tentative eye contact with her for the first time. "They're the trustees, ma'am. Agatha Roundtree worked with Debby, as did the other two, Silvia Peacock and Greg Jamieson. The four of them basically ran the charity."

Jenny was nodding. "So we leave them on the list?"

"Actually, no," continued Trent.

Felicity raised an eyebrow. "Why's that?"

"Greg Jamieson and his new wife, Beccy, attended the party, but they'd just got back from their honeymoon in the Caribbean. When I questioned him, Greg was upset about Debby's disappearance, but he hadn't seen her for three weeks prior to the party, and Beccy had only met her once or twice at the pub. I don't think he had any motive to murder her."

"What about Silvia Peacock?" Rob asked.

"She's just had a hip replacement, so was out of action the month before the party. In fact, she attended on crutches."

"Definitely cross her off, then." Jenny blew a stray hair out of her face. "No way she could have done it on crutches."

Felicity tended to agree. "We can always revisit them later, if needs be," she added.

"Who's next?" Harry scanned the board. "Zeke Hamlin. That's quite a name."

"He's a pianist," said Rob. "Apparently, he was something of a child prodigy."

Harry scoffed. "Figures, with a name like that."

"Except he's in his twenties and playing random gigs," Will pointed out.

"Is he short of cash?" Felicity wondered.

"Possibly, although he's a student at the Royal Academy of Music. That's not cheap." Rob rubbed his chin.

"Could he have got a scholarship?"

"I'll look into it." Jenny made a note on her iPad.

"Is there anyone else?" Felicity asked. They'd got to the end of the official guest list.

"There's Lily, Roman Petrovic's housekeeper." Rob took the marker from Jenny and wrote Lily's name on the board. "She helped at the party."

"What about Roman Petrovic himself?" Felicity frowned. The name sounded vaguely familiar, but she couldn't place it. "He owns the manor house, right? What's it called again?"

"Hollyhock Manor," Rob said. "It might sound grand, but it's a creepy stone mansion set back from the river. There are surveillance cameras all over the place, and I definitely saw at least one guard patrolling the grounds. Petrovic is a shady character, all right."

"Russian?" she guessed.

"Serbian. No one knows how he made his money, but the rumour is it's from arms dealing. He's one of the charity's biggest supporters, which is why he hosts the annual Christmas party."

"Why does he care so much?" Felicity was intrigued.

"Lily, the housekeeper, thought it had something to do with his late wife." Rob paged through his notebook. "I looked her up last night. Her name was Nina Petrovic. She had something called hypertrophic cardiomyopathy and was on the waiting list for a transplant. Unfortunately, she died before they could find a donor."

"Ah, I get it," Felicity mused.

"He's been a patron ever since."

"Okay, great." She smiled around the group, but only got a few nods and a grimace in return. "You've got a lot to be getting on with, so I'll leave you to it. Keep me posted on your progress." She glanced at Trent. "It's good having you on the team, Constable."

Trent flashed her a shy smile. "Thank you, ma'am."

Felicity left them to sort out who would question who and went back to her office. There was some paperwork she had to do before catching an Uber to Victoria Embankment, where she was meeting the man she answered to, Assistant Commissioner Matthew Gray. Sadly, their budget didn't extend to black cabs anymore.

An hour later, through the glass walls of her office, she saw DCI Miller come out of the incident room. He was wearing his long winter coat and feeling in his pockets for his keys. Felicity grabbed her briefcase and charged after him. "DCI Miller."

He turned, albeit rather reluctantly.

"You heading to Westminster?"

"Yeah, I've got a two o'clock appointment with Sir Ainsworth."

"I'm not telling you how to do your job," she began, and immediately saw him stiffen, but she pushed on. "Please tread lightly on this one. The last thing we need is for Westminster to get the hump with us. It's not going to take much . . ." She didn't finish.

He nodded, and his tone softened. Miller was intuitive, and he knew the stress she, and the department, had been under since his suspension. The threat of closure was real. "I know. Don't worry. Sir Ainsworth seemed amiable on the phone." However, he hadn't experienced Miller's sharp tongue and steely glare yet.

He must have clocked her nervous look, because he said, "I'll go easy on him. I'm not going to rock the boat any more than I have already."

She exhaled, relieved, and watched as he shot her a parting nod and took the stairs. She waited for the elevator. Their careers depended on a successful conclusion of this investigation. They had to find Debby Morris's murderer, and they had to get it right the first time. There was no room for error. The Police Commissioner, heavily influenced by the Assistant Commissioner and Mayor Raza Ashraf, was waiting for them to screw up, and she'd be damned if she was going to let that happen.

"Not on my watch," she muttered to herself, as the doors pinged open.

CHAPTER 15

"I don't have long," Sir Ainsworth said as he crushed Rob's hand in his beefy one. They'd met outside the House of Commons on Westminster Bridge Road, which was crowded with die-hard tourists and harassed parliamentary workers. "Do you mind if we grab something to eat while we talk? I'm famished."

"Of course." Rob looked around but saw nothing but black taxis, London buses and people. He had no idea where to go for lunch. Did the MP want a sandwich bar or something posher? Takeaway or eat in?

"There's a rather good coffee shop around the corner," he said, saving Rob from having to make a suggestion. "Follow me." The MP strode off, his long coat billowing out around his ankles as he walked.

Leland Ainsworth was a tall, robust man with a ruddy face, a trim beard and a belly that hinted at too much of the good life. He had a loud voice that rose above the din of the traffic, probably honed from years of projecting from the back benches. He was especially fond of campaigning against the extra runway at Heathrow, or for increased protection of the green belt, both issues dear to his constituents' hearts.

"Goddamn awful thing finding her body like that," he said, once they'd ordered and sat down. "She was a lovely woman. Very bright, if I remember correctly."

"You knew her well?"

"Not well, no. But I knew her."

"Did you speak to her at the party?"

"Oh, yes. We had a rather enlightening discussion about organ donation. Did you know that most people wait an average of three to five years for an organ?" He shook his head. "It's a bloody tragedy." Rob wasn't sure if he meant the waiting times or what had happened to Debby.

Sir Ainsworth picked up his baguette. "Do you know who killed her?"

"Not yet." Rob had to admit the baguette looked damn good, but he couldn't eat and interrogate a suspect at the same time.

"I'm happy to help in any way I can." He took a monstrous bite.

While he chewed, Rob got up to collect their coffees. Back at the table, he asked, "Do you recall what time it was you spoke to Debby?"

"Not precisely, I'm afraid, but it was somewhere in the middle of the evening. We were standing by the canapés when she came up to me and thanked me for my support. The Lifegiving Foundation was our selected charity last month."

"What does that mean?" asked Rob. "Your selected charity."

Sir Ainsworth chewed, swallowed, then reached for his Americano. "Every month, we select a charity to promote. I introduce the founder at a charity evening at the Town Hall; they give a speech and raise awareness in the constituency. They also get a small donation from the council. It's a good thing."

Rob didn't doubt it.

"Who spoke on behalf of the charity? Was it Dame Constance Blanchard?"

"Yes. What a fabulous woman. Terrific voice. I heard her sing once at the Royal Albert Hall." He scoffed. "Decades ago, now." Rob remembered she'd been an opera singer before becoming a philanthropist.

"Did Debby Morris seem upset to you?" Rob asked.

"Good Lord, no. She was in good spirits. It was a fun party, but then Roman's always are."

"You've been to one of his parties before, have you?"

He paused, baguette in the air. "We had my re-election celebrations at the manor house last year. Didn't I say?"

"No, you didn't."

Ainsworth gave a nonchalant shrug. "I consider Roman a friend, as well as a supporter of the Conservative Party."

"Roman Petrovic supports a lot of different organisations."

A sharp look. "He's a caring constituent."

"I'm sure he is. Okay, let's get back to Debby Morris. Did you notice her talking to anyone else that night?"

"Plenty of people. It was a small, intimate gathering and the guests were there to have a good time. I went as Father Christmas." He gave a very realistic *ho-ho-ho*. "It seemed most appropriate." Looking at him, Rob had to agree. He'd make a great Santa.

"Did you see her talking to anyone in particular?" pressed Rob. He was beginning to fear this was a waste of time.

Ainsworth thought for a moment. "After I spoke to her, that Assistant Commissioner chap came up and introduced himself. We had a short discussion, but then I left them to it."

Rob frowned. He didn't remember seeing an assistant commissioner on Chloe Brooke's list. "What sort of assistant commissioner?"

"From the Met, man. Your lot."

Rob's eyes widened.

Shit. The *Assistant Commissioner?*

Now he was definitely interested. "Matthew Gray was at the party?"

"That's what I'm telling you, yes." Sir Ainsworth frowned and scratched his head. "Although, I always thought his wife was a blonde."

* * *

Rob called Chloe on the way back to Putney. It rang for some time before the assistant answered. "Frosted Lemons Events; how can I help you?"

"This is DCI Miller. I'd like to speak to Chloe Brooke, please."

A slight pause. "One moment, Detective Chief Inspector." He was left hanging for about three minutes while the assistant transferred the call and, no doubt, warned Chloe about who was on the line. Rob would have much preferred visiting in person, but didn't have time to get out to Bisham today.

"Hello, DCI Miller. How can I help?"

"Chloe, you can tell me why you left Assistant Commissioner Matthew Gray off the guest list." And therefore, the suspect list.

"Oh, did I?" She sounded surprised.

"Yes, you did. I believe he was at the party?"

"That's right, he was. How silly of me!"

He frowned. Was she telling the truth? Was this a genuine mistake? "Was there a reason you failed to mention him?" he pressed.

"Not at all. It simply escaped my mind. I apologise. Things have been crazy around here, and I thought I'd listed everybody, but obviously not."

He hesitated. "Okay, thank you, Chloe. I'll be in touch."

* * *

"Did she say why she'd left him off?" Jenny wanted to know once he got back to the office.

Rob shook his head. "Claims it was an honest mistake."

"Do you believe her?"

"I'm not sure. Maybe."

Jenny groaned. "Mayhew is going to love this."

Rob rolled his eyes. It was bad enough that Sir Ainsworth was on the list, but her direct boss, Matthew Gray . . . That was tricky.

"Where is she?" He perched on the end of his desk and gazed across the squad room. Her office was empty. "I'd better tell her."

"Head office," Jenny said. "In fact, I think she's meeting with Gray this afternoon." She raised her eyebrows. "Are you going to tell her now, before she meets him?"

Rob pondered this. "It might not be a bad idea. Firstly, she's not here to yell at me, and secondly, she can gauge Gray's reaction. If he mentions the party, which he ought to do, of course, he's on the level. If he doesn't, well . . . that gives us something to think about."

"Doesn't necessarily mean he's got anything to hide," Jenny pointed out.

"Doesn't it?" Rob's stomach gave a loud rumble.

Jenny tutted. "When did you last eat something, guv?"

"Can't remember." Lack of food was making him grumpy.

"The canteen has sandwiches, you know."

He nodded, still thinking about Mayhew and Matthew Gray.

Jenny sighed. "He might just be trying to distance himself. The Assistant Commissioner of the London Metropolitan Police Force wouldn't want it to come out that he was at a party where one of the guests turned up dead. Doesn't look good. Questions will be asked."

She was right. Questions like: Was someone at the party responsible? Had he been socialising with a killer? It could get ugly.

Rob made a decision. "I'm going to give her a call."

"Go get some food while you're at it," Jenny coaxed.

Rob walked towards the elevator. "Okay, I'm going." He held up his phone. "Wish me luck."

CHAPTER 16

Mayhew had just climbed out of the Uber when her phone buzzed. She reached into her bag and pulled it out.

DCI Miller.

Frowning, she answered it. What could he want? She'd only just spoken to him. "Miller? I'm at Scotland Yard. Is this urgent?"

"It is, ma'am. I think you're going to want to hear this."

She stopped walking. The two armed guards outside the entrance eyed her, but she turned around and walked into the small public garden outside before replying. "What is it?"

"Matthew Gray was at the Christmas party in Marlow the night Debby Morris disappeared."

Felicity felt the ground tilt a little under her feet. Reaching out for a nearby bench, she sat down. The bronze statue of Lord Trenchard, Marshal of the Royal Air Force, stared nobly down at her. "Are you sure?"

"A hundred per cent, ma'am. Sir Ainsworth mentioned it and I've just confirmed it with Chloe Brooke, the event planner. She forgot to add him to the guest list she sent us."

"Is he a suspect?" Her voice was a whisper.

"Not yet, but you might want to see if he mentions it without being prompted."

DCI Miller was wily; she'd give him that much. She understood what he meant. Update Gray on the Debby Morris case and see if he offered up the information. If not, she'd have to confront him with it.

She gazed up at the statue. *Do the right thing,* it seemed to be urging her. The right thing, however, made her day a lot more complicated. "Okay, thanks for letting me know."

After showing her Met Police ID to the guards, and going through a security monitor, she was allowed inside the classical stone-fronted building that housed New Scotland Yard. The Assistant Commissioner's office was on the third floor, facing the river. His view was rivalled only by the Commissioner's himself, who had the office directly above.

How nice to gaze out over the restless Thames every day, Felicity thought wistfully as she waited for the elevator. Her office overlooked Putney High Street, which didn't come close to Victoria Embankment. Her desk, however, faced the bullpen. She liked glancing up occasionally and seeing her teams at work. Queen Bee in a hive of workers.

Felicity was a control freak; she knew that. Delegating was hard for her, but she satisfied the compulsion by knowing what was going on with all three of her murder squads. Miller, Galbraith and now Linden. Three solid DCIs. Three great teams. She'd learned a long time ago that in order to succeed, she had to surround herself with good people. A rising tide and all that. As Superintendent of the Putney department, she felt she had found that and was determined not to lose it.

DCI Miller kept her on her toes. There were times when she knew he was withholding information. Whether he eventually told her or not depended on the outcome of the case and his mood at the time. She'd learned to trust his judgement over the last year and a half, but this recent case had shaken her faith in him. Like the wife of a cheating husband, she had become super vigilant, something she did not enjoy. It was a step too far, even for her. Trust was everything in this job. You had to trust your team.

The elevator pinged open, and Felicity stepped out on to a carpeted landing. Directly in front of her was a reception desk with a mature woman in her fifties sitting behind a computer.

"Good afternoon, Ellie."

The Assistant Commissioner's executive assistant smiled. "Hello, Felicity. Matthew's not quite ready for you yet. Do you want to take a seat? I'll let him know you're here."

"Thank you."

Felicity eased down on a leather couch, but she was too uptight to relax. She knew Ellie fairly well, having been reporting to Matthew Gray for the last year and a half, ever since she'd taken the job of Acting Superintendent of the Major Investigation Team. Now Superintendent, she had weekly briefings at Scotland Yard. Sometimes the Commissioner sat in on their meetings too, which always gave her a kick. Although recently, it had only been to voice his displeasure at the way the Soho case was handled.

Taking a deep breath, Felicity took out her compact and checked that the lipstick she'd applied in the Uber wasn't all over her teeth, then she perused the folder in her lap. With a suspect list including a dame, an MP, minor celebrities, artists and arms dealers, the department had their hands full. There was no way this was going to be kept on the downlow. The media would be all over it like flies on—

"He's ready for you now." Ellie stood up. "If you come this way, I'll show you in."

Protocol. Felicity knew the way to Matthew Gray's office blindfolded, she'd done it so often. Still, his EA led her down the plush corridor with its recessed lighting and cream walls, to the end office. She knocked on the door.

"Come," intoned a voice.

Ellie pushed it open. "Superintendent Felicity Mayhew, sir."

"Thank you."

Ellie stood back to let her enter. The routine never changed, but that was government for you. It had to be by the book.

"Assistant Commissioner." Felicity broke into a smile as she entered, her heels sinking into the deep-pile carpeting.

He didn't get up. Instead, he waved to the chair opposite. "Felicity, please take a seat."

Behind him, through the window, dark clouds were gathering. It looked like it was going to bucket down. Felicity sat. A frisson of nervous excitement made her shiver. It had been a while since she'd done any interrogating. She'd forgotten what it felt like to face a potential suspect, trying to outmanoeuvre them.

"How have you been?"

"Good, thank you. Yourself?"

"You know." He nodded to the pile of paperwork on his desk.

She returned a sympathetic smile. "Tell me about it." Driving a desk wasn't a fun job, but it paid better than doing actual police work. One of life's little ironies. The higher you got, the less you did.

"Your team behaving themselves?" It was a fair question, considering what had happened.

"So far." She smiled, genuine this time. "We're neck deep in the Debby Morris investigation."

"Ah, yes. Debby Morris. She's caused such a stir. Chief Superintendent Wallace is up in arms about the pictures of her body being removed from the river plastered all over social media. We're looking into that, by the way. We're tracking down the culprit, and I'm thinking about charging them with interfering with a police investigation. It's not on."

It was what it was. Masking it wouldn't change anything. "That's social media for you," she said with a wry grin. "Nothing's sacred anymore."

"True." He sat back and studied her. "So, what have you got for me?"

"We've been given a list of guests who were at the party the night Debby Morris disappeared," she began, watching him for a reaction. He didn't so much as twitch.

"Any leads?"

"Not yet. My guys are looking into it. The preliminary post-mortem report showed evidence of blunt force trauma to her head."

He leaned forward. "She was attacked before she drowned?"

"Yes, sir. It looks like it. There are also bruises on her back where she was held down under the water."

"Jesus." He shook his head.

Still nothing.

Felicity took a deep breath. "I was wondering if you noticed anything unusual, sir."

"Excuse me?" He frowned.

"You know, at the party."

There was a long pause, then the Assistant Commissioner cleared his throat. "Um, no. I'm afraid I didn't notice anything strange at the . . ." He stopped. "How did you know I was there?"

"Sir Ainsworth mentioned it. Chloe Brooke, the event planner, mistakenly left you off the list of guests that she gave us."

He looked annoyed. "Did she now?"

"I don't suppose you spoke to Debby Morris at all?" Felicity kept her voice casual. "It would really help if you could give us your professional opinion on her state of mind that night."

Matthew Gray sat up straight and puffed out his chest. She'd given him a chance to save face, and he was going to take it. "I only spoke to her very briefly," he said. "It was shortly after I arrived. Agatha Roundtree, who I was at Oxford with, introduced us."

Felicity felt a surge of relief. "So, you didn't know her prior to the party?"

He shook his head. "Never set eyes on her before. Nice lady, though. Such a tragic turn of events."

"Was she upset or angry when you spoke to her?" Felicity asked, the interrogation techniques coming back to her. Body language, read the room, look for visual cues. Her instructor at the police academy had told her she was a natural, but then she'd always found it easy to manipulate people.

"Not when I spoke to her," he replied, "but it was the start of the evening."

"You didn't speak to her again?"

"No, I didn't." He hesitated. "Felicity . . ." It wasn't often he called her that. "Can I be blunt?"

"Please do. You know I always appreciate your candour."

"I asked Chloe Brooke to keep my name off that list," he said slowly.

"You did? Why?"

"Because I wasn't there with my wife."

Felicity stared at him, momentarily stunned. "I see."

She didn't. How could he be so stupid?

"If Rachael was to find out . . ." He broke off. "Well, you can imagine."

"Indeed." Rachael Gray, or Rachael Huntington-Gray, as she was formally known, was the daughter of Lord William Huntington and heir to a substantial fortune. Felicity shifted in her chair. She'd never felt so uncomfortable in her life.

"Can I count on your discretion?" He fixed his gaze on her.

"Of course." What else could she say? He might be a cheating bastard, but he was still her boss. Her direct supervisor, at that. "It won't go any further," she promised, but hated herself for saying it.

"Thank you, Felicity. I consider this a great personal favour. It won't be forgotten."

There was that, at least. God knew she might need his help one day. She got to her feet. "I'd better be going."

"You're a good officer, Mayhew. You've got a bright future ahead."

She smiled. It hurt her cheeks. "Thank you, sir."

She smiled at Ellie, and again at the guards as she left. Deciding not to catch an Uber back to Putney but instead take the ferry, she walked down on to the wooden pontoon.

The water smacked against the underside of the jetty, while the cold air pricked at her face, making her eyes sting. She was one of a handful of commuters, waiting for the boat to pull up at the dock.

Felicity stood to one side, enjoying the icy tentacles as they clawed at her skin. At least she didn't have to smile out here. Nobody in their right mind would smile in this weather. She pulled her coat around her and stared into the murky depths of the Thames.

Secrets.

Everybody had secrets.

CHAPTER 17

Rob got back to the office to find the rest of the team hunched over Harry's desk. "What's going on?"

Jenny glanced up. "Harry was looking into Chloe Brooke, and you'll never guess who she hosted a party for last summer."

"Who?"

"Dream Designs."

He scowled, remembering. "Isn't that the firm Ian Morris works for?"

"Correct." Her eyes were shining.

Rob thumped Harry on the back. "Good work, DS Malhotra."

"Neither of them mentioned anything about it in their previous statements," she added. "I've just been through them again."

"Where is Trent?" Rob asked.

"He's gone back to Marlow," Jenny said. "He wasn't sure if you wanted him to stick around."

Rob tsked. He'd assumed Trent would stay, but hadn't made it clear. That was his fault. "Well, since he's out there, he can come with me to talk to Ian Morris."

"Guv, I've also found something," Will said, from his desk. They turned to face him. "I've been looking at Ian

Morris's phone records, and he had several incoming calls from Chloe Brooke around the time of last summer's party."

"That makes sense," said Rob. "They were probably discussing the arrangements."

"They carried on for a while afterwards." Will glanced back at his screen. "She called him every day for weeks after the party."

"Any messages?" It was often easier to see what was going on from text messages these days. Young people barely picked up the phone and spoke to each other anymore.

"No. I'm thinking they were using WhatsApp, as it's encrypted." Using the app meant no one, not even WhatsApp itself, could read messages sent on its platform. "They don't store messages, nor do they keep transcripts of them."

Damn. Rob flexed his jaw as he paced up and down. "Okay, we need to speak to them about this, but separately."

"You want me to talk to Chloe?" Jenny volunteered.

Rob decided to revise his previous suggestion. "I think you and I should talk to Ian Morris. He'll be the tougher nut to crack. We'll get Trent to talk to Chloe. Will, stay on the phone data. I want to see Chloe's call logs, too." The techie nodded.

Rob turned back to Harry. "Are you and Celeste still looking into the other guests?" He'd asked them to run background checks on everybody at the party, regardless of whether they knew Debby Morris or not.

"Yep, I've found a few things, but nothing major."

"Like what?"

"Agatha Roundtree, one of the trustees, was arrested when she was eighteen for a drunk driving incident."

"Oh, really? Anyone injured?"

"No. She drove her car into a bollard coming off Hammersmith Bridge. You know how tiny those gaps are?" Everyone who'd ever driven over Hammersmith Bridge knew how hard it was to squeeze a decent-sized vehicle through without scraping it on one side or both. He nodded.

"Anyway, she had to pay a fine, plus damages, and got six points on her licence."

"No jail time?"

"Nope."

Rob shrugged. "Probably not important. Anything else?"

"Not as yet. I'll keep digging."

He nodded to Jenny. "Right, let's get going. We've got a suspect to interview."

* * *

Ian Morris looked suitably guilty, but put up a good defence. "So what? Chloe organised our company's tenth anniversary bash. It's no big deal." They were standing in his second-floor studio in Marlow, just off the high street. Situated above an off-licence, it consisted of a small outer office and two larger studios which would have once been bedrooms. Ian's partner was out, and the assistant was apparently off sick today, so Ian was there alone.

Rob cut to the chase. "It is, if you were having an affair." Jenny glanced across at him, surprised by his direct approach, but Rob wasn't in the mood for subtle. This guy had lied to him and wasted his time. He didn't appreciate either of those two things.

Ian's pupils dilated. "We were not having an affair."

"Your phone data begs to differ." Rob placed the sheets of paper on the drafting table in front of him. Lines and lines of highlighted rows. "And those are just the phone calls. Don't get me started on the texts."

Ian swallowed. He probably didn't know they couldn't get hold of the WhatsApp messages.

"Shall I read some of them?" Rob opened the folder he was carrying and glanced down. Jenny peered over his shoulder.

"Okay, okay." Ian held up his hands. "We slept together, but it was only a couple of times. It was a mistake, okay? I ended it after a few weeks."

Rob glanced down at his notes. "Seven weeks, to be exact."

Ian coloured. "She kept trying to contact me after I'd ended it."

That much, at least, appeared to be true. Will had sent over Chloe's call logs on the way to Marlow, and her last flurry of calls had gone unanswered.

"Did Debby see them?"

"God, no." Ian paled. "I ended up blocking Chloe's number, so they didn't come in. The things she was saying." He shook his head.

"Like what?" asked Jenny.

"Well, you know . . ." He glanced at the folder.

"We'd like to hear you explain them in your own words," she said.

He sighed. "Why does any of this matter? Debby's dead. She isn't coming back."

"I know, but in order to find out who killed her, we need to know what your relationship with Chloe was like."

He gasped. "You don't think Chloe—"

"We don't think anything at this stage," Rob explained, as patiently as he could. "We're still gathering all the facts."

"Oh, okay." Ian exhaled, relieved. "Well, she kept saying she missed me, that we were meant to be together, that I should end my relationship with Debby."

"She actually said that?" Jenny glanced at Rob. "That you should end it with your wife?"

"Yes. I told her the whole thing was a mistake and I loved my family, but she said I was fooling myself. What we had was special. A once-in-a-lifetime love. That sort of crap."

"You obviously didn't feel the same way?" Jenny tilted an eyebrow.

"No, of course not. I never meant to . . ." He hung his head. "Debby and I were having some problems. I was stupid, and I regret it now."

"What problems?" asked Rob.

"That's private."

"Not anymore. Not if it pertains to Debby's murder."

"It doesn't."

Jenny turned to Rob. "Maybe we should take him down to the station and discuss this more formally?"

Rob pretended to think about it.

"Okay, for God's sake!" Ian exploded. "I was trying to protect her dignity. Debby loved her job, but it took up a lot of her time, and the twins are hard work. She lost interest in sex. We hadn't been intimate in months."

"Did you talk about it?" Rob asked.

"I tried, but you can't force these things."

That much was true.

He looked forlorn. "I tried to talk to her about it, I swear I did, but she clammed up. I was feeling lost, and so the night of our company party, I had a bit too much to drink and blurted everything out to Chloe."

Rob could understand how that might happen. Ian had been lonely, unable to talk to his wife about their intimacy problems, and Chloe would have been a caring listener.

"Do you think Chloe told Debby about your affair?" Rob asked. Both women had been at the Christmas party, one organising it, the other a guest. Their paths would definitely have crossed.

"I-I don't think so." He gnawed on his lip. "I bloody hope not."

"Say she had," Rob speculated. "How would Debby react?"

He hung his head. "I honestly don't know. I felt like . . . I felt like I was losing her."

Rob felt a pang of sympathy for Ian Morris, even though he was the one who'd been unfaithful. If Debby had been able to talk to him about their problems, this might not have happened.

"Okay, thanks for talking with us." He tied up the interview. "Once again, we're very sorry for your loss." It wasn't just Debby's death he was talking about. It was everything. The breakdown in their relationship, the inability of his wife to open up, and finally her murder. A downward spiral that ended in disaster.

Once they got outside, Rob turned to Jenny. "Let's see how Trent's getting on with Chloe."

CHAPTER 18

PC Trent pulled up outside Chloe Brooke's house. He'd gone to her office first, but her assistant had said she was working from home today, as there was a function tonight.

The modest bungalow was located behind Great Marlow School, off Little Marlow Road. In summer, this area was leafy and green, with birds chirping in the trees and kids hanging out after school, but right now, it was barren and stark. Nobody wanted to hang around outside in the frigid temperature.

It was late afternoon, and the lacklustre sun was beginning to sink, giving up on a day that hadn't given it an opportunity to shine. Dark clouds were already moving in, bringing a damp heaviness with them.

Beside the house was a short driveway, but Chloe's racing-green Mini was parked in it, and behind that, a white transit van with a Frosted Lemons decal on the side. Trent parked on the street.

DCI Miller had been fairly specific: push her about her affair with Ian Morris. Find out why it ended, and if there was any lingering resentment.

Wow. An affair. Trent hadn't seen that one coming. Chloe Brooke was a glamorous event planner, vibrant and extroverted, while Ian struck him as a quiet creative, hard-working and committed to his family. Who would have thought they'd end up together?

As he got out of the patrol vehicle, a worried-looking couple came running up the driveway.

"Can I help you?" he asked.

"Has something happened?" the woman asked.

Trent frowned. "Why d'you ask?"

"We heard screaming," the man said. "We thought it might be Chloe, so we rushed over."

"We're her neighbours," the woman added.

Trent sprang into action. "Stand back." He raced up to the front door. Pushing the buzzer, he called, "Miss Brooke? It's the police."

There was no answer, so he tried the door. Locked.

"Miss Brooke, don't be alarmed. I'm coming in." He stood back, surveyed the door, then gave it a firm kick with his steel-toed shoe. The flimsy lock gave out and the door swung open.

"Miss Brooke?"

Still no answer.

"Chloe? Are you home?"

There was a scraping sound and a loud bang. It was coming from inside the house. What the hell was going on? He moved down the hall. "Chloe?"

A screech of tyres behind him made him turn. Seconds later, DCI Miller and DS Jenny Bird entered the house.

"What's going on?" DCI Miller demanded.

Trent didn't mince his words. "Neighbours heard screaming."

They proceeded gingerly, truncheons in hand. Trent, his heart thumping, proceeded down the hallway to the kitchen, while DS Bird broke off into one of the bedrooms and DCI Miller took another.

"Clear," DS Bird shouted.

"Clear," came DCI Miller's deep voice.

Trent rounded the corner into the kitchen and came to a halt. "Oh Jesus," he muttered, before his knees gave way and he fainted.

* * *

Rob heard the crash as Trent hit the floor.

What the hell?

"Jenny!" He raced down the corridor.

"What happened?" She came out of the bedroom.

"He passed out." Rob stepped around the dazed police officer, as Jenny bent down to make sure Trent was all right. The young constable stirred.

Rob entered the kitchen and froze.

Please, no.

Chloe Brooke lay on the floor, blood running down her neck, soaking her cream silk blouse. It pooled under her on the terracotta tiles. Her throat had been cut, the wound glistening in a macabre grin.

"Chloe!"

The world began to spin. It was suddenly difficult to breathe. Rob stumbled forward towards the woman on the floor, dropped to his knees and put his hands over the gash to stem the blood. He couldn't feel a pulse.

"What is it?" Jenny took one look at Chloe's body and her hand flew to her mouth. "Oh God. Is she . . . ?"

Rob, still kneeling beside the body, gave a weak nod. "We're too late."

"Fuck!" Jenny pulled out her phone and dialled 999.

Trent, who'd regained consciousness, got unsteadily to his feet. "Sorry about that. I've never fainted before."

Rob barely heard him, or Jenny as she spoke to the emergency operator. It was all white noise, roaring in his head, just like when Jo had been attacked. Another kitchen. Another woman with her throat slashed.

Get a grip!

This was not Jo. This was Chloe.

Not. Jo.

He tried to slow his breathing. In through the nose, out through the mouth, like the police therapist had told him. Repeat. Slow it down. There was so much blood. He glanced at his hands, sticky with it. A wave of nausea hit him, and he began to gag.

Jenny took one look at his face and hauled him to his feet. "Get away from the body, guv."

"I'm okay," he rasped, but let her lead him to the sink.

"Wash your hands." Her voice was gentle, yet firm. "Have some water."

Gulping down air, he focused on the task in front of him. Turn on the tap. Soap. Rinse. By the time he was done, he felt marginally better. The noise in his head had gone.

"Who on earth would do this?" Jenny looked around. "There's no knife, he must have taken it with him." Rob felt an icy draft and realised the back door was open.

"He left this way," Trent said. "I heard it banging as I came in."

"It must have just happened." Jenny's gaze dropped to the woman on the floor. "Seconds before we got here."

"He could still be in the vicinity," Rob said.

Trent darted towards the door. "I'll go. I might still be able to spot him." Before either of them could say anything, Trent had charged out of the kitchen and across the back lawn.

CHAPTER 19

PC Trent sped out into the garden. A fence on either side separated the property from the neighbours, but it was too high to climb over, so the killer must have gone out the back gate situated at the end of the garden.

Trent raced across a leaf-strewn lawn in dire need of mowing and over a flower bed brimming with weeds, until he got to the gate. It was ajar, but the bottom edge was stuck on a jutting paving stone. With a heave, he pulled it free and burst out into a park about an acre across. Empty, with threadbare trees dotted haphazardly over it, it didn't look like it could hide anyone, and yet Trent couldn't spot the killer.

Wait. He squinted across the park.

There!

At the far end, he saw a figure in black running like the clappers. That must be him. That must be Chloe's killer.

Adrenalin pumping, Trent sprinted after the man in black. He zigzagged through the trees, feeling the grass give beneath his feet. It was wet and soggy, and would become more so once the rain started. Even as he ran, he felt a few spits on his face. Any moment now.

He leaped over a dead rose bush, around an ancient oak, its trunk wider than his kitchen table, and continued after the fleeing man. A low stone wall marked the end of the park, and the man disappeared through it.

Come on . . .

Trent charged through the gap and found himself in a wide, open meadow with long grass the colour of pinewood. He looked around, breathing heavily. Where the hell did he go?

Straining his eyes, he spotted a black speck on the southern side, heading toward the river. Yes! That was him. Maybe he could catch him.

Trent took off again, his arms pumping as he ran, his breath evenly paced. He'd been a good sprinter at school — fast, with stamina; he outran most of the boys in his year at sports day. This was no different. He was back on the school pitch, tearing down the track. That medal was his.

Trent could see the man better now. A dark hoodie hid his face, but he was about the same height and build as DCI Miller, with long legs that sent him leaping like a gazelle over small bushes.

Where was the guy going? Did he even know, or was he just running blind, hoping to get away in the fading light? It was nearly dark now, and only the straw-coloured heath made the man in black visible. Another ten minutes or so and it would be too dark to see.

The river.

That's all that lay at the south end of this field. Trent had walked here before, on his days off. Exploring the area, clocking up the steps. A bobby on patrol couldn't afford to be unfit or get lost. Trent took his job very seriously. All his life he'd wanted to be a police officer, ever since he'd found out his father had been one.

The father he'd never known.

Trent had the killer trapped. There was nowhere to go, not unless the man could take flight over the water. The towpath would be in complete darkness. Treacherous to those who didn't know the way, and impossible to traverse in the dark. He came to a stop, panting heavy, misty gasps.

I know you're here.

Trent tried to get his bearings. They were somewhere near the river towpath. An undefined green part of the map where the contour line stopped and foliage crawled across the path into the river. Trent squinted into the deepening darkness but couldn't see him.

Bugger.

He walked one way, then the other. Listening for movement. The crunch of gravel or the rustle of a bush. There was nothing. Only a whispering silence, punctuated by the occasional hoot of an owl.

So close.

Then he heard a splash.

No way.

Trent raced to the riverbank just in time to see the white fringes of water as the killer swam strongly across the Thames.

"Holy shit," he whispered. The water must be sub-zero. The guy would freeze his nuts off. Yet on he went, stroke after stroke, until he reached the other side. The Thames was easily twenty-five metres wide in this part, so that was no mean feat. There was a scramble as the killer pulled himself from the water. Reeds breaking, grass tearing, and he was out. The man kept his head down, his face unidentifiable across the dark expanse, and then he was gone.

Trent stared at the spot where the killer had stood, his heart pounding. A big wet splodge fell on his forehead, and then the heavens opened.

* * *

"He did what?" Rob stared at Trent, who was soaked through. He'd walked back to Chloe's house in the deluge.

"He swam across the river. I swear, guv, I saw him do it."

"Bloody hell." Rob glanced at Jenny.

She was as surprised as he was. "He'll freeze to death, surely?"

Trent shook his head. "He made it. The perp's a strong swimmer."

"He must be, to make it across in this weather." Rob exhaled. "There's no point in calling for a search party. He'll be long gone."

A crime scene photographer danced around the body taking photographs. The flash was giving Rob a headache. His initial panic attack had resided, and he was back in control of his emotions. Thank God for Jenny. For a moment there, he'd completely lost it. He'd been back in his own kitchen, kneeling beside Jo, desperately trying to save her life.

Rob had thought he was over that. Six months of therapy, long walks with Trigger, time spent with his family. It ought to have been enough, but after today, he knew the incident would always haunt him. The trauma had hacked a path in his subconscious, and it couldn't be repaired or patched up. It had shaped who he was.

"It does narrow down our suspect list," Jenny commented wryly. She was right about that. Very few people would have made that swim.

The paramedics appeared with a gurney. They lifted Chloe Brooke on to it, gently folding her hands on top of her chest. Rigor hadn't set in yet. The bleeding had stopped, now that life was extinguished, leaving a wine-coloured smear on the floor. Rob turned away.

"Did you find anything here?" Trent asked. He too, was avoiding looking at the bloodstain.

"Not yet. We're going to search the place, but they haven't given us the go-ahead yet. We're waiting for forensics to finish up." Trent's gaze shifted to Chloe as she was wheeled from the room.

"You feeling better?" Rob asked the young PC, who was beginning to shiver. Despite the fainting spell, he'd shown that he had guts. Going after the perpetrator like that, putting himself in danger, all in frigid temperatures.

"I'm good." His hand trembled as he pushed a damp lock of hair off his forehead. "I'm just sorry I lost him."

"Go home and get warm," Rob told him. He didn't want the kid to get pneumonia. "We'll reconvene tomorrow at the office. Be there at eight sharp."

"Yes, guv."

The PC turned and hurried back to his vehicle. Rob met Jenny's eye. "I like him."

She smiled back. "I know."

CHAPTER 20

"Your prime suspect is dead?" Mayhew rubbed her eyes, then wished she hadn't. The make-up she'd applied so liberally this morning to conceal the dark shadows was making them sting. Thanks to bloody Matthew Gray, she'd had a torturous night's sleep, tossing and turning until the early hours, when she'd given up, got dressed and come into work.

Her professional aspirations were wrestling with her conscience. On the one hand, she wanted to protect her boss, because if she didn't, he had the power to make her life a misery. On the other hand, she couldn't just pretend he hadn't been there. There were eyewitnesses, for God's sake. People who'd seen him with his girlfriend. Part of her wanted to tell him that if he was foolish enough to take his mistress to an event like that, instead of his wife, then he ought to suffer the consequences.

God forbid they ever had to interview him formally, or if any of the other guests mentioned his plus-one in their statements. It would be impossible to keep it out of the case notes. Of course, she'd be the one with egg on her face for covering it up in the first place.

Dammit.

She was supposed to be rooting out police corruption, not subscribing to it. Sighing, she blinked rapidly to quell the stinging.

"Are you okay?" DCI Miller gave her an odd look.

"Fine, just tired. Did you find anything at the victim's home? Any indication of who did this?"

Miller shook his head. "Nope. Chloe Brooke was about to leave for an event. She had a kitchen full of vol-au-vents, a refrigerated van full of profiteroles and multiple crates of Prosecco, but nothing that could tell us who did this to her."

"What did forensics say?"

"Neither the front nor the back door was forced, so we think she let her killer in. In fact, the front door was locked from the inside, which means she felt comfortable enough letting him in and relocking it."

"Interesting." Felicity thought about this. "And Debby Morris's husband, the man she had an affair with, was being interviewed by you at the time, so we can rule him out."

"Not quite." Rob frowned.

Felicity gave him a questioning look. "No?"

"Well, it's true we interviewed him and he confirmed their affair. After that, we went to Chloe Brooke's office to talk to her, but she wasn't there. We spoke with her assistant, got her home address and diverted there, where we met Trent, who'd done the same thing."

She frowned. "You're saying Ian Morris had time to get there before you?"

"If he knew where she was, then yes. It would be cutting it fine, but theoretically he could have gone straight to her house and murdered her, while we were faffing around at her office."

"Have you spoken to him since then?"

"Not yet. By the time the paramedics had taken the victim's body away and we'd searched the house, it was too late to go back to check on Ian Morris. To be honest, we didn't consider him — I didn't consider him — until I got home and started replaying the events in my mind."

Felicity gave a stiff nod. "Maybe you should question him again."

"We will. I'm heading out there right after the briefing."

"Keep me posted."

"Will do. Hey, how'd it go with the Assistant Commissioner? So much has happened, I forgot to ask."

She didn't meet his gaze. "Fine. He admitted to being at the party."

"Did he speak to Debby Morris?"

"He said he was introduced shortly after he arrived, at the start of the night. He didn't speak to her again after that."

Rob gave her a sharp look that made her gut tighten. "Can we rule him out?"

He was asking for her professional opinion. Every fibre of her being wanted to tell him about the mistress, but what good would that do? Gray had been with another woman. So what? That wasn't a crime. Instead she said, "I'd say so. I don't think he's involved in this."

"Okay, fine." His expression relaxed. "So, Chloe leaving him off the list was a genuine mistake?"

"Looks like it."

Felicity turned and walked away before he could see she was lying.

* * *

"Everything all right?" Jenny raised her eyebrows as Rob walked back to his desk.

"Yep, I think so." He tilted his head toward Mayhew. "She gets weirder by the day, I swear."

"She's got a lot going on," Jenny replied, surprisingly loyal. "It hasn't been easy since you've been away. She's had to put out a lot of fires."

"I know I made things difficult for all of you." Rob gave a little shake of his head. "I still can't believe I didn't see it." He wasn't talking about this investigation.

"Don't beat yourself up." Jenny patted him on the shoulder. "Tony fooled us all, including Mayhew. It was her head on the block. Raza Ashraf was here with the Commissioner, discussing what to do. I don't know how she did it, but somehow, she talked them out of closing us down."

Rob exhaled. "I knew it was bad, but not that bad."

"Yeah." Jenny pursed her lips. "She might be a prize bitch sometimes, but she saved our necks."

"I'll bear that in mind next time she pisses me off."

Jenny grinned. "Let's go in. Everybody's waiting."

They walked into the incident room, which was absolutely freezing. "Radiator's bust," complained Harry, as Jenny shivered and rubbed her shoulders.

"Celeste, can you get on to maintenance and ask them to fix it?"

"Already did," replied Celeste, wearing a thick woollen scarf. "They're sending someone up."

"Let's get started," Rob said. "I've got to get back out to Marlow to interview Ian Morris. Trent has taken him into custody."

In response to the blank stares around the room, Rob said, "Chloe Brooke was murdered last night."

There was a shocked murmur.

"H-How?" stammered Celeste.

"Her throat was slit. The assailant got away, but we arrived at the scene shortly after it happened. PC Trent went after the perpetrator, but he jumped in the river and swam away."

"Sorry, did you say *swam*?" Harry stared at him.

"Yeah. The water must have been freezing because the atmospheric temperature was about four degrees Celsius at that point."

"Kinda like in here," murmured Harry.

"That does narrow it down," remarked Will, just as Jenny had said the day before. "How many of our suspects can swim across the Thames?"

"Not many," replied Rob. "It's fairly wide at that point, and choppy on account of the squall. Chloe's killer must have been an experienced outdoor swimmer to have handled that."

"How does one even check that?" Celeste looked around the table. "There won't be any record of childhood swimming lessons."

"Unless they competed," said Will.

"Open-water swimming is a thing," Harry volunteered. "We could check the lakes around Marlow to see if any of our suspects were regulars."

"Good idea," said Rob. "Let's start with Ian Morris."

Harry nodded. On the whiteboard, someone had rewritten Ian Morris's name and put it at the top of the list. As of now, he was their prime suspect.

"Do you think Ian murdered Chloe?" Celeste asked.

"It's possible," Rob replied. "Although the timing is tight."

"My money was on Chloe murdering Debby Morris." Jenny threw her hands in the air. "Turns out I was wrong."

"She did appear to have a strong motive," Rob agreed, and told the others what her husband had said about Debby's disinterest and his subsequent affair. "Chloe wanted a relationship, but Ian didn't."

"It's a bit *Fatal Attraction*," said Harry, who liked his movie references.

"Let's bring up a map of the area." Rob turned to Will, who tapped away on his laptop, then turned it to face the table.

Rob leaned forward. "This is where Ian lives. He'd have to get across town on foot to Chloe Brooke's house in . . ." He glanced at Jenny. "How long were we at her office for?"

"Ten minutes," Jenny supplied. "Add on another ten to fifteen minutes for driving time."

"He'd have to get from here to here in, say, twenty-five minutes max."

"Is that possible?" Will frowned at the map.

"To get there, slit her throat and escape out the kitchen door, just as we walked in the front. I don't know."

Harry frowned. "It's cutting it fine."

Rob shook his head. "We were so damn close. Five minutes earlier, and we'd have got him."

"Don't." Jenny shook her head. "Don't do that. We couldn't have known."

He sighed. She was right. There was no point in thinking about the "what ifs". What was done was done.

"Trent was there already, don't forget," Jenny pointed out.

"Yes," Rob looked up. "Make that twenty minutes, because Trent arrived just before us."

"Ian Morris could have cycled," Harry said.

Rob pointed at him. "That's true. Let's look for a bicycle at his house."

"We'll need a warrant," said Jenny.

"No problem. I'll sign off on it."

"Did Trent see anything?" Celeste asked.

"No, but the neighbours heard screaming. Trent said he was about to enter the premises when they ran up the driveway."

"They didn't see anyone?" Harry asked.

"No, we spoke to them last night. All they heard was Chloe screaming. That's why they came over."

"I didn't notice a bicycle outside the house." Rob thought back to when they arrived. "But that doesn't mean he didn't toss it in the bushes or somewhere before he went in."

"He could be planning to go back for it," Harry pointed out. "It might still be there."

"We'll check." He nodded to Jenny. "Get Trent over there once Ian Morris is in holding."

She fired off a text message.

"Okay, guys. I'll leave the swimming angle with you. Also, the contents of Chloe's office and home study will be delivered here today. We need to go through everything with a fine-tooth comb. There might be something there that will give us a lead."

"If Ian isn't guilty," remarked Harry.

Rob nodded. "Yes, if Ian isn't guilty."

CHAPTER 21

Trent parked outside Chloe Brooke's house and climbed out of the car. He shivered as the cold snuck beneath his yellow high-vis jacket. It was time to haul out the thermals. Up north, they were an integral part of winter attire, but he hadn't thought he'd need them down south.

Trent stood beside the police vehicle and looked around. DCI Miller had been clear. Search the outside of the property for a bike, or any form of transport. The theory was that Ian Morris had run or cycled across Marlow to Chloe Brooke's house after they'd interviewed him, and slaughtered her.

He pondered that for a minute. Twenty minutes wasn't a lot of time. Still, it was possible. You could jog around Marlow in half an hour. The town wasn't that big.

But it wasn't just getting here. The suspect would have had to have knocked on the front door, been admitted and followed Chloe to the kitchen, where he'd slit her throat with a kitchen knife — a messy business, he now knew — before vanishing out the back. All in twenty minutes? Now that was less likely.

Unless, as DCI Miller supposed, he had transport.

Trent walked up the short driveway, then peered over the hedge into the neighbour's property. No bike there. No other foliage in front of the house in which to hide a bike. He tried the garage, but it was locked. Chloe's Mini and the transit van were still parked in the drive. He wondered what had happened to all those little nibbles she'd had lying around. They'd looked quite good, and if he hadn't been queasy from all that blood, he might have tried a couple.

Nothing here. Time to check the back. The killer could have come in that way. The back door was open, but forensics said there was no evidence of forced entry.

He walked around the corner, through an ancient stone archway, and into the park that led to the back of the property. As he did, he envisaged the man he'd chased. Head-to-toe black, lean, athletic. Not the same physique as the stocky Ian Morris. Still, if DCI Miller wanted him to search for a bicycle, he would.

The park was deserted. There weren't even any birds in the trees, it was that cold. Nobody in their right mind wanted to be out in this. Trent strode up the meandering path till he was parallel to the back gate of Chloe's house. The statuesque old English oaks groaned over him, watching as he pulled back branches and peered into bracken and thistly bushes. There was nothing here. As much as he respected DCI Miller, he thought he was grasping at straws with this one.

An ancient stone wall, about chest high and covered with ivy and any other plant that had decided this was a good place to put down roots, ran along the opposite side of the park. He'd once read something about the land being part of the feudal system, divided up to be worked by the farmers. The foliage covering it was thick and lustrous, and could probably be torn away from the wall.

A spark of adrenaline made his heart beat faster. Could he be on to something? He walked across to the wall. It was about forty metres long, nearly the entire length of the park. Luckily, he was wearing gloves. Trent started in the middle and pulled back the foliage until he saw the stonework. It was thick, like a leafy green curtain, camouflaging anything behind it. Moving to the right, he worked his way to the south side of the park. Nothing. Maybe he was barking up the wrong tree, so to speak. He sniggered at his little joke.

Back to the middle. This time, he worked his way to the left, pulling at anything that bulged. He was ten metres along when he found what he was looking for. A rusty old bicycle. Trent stared at it for a long time, then took out his phone and called DCI Miller.

* * *

While Trent was fumbling through the hedgerow, Rob and Jenny were searching Ian Morris's home. Apparently, his mother had come to collect the kids when Trent had arrested him, and there were remnants of their presence all over the house. Toys discarded in a hurry, crumbs on the couch, the TV on in the front room. It was like someone had plucked the occupants out, leaving everything as it was.

"You can't help but feel sorry for the guy." Jenny carefully lifted the cushions off the couch. "I mean, if he's innocent, this is going to hurt him."

"What if he's guilty?" Rob walked past her into the open-plan kitchen. The house was a standard, two-up two-down with the kitchen–living area downstairs and the bedrooms upstairs.

"Then he deserves everything that's coming to him." Jenny stood up. "Nothing here."

Rob opened the dishwasher and peered inside, but he couldn't see a knife that matched the size and shape of the one used to cut Chloe's throat. You wouldn't think a suspect could be so stupid as to bring the murder weapon home with him, but he'd once had a case where the perp had washed it in the dishwasher. It got the blood off, but the dimensions were an exact match, right down to the tiny striations on the side from wear and tear.

The kitchen was a mess, with a dirty pot lying in the sink, a used mug by the kettle and porridge oats scattered on the countertop. Rob looked around. In a small utility room off the kitchen, he found a washing machine, a basket of dirty laundry and various tiny pairs of muddy boots and trainers.

"I'm going upstairs." Jenny poked her head over the bar counter into the kitchen. "Where are you?"

"Down here." He paused. "What did Trent say the man he chased was wearing? Black trousers?"

She appeared in the doorway. "Yeah, and a dark hoodie. You found something?"

"I'm not sure. There's a lot of dirty laundry in here. Most of it in kids' sizes."

"Tip it out," Jenny suggested.

So he did. All over the floor.

"It would be soaked through," Jenny said. "After his swim."

"I suppose the river would have washed off the blood," Rob remarked.

"What about the machine?" Jenny asked. "Have you checked in there?"

He hadn't. Rob bent down to pull open the door, but it was suction-locked. He hit the off switch, and when the light turned from red to green, he pulled open the circular door.

Reaching inside, Rob grabbed the damp items of clothing and pulled them out. Multiple T-shirts, underwear, and a pair of black denim jeans. He held them up. "What do you think?"

Jenny frowned. "I don't know. Jeans weigh a ton when they're wet. He'd have to have been a really good swimmer to get across in those."

"Hmm . . ." Rob reached back inside and pulled out a few more items. He found a pair of black jogging bottoms and a navy-blue hoodie.

Jenny stared at the clothes. "Now, they fit the description."

Rob nodded. "Could be we've found our man."

* * *

Rob sat facing Ian Morris in the interview room at Marlow Police Station. There was no live feed like they would have at bigger Thames Valley stations, but there was a camera in the corner and a digital recorder on the table. It was good enough. Rob pressed the record button and introduced himself. "DCI Miller from the London Met's Major Investigation Team." He nodded to Ian, who sat stiffly opposite him, his hands in his lap. "Please state your name for the tape."

The father of two said, "Ian Morris." his voice was hoarse, like he'd been shouting. A glass of water sat on the table in front of him, and he took repeated sips. Nervous or just worn out? Maybe both.

"Ian, you're being questioned in relation to the murder of Chloe Brooke."

He stifled a sob. "I didn't kill her. I didn't even know she was dead."

"Then it should be easy enough to prove." He kept his voice light. Hope flickered in Ian's face. If the guy was guilty, he was a terrific actor. Rob began to get the first stirrings of doubt. "Let's start with what you did yesterday after we spoke to you."

He threw his hands in the air. "Nothing. You left, I cleaned up around the house, then went to fetch the kids from my mother's house. We got home at six."

Rob thought about that. They'd left Ian's house at roughly three fifteen and reached Chloe's office shortly after that. By the time they got to her house, it was nearly twenty to four. Chloe was already dead when they arrived. Trent reckoned the chase had taken the better part of half an hour, and then he'd walked back in the driving rain. By that stage, it was almost five o'clock. If Ian had swum across the river, there'd still have been time for him to get home, change his clothes, load the washing machine and go fetch his kids from Henley-on-Thames, a twenty-minute drive away.

"Do you own a bicycle?" Rob asked.

Ian looked confused. "Debby had one. It's in the shed in the garden."

"But not you?"

"No."

"Can you describe the bike?"

"Pale green with a brown basket on the front."

It wasn't the same bike. Rob slid a photograph across the table. "Do you recognise this bicycle?"

"No. What is this? I told you; I don't have a bike."

"Why don't you have one?"

He shook his head. "Because . . . I don't like cycling. I've got knee problems. If I want to go somewhere in the town, I'll walk, otherwise I'll take my car."

He could have stolen it or found it somewhere. It was an old rusty thing, but it still worked. Forensics were analysing it for recent prints and DNA.

"Did you speak to Chloe yesterday, after we left?"

"No. I haven't spoken to her in weeks."

"You didn't go and visit her after we left you yesterday?"

"Absolutely not. I told you: I went to fetch the boys."

Rob got up, walked to the door and opened it.

"That it?" Ian sat up, surprised.

"Unfortunately not." Rob took the two black bags that Jenny handed him and went back to the table. Opening the first, he took out the pair of damp joggers and laid them on the table. "Is this item yours?"

Ian tilted his head to the side. "I don't know."

"It's a pair of tracksuit joggers with a size thirty-six waist."

He tilted his head. "They could be. I do own a pair like that."

"What about this?" Rob pulled the navy hoodie out of the bag and laid it on top of the joggers.

Ian stared at him as if he were mad. "Yes, that's mine. Why are you—? What have my clothes got to do with anything?"

"Were you wearing these yesterday?" Rob asked.

"I don't understand." He ran a hand through his hair.

"Please, just answer the question."

"Um, no. I didn't wear them yesterday."

"Are you sure? They were in your washing machine."

"Why are you pulling clothes out of my washing machine?" His eyes searched Rob's face for answers. "Is that even legal?"

"We had a search warrant," Rob said. "Which makes it legal."

"I'm sorry, I still don't—"

"When did you wear them last?" Rob cut in.

"The day before yesterday, I think. I don't know. I can't be sure."

"But you're sure it wasn't yesterday."

"Yes, I'm sure it wasn't yesterday. That stuff's been in there for at least a day and a half. I didn't get a chance to hang it up this morning before PC Trent arrested me." He glared at Rob.

That did sound feasible. It was just plain black jogging bottoms and a hoodie, after all. Found in any high-street clothing store. "Ian, can you swim?"

Ian, totally confused, just blinked at him.

"Ian?"

"Um, yeah, I can swim."

"Are you any good?"

"I'm all right. I wouldn't win any medals or anything."

Rob studied him. The flustered complexion, the confusion, the bewilderment. This wasn't the behaviour of a man who'd just killed his girlfriend. Besides, Trent had said the man he'd followed was taller, lankier than Ian Morris.

Rob got up. "Thanks for your time, Mr Morris."

"Are we done?"

Rob gave a terse nod. "Yeah, now we're done."

CHAPTER 22

"It's not enough," Rob said simply. They were standing in the booking area at Marlow Police Station discussing Ian Morris's arrest. "We're going to have to let him go."

"But the clothing?" Jenny said. "And the bicycle?"

"It's not definitive. We can't prove any of it. I also don't think he's that strong a swimmer."

"Maybe SOCO will find something on the bike," Trent said hopefully.

"He claims it's not his." Rob shook his head. "Let's release him. We know where he is if we need him."

"What if he runs?" asked Trent.

"He won't. He's got the boys to think about. He's all they've got."

Once a thoroughly disgruntled Ian Morris was released, Rob and Jenny drove back to Putney.

"I'm calling it a day," Rob said, after he'd dropped her at the office. A quiet evening at home with Jo and his son was what he needed. "Don't work too late."

"I won't." She gave him a wave. "Have a good evening, guv."

* * *

Rob got home to find Jo giving Jack his supper. Trigger was curled up on his bed, face hanging over the edge, watching them with mournful eyes. The fourteen-month-old sat in his high chair playing with his bib as Jo spooned a chicken-and-vegetable mush into his mouth.

Rob kissed Jo on the cheek, then walked around and kissed Jack on the head. He giggled and looked up. "Da-da."

Rob smiled. It was amazing how two little syllables could make everything right in the world.

"You okay?" Jo asked, as he sat down. He loved that she could read him with one glance.

"I've been questioning Debby Morris's husband in Marlow." The unsettled feeling he'd had since he'd spoken to Ian had intensified. "I don't think he did it."

"You should trust your gut."

A moment of insecurity. "What if I'm wrong? Look what happened with Tony."

She flinched. "Forget about Tony. He's a psychopath. You can't read a psychopath, because they don't adhere to any of the normal patterns. If he'd been wired normally, you'd have picked up on it."

Rob got up and gave her a hug. "You always know what to say to make me feel better. Here, let me take over."

Jo handed him the spoon, then sat down where he'd been sitting. "He was cleared of murdering his wife, wasn't he?"

"Yeah, his alibi held up."

"Are you sure the same person killed Debby Morris and Chloe . . . ?" She raised her eyebrows.

"Brooke," he supplied. "I don't know. What are the chances of there being two killers in Marlow?"

"Of there being two separate killers?" Jo shook her head. "Zero chance. But two interconnected killers . . ." She shrugged.

Rob turned to face her. "What are you thinking?"

"Okay, hear me out. You've got one man and two dead women."

"Yeah."

"What if it's a classic love triangle?"

He scowled. "I'm not following."

"What if Chloe murdered Debby because she wanted Ian all to herself, but then, somehow, he found out about it, and consumed with rage, killed her?"

"Logically, it makes sense, but after interviewing him for the second time . . . I'm not sure he's the 'consumed with rage' type."

"People hide things."

"They do, but Chloe's killer also swam across the Thames in the dark. I can't see Ian doing that."

"You get my point, though," Jo said. "Connected, but not the same person."

He did.

Much later, after they'd eaten and Jo had gone up to have a bath, Rob opened his laptop and Googled Ian Morris and "swim" or "swimming". Maybe he'd missed something. Ian could be lying about being an average swimmer. Nothing came up. No references to any type of swimming in Ian's past. On a whim, he called Ian's mother, Ruth.

"I'm sorry to call so late," he said, once he'd introduced himself. "But I was wondering if I could ask you a question about Ian?" He waited while she gave him an earful about her son's arrest earlier today. Rob said he was only doing his job, and Ian had been released. No harm done.

She snorted. "I wouldn't say that."

He decided not to ask her what she meant. "Mrs Morris, is Ian a good swimmer?"

"What?"

"It's a strange question, I know, but is Ian a strong swimmer?"

"Not especially. We took him for some lessons when he was younger, but he didn't keep it up."

"You don't think he's capable of swimming across the Thames, then?"

"Good heavens, no. He'd sink before he got halfway."

"Okay, thank you, Mrs Morris. Once again, I'm sorry to have disturbed you."

Jo's theory was a good one, but unless Ian had been having secret swimming lessons, he wasn't their man.

* * *

Rob got to the office at the usual time the next morning. Most of the team was already there. He hung his coat on his chair and was about to grab a coffee from the machine in the waiting room when Celeste beckoned him over. "Guv, you need to see this."

"What's up?" He diverted to her desk.

She pointed to her screen. "I've been looking at CCTV footage in Oxford, outside the hotel where Ian Morris stayed." At Rob's surprised look, she added, "I put the request in days ago and forgot about it. It didn't seem important until now."

"What did you find?"

"Well, you know Trent said he was in his room all night?"

"Yeah."

"He wasn't." She gave an impish grin. "He left at nine forty-five and only got back at one in the morning. He was gone for three hours and fifteen minutes."

Rob stared at her. "You're serious?"

"Yes, look, that's him."

Rob leaned in to look at the video, which she'd paused. A dark street. A dim street lamp. A man in jeans and a leather jacket. That was Ian Morris leaving the hotel.

"Holy shit," he muttered. "Why didn't the system register his return?" Trent had said the last known entry was at 9.26 p.m.

"I don't know, guv. He must have found some way to circumvent it, or the receptionist made a mistake." A thought occurred to her. "Maybe he left his door ajar, prised it open somehow, so he didn't need to use his key card to get back in?"

"It's possible." Rob exhaled noisily. "Either way, Ian Morris's alibi for his wife's murder just fell through."

"What do you want to do?" Celeste glanced up at him.

He scratched his head. "Is three and a quarter hours enough time to drive back to Marlow and kill your wife?"

"An hour each way," Celeste said knowingly. "An hour and fifteen to do the deed."

"He wouldn't have known what time she'd leave the party, though." Rob began to pace as the thoughts tumbled through his head. "Or did he? Maybe she'd told him she'd leave at midnight?"

"There's something else," Will, who'd been half-listening, said from his desk. They turned to face him. "I found an insurance policy in Debby's name. If she dies, her husband gets a two hundred and fifty grand payout."

"That's a lot of money," Jenny said, coming over. Her eye caught sight of the picture on Celeste's screen. "Is that Ian Morris?"

Celeste filled her in.

"Well, I'll be . . ." Jenny gazed at the shadowy image on the screen. "He bloody did it, didn't he? The weasel killed his wife."

"Unless he has some other reason for leaving the hotel," Rob said.

"At that time?" she scoffed. "Where could he be going?"

"Another woman?" Was there such a thing as a love rectangle? "That's the most logical conclusion."

"He's not even that good-looking," Jenny murmured. "Besides, he'd just ended it with Chloe. Would he be seeing someone else so soon?"

"Especially after what happened with her," Rob pointed out.

"Okay, so say he did kill Debby." Jenny narrowed her eyes thoughtfully. "He must have sped back to Marlow, gone to the park to lie in wait, then hit her on the head as she walked past."

"She would have collapsed unconscious," Rob picked up her train of thought. "At which point, he dragged or carried her unconscious body to the pontoon, lowered her into the water and held her under until she drowned."

"Barbaric," hissed Celeste. "She was his wife."

"We've got to find out where he went that night," Jenny said. "I'll check the ANPR database. We might be able to pick up his vehicle."

"I'll check other cameras in the area," Celeste said.

Rob scraped a hand through his hair. "Get Trent to arrest him and bring him to Putney nick for questioning. I'll be damned if I'm driving out to Marlow again."

Jenny swiped at her phone. "Will do, guv."

* * *

Felicity watched the interrogation on the live stream from her office. DS Bird was one of their best interviewers, which was why she was still a DS and not a DI or a DCI. Certain skill sets demanded you remain at a specific rank, and while Felicity had always aspired to reach the top of her chosen career, DS Bird was more interested in the human aspect of policing. A waste of talent, in Felicity's option, since DS Bird was a damn fine detective, if a little frumpy. Still, it wasn't her place to judge.

DCI Miller had opted to sit this one out. His excuse was he'd interrogated the suspect yesterday, and it was too soon. A different approach was needed. Perhaps he was right. He, too, was watching the live stream on the incident room flat-screen, along with the rest of his team. They hadn't invited her to join them. Not that she needed an invitation, but she didn't want to gatecrash their little party.

Ian Morris looked furious. Shoulders taut, back straight, hands crossed on the table in front of him. No wonder Miller had asked DS Bird to take this one. She was going to get an earful from the suspect as soon as she walked through that door.

Felicity was right.

"How dare you do this to me again! My mother is about to have a nervous breakdown, and what are my boys going to think?"

"I'm sorry," DS Bird said, in a soft voice. "PC Trent was following orders."

Some of the fight went out of him at her calm, measured response. Water on the flame. "Whose orders? Because I want to speak to them. I want to issue a complaint. This is completely uncalled for."

She sat down opposite him. "You're perfectly entitled to do that. The order came from DCI Miller, who is leading this investigation."

Ian Morris's face turned puce. "That man has a problem with me. He's been gunning for me right from the start. I've answered all his stupid questions, even gave him the keys to search my house, and yet he still hauls me in here for another round of questioning." He scoffed. "Don't you have anyone else you can put the blame on?"

"No, actually. You're our prime suspect."

Ian Morris stared at her, then slumped back against his chair. "Why? I didn't do anything wrong."

DS Bird placed a photograph on the table in front of Ian. "Is this you?"

The suspect turned ashen. "Where did you get this?"

"From the CCTV camera in Arlington Road, Oxford. That is you, isn't it?"

Ian Morris gave a minute nod.

"This photograph was taken from the video at 10.33 p.m. the night your wife was murdered. Would you care to tell me where you were going?"

"I can't." It was a whisper.

Felicity could see DS Bird studying him across the table. The thin layer of perspiration on his forehead glistened in the fluorescent lighting. His hands, at first loosely clasped, were now white-knuckled balls of steel.

"Where did you go, Ian?" DS Bird asked again.

The suspect, mouth firmly shut, shook his head.

"Did you drive back to Marlow and murder your wife?" DS Bird was going in for the kill. Felicity watched the suspect, intrigued. This was better than any soap opera.

"No."

"The same CCTV camera shows you re-entering the hotel at around one o'clock in the morning."

He licked his upper lip, sweating profusely now. A guiltier man she'd yet to see. "I didn't kill Debby. I loved her."

"And yet here you are leaving your hotel on the night she was murdered, with no explanation as to where you were going. How do you expect us to believe you *didn't* kill her?"

Felicity found she was nodding at the computer screen. DS Bird was doing an excellent job of pinning him into a corner.

"You were frustrated." Her voice remained even. "Debby was neglecting you. You felt like you were losing her. Your business was in trouble, and you thought you could cash in on the insurance policy."

Felicity gasped. This was the first time she'd heard about an insurance policy.

"It's not true. That money is for the boys' education," Ian Morris was saying. "We both took out identical policies, so that if anything ever happened to one of us, the other would be okay."

"Still," DS Bird was saying, "you knew if she died, you'd receive two hundred and fifty thousand pounds."

"The same could be said for her," he argued.

"But you got there first."

"It's not true." He slammed his fist down on the table. "I didn't kill her, and I sure as hell didn't kill that psycho Chloe either. You guys have the wrong man."

"Then prove it," DS Bird said. "Tell us where you went for those four hours."

He looked pained. "No comment."

Every answer from there on out was the same. *No comment.* Eventually, Felicity left her office, walked down the aisle between desks to the suite of boardrooms. She knocked on the door of incident room 1.

Rob opened it. "Superintendent, what can I do for you?"

"I'm watching the live feed. You can tell DS Bird to charge that man with the murder of Debby Morris."

CHAPTER 23

"He wouldn't say where he went," Rob told Jo that evening. It had been bugging him ever since Ian Morris had been charged with Debby Morris's murder.

She stopped chopping tomatoes and glanced up at him. "You don't think he killed his wife?"

Rob sighed. "I don't know. If he didn't, why won't he give us his alibi?"

"He could be protecting someone. Another woman?"

"He's already had one affair."

She scoffed. "You know what they say about a leopard, right?"

Rob turned to her. "He even used chewing gum to keep the door from locking. We sent a forensic tech to the hotel to have a look. She found gum residue in the hole. That's why his key card didn't register when he got back to the hotel. It was a deliberate attempt to deceive us."

"He's definitely hiding something," Jo murmured.

Rob switched the oven on. "But is it murder?"

Jo waved the knife in the air. "Maybe he did kill her and doesn't want to implicate himself by admitting it."

"Hmm . . ." It was a possibility. "Maybe I'm reading too much into it. Maybe the guy is just a murdering scumbag."

"I think Mayhew's right to charge him," Jo said. "If he's innocent, let him prove it. The evidence is stacking up now."

"For Debby's murder."

Then again, there were still things that didn't make sense. The timing, for one. How would Ian have known when Debby would leave the party? It was a freezing night. Had he hidden in the park, waiting for her to walk past? How did he know she wouldn't take a cab? Or get a lift? How would anyone know, for that matter — unless they saw her leave because they were at the party.

Ian wasn't at the party.

"What about Chloe's murder?" Jo asked. "Are you going to charge him with that too?"

"Maybe. He had a similar outfit in his washing machine to the one the perpetrator was wearing the day she was killed. Unfortunately, it had been laundered, so we can't tell whether it was ever in the Thames."

"That's circumstantial," she pointed out.

"Yeah, but he had a motive. Chloe wouldn't take no for an answer. He had the opportunity. There was enough time to get to her house before we did."

"Only just," said Jo.

"True, but considering his refusal to say where he was on the night of Debby's murder, it might swing the jury to find him guilty of Chloe's. too. Ian Morris is in a lot of trouble."

"Is there any chance he's innocent?" Jo asked quietly.

"Well, his prints weren't on the bicycle we found outside Chloe's house. But if he is innocent, he'd better start talking," Rob said. "And fast. His indictment is tomorrow, and then a court date will be set. After that, it's out of our hands."

"You could find the real killer," Jo said. "I mean, if you don't think he did it."

Rob paused.

"Mayhew wants a win on this one, and Ian Morris looks good for it."

She put a hand on his shoulder. "You must do whatever you think is best."

While he knew she was right, he couldn't stop pondering it. It was the early hours when he came to a decision. Only then was he able to get some sleep.

* * *

"We're going to keep going," he told the team the next morning. Trent was there too, huddled around the boardroom table. "Until we know for sure that Ian Morris is guilty, we're going to treat it like an open case."

"Mayhew's not going to like that," Jenny warned, glancing towards her office.

He shrugged. "I know, but let's pretend we're preparing for trial. Ian Morris will get his court date today, and we're going to have to present the case to the prosecutor. She won't know we're still looking at the other suspects."

"*Do* we have any other suspects?" Harry asked.

"We have a whole list," Rob reminded them. "Listen, I was thinking. The only way Debby's murderer knew she would be in that park at that time was if he or she followed her. That means the murderer must have been at the party." There were several nods of agreement.

"We need to look into everyone on that guest list again," Rob said, "including the ones we discounted before because they didn't know Debby. Let's try to find a connection."

He turned to Trent. "Why don't you go and speak to the housekeeper, Lily, again? See if she noticed anything else."

"Oh, okay. Yeah. I can do that."

"The contents of Chloe's office arrived this morning," Celeste said. "I'll tell them to bring it up so we can start going through it."

"I'll help," Jenny said. "It's too big a job for one."

Rob nodded. "Will, you and Harry see what you can dig up on the guests. Look at their social media profiles, blogs, YouTube videos, anything you can find. Try to find links to either of the two victims." They both nodded.

"What are you going to do?" Jenny asked.

Rob tapped a name near the top of the list. "I'll take Roman Petrovic. I'm sure he's got a few skeletons in his closet."

A hard knock on the glass door made them all jump. "What are you guys doing in here?" It was Mayhew, in all her fiery glory.

"We're just finishing up," said Rob. "Divvying up the tasks for the CPS."

She gave a curt nod, her eyes roaming over the whiteboard. "Okay, good. Let me know if you come across any issues."

"Will do."

"I don't want to fuck this up, Miller," she said. "Our heads are already on the block. Make sure it's airtight."

He glanced at the others. "Yes, ma'am."

A nervous nod, and she stalked back to her office.

"Are you sure about this?" Jenny whispered, once she'd gone.

"You heard her," Rob said. "No fuck-ups. Imagine if we book the wrong man? How's that going to look on our record?"

Jenny arched an eyebrow. "You've got a point."

"Let's get to work, team." Rob patted Trent on the back as he walked past. "Call me as soon as any of you have anything."

* * *

Felicity stared out of her corner office at DCI Miller's team. Heads down, concentrating hard. No office banter. No glib comments. They were up to something; she could smell it. She just didn't know what.

Preparing the case for the trial is what one would expect at this stage of the game. So why did she get a nervous flutter every time one of them glanced up at her?

A short time later, several boxes of paperwork were delivered to their incident room. Confused, she went to see what they were.

"The contents of Chloe Brooke's office." DCI Miller waved a hand at the boxes. He'd intercepted her in the corridor. "I thought if we could tie Ian Morris to her murder, we could close both cases."

Felicity gave a quick nod. She'd known there was something else. Closing both cases would be a coup, especially since the media were constantly hounding her for an official update. Once Ian Morris appeared in court, there'd be a frenzy of press attention. Debby's murderer, her cheating husband. If nothing else, it made for good reading.

If Ian Morris was charged with both Debby and Chloe's murders, they could put the whole investigation to bed. The Commissioner would be happy, and it would show her department hadn't lost their touch. She might even get a commendation. "Is he good for it?"

"That's what we're trying to find out. He certainly had a motive, and the opportunity. We know Chloe Brooke knew her attacker because she let him into her house. And we found similar clothing to what the killer was wearing in his washing machine."

Felicity had already read the case notes. "Okay, good. I want you to give a statement to the media tomorrow about Ian Morris's arrest. I've had the press on the phone all afternoon."

Rob stiffened. He'd made it very clear he didn't like appearing in front of the cameras. Well, as a DCI, he'd have to get used to it. It was part of the job. "If we could wait a couple of days, it would be better," he began. "That way we can say we're charging him with both murders."

Felicity shook her head. "No can do. We don't want to look impotent. They know something's going down, and when Ian Morris is led into court tomorrow, it's going to be obvious. We've got to be ready with a statement. Ten o'clock tomorrow. Don't forget."

CHAPTER 24

At ten o'clock the next morning, Rob stood outside Scotland Yard in his official Metropolitan Police uniform and read a prepared statement. Short and sweet: he confirmed that they had arrested and charged Ian Morris for Debby Morris's murder.

As the cameras flashed and the breaking news feed went out across the networks, he met Mayhew's eye. She stood beside him, silently endorsing her department's decision. Once you put it out there, you couldn't take it back. If they found anything else, anything that would dispute the current hypothesis, Mayhew would have egg on her face. It wouldn't look good for the Major Investigation Team, who were already under scrutiny from the powers that be.

"What evidence do you have, DCI Miller?" a journalist with the BBC called out.

"Is Ian Morris also responsible for Chloe Brooke's murder?" asked the *Independent*.

"No comment at this time." Rob turned and marched back inside the building. The armed guards slammed shut, shoulder to shoulder, in front of the doors like a muscular security gate, and the reporters backed away.

“Well done,” came a deep voice. Rob looked up to see the Police Commissioner standing in the lobby. They shook hands. “I’m glad to see you back at the helm.”

“Thank you, sir.”

Mayhew had a car waiting out the back. The jumble of reporters made it impossible to leave via the front exit. “Let’s get back to Putney.”

With her auburn hair cascading around her face, sparkling eyes and flushed cheeks, she looked almost pretty. This was a big win for her. Rob hoped Ian Morris was guilty — because, if not, they’d destroyed a man’s life, and possibly their own careers as a result.

* * *

As soon as Rob walked into the squad room, he could tell something was up. Jenny and Celeste were hovering around his desk, talking in low voices. He waited for Mayhew to go back to her office and then whispered, “Caffè Nero. Ten minutes.”

When Will and Harry made to move, he shook his head. “We can’t all go, else she’ll get suspicious.” They sat back down again. Rob glanced at Mayhew’s fishbowl. She was on the phone, her back to them.

Ten minutes later, Rob walked into Caffè Nero. He ignored the coffee queue and headed straight to where Jenny and Celeste were seated. The aromatic high-street coffee shop served as a backup meeting place when they needed privacy.

“What’s going on?” he asked.

“We’ve been going through Chloe Brooke’s office contents,” Jenny began, a coffee and croissant on the table in front of her, “and we’ve found a couple of things that might have a bearing on the case.”

“Like what?”

“Well, for starters, her business wasn’t doing too well.”

“Oh?”

"The last few years hit her hard. Her net profit was down year on year, and while she wasn't in debt, she was only just breaking even."

"Okay, so money was tight."

"There's something else." Jenny paused.

Rob raised an eyebrow.

"Will was looking into Zeke Hamlin's background and found an old school photograph online."

Rob went blank for a second, then clicked his fingers. "The pianist?"

"Yes, he played at the party. Remember, we had him on the whiteboard, but he was at the bottom of the list."

"I remember. Okay, so what's the relevance of the school photo?"

Jenny slid a print-out of the photograph across the table. "That is Zeke Hamlin," she said, pointing to a short, slim boy of about thirteen. She paused, then stabbed at the photograph again. "And that . . . is Debby Morris."

Rob stared at her. "Debby and Zeke were at school together?"

"Yeah, they were several years apart, but they could have known each other."

"How did we miss this?"

"We never thought to look."

"Which school is it?" Rob peered at the faded name at the bottom of the photograph, trying to make it out.

"Reading Blue Coat."

"Okay." Rob thought quickly. "We need to talk to him as soon as possible. The universities will be closed for Christmas break. Do we know where he lives?"

"He's got student digs in Kensington," Celeste supplied. "I'll find out."

"One more thing," Jenny said, before Rob could get up.

"I'm not sure I can take any more surprises."

She grinned. "Guess who paid his school fees?"

"It wasn't his parents?"

"No." Jenny lowered her voice. "It was Dame Constance Blanchard."

* * *

Rob and Jenny met Zeke in a café in Kensington near to the Royal Academy. They found him at a table at the back, reading a score, his long legs stretched out into the aisle.

"DCI Miller and DS Bird," Rob said, before they sat down. "Can I get you anything?"

"No, thank you." His long musician's fingers were wrapped around a cup containing something herbal.

Once they'd got yet another coffee, they rejoined Zeke, who'd put away his music and was gazing at them curiously. "You said this was about Debby?"

"Yes. We believe you knew her?" Jenny was leading this conversation. She had a way with youngsters that Rob had yet to muster. He was more useful as an intimidation tactic.

"We were at school together." He shook his head. "I can't believe she's dead."

"Did you know her well?" Jenny asked.

"Yeah, I'd say so. She was in my tutor group and took me under her wing."

At their blank faces, he elaborated. "We had this vertical tutoring system where you're grouped with students from other year groups. It gives the younger kids a chance to ask questions and the older ones a chance to be mentors."

"Ah, okay." Rob nodded. They didn't have anything like that at his school. It was more of a dog-eat-dog kind of place.

"She was nice. I'd come from a South London state primary, so it was all foreign to me."

"I'm sure. Why did you change schools?" Jenny cocked her head to the side, feigning ignorance. This was where Dame Constance Blanchard made an appearance.

He hesitated. "My parents came from Jamaica. They owned a hair salon in Wembley. There was no way they could afford to send me to an independent school, but with my music . . ." He tried again. "I got a sponsor."

"Dame Constance Blanchard?"

Dark eyes blinked at them. "Yes. How did you know?"

"She's listed as the person who paid your school fees, and who still provides funding for the Royal Academy of Music."

"That's right. She's been extremely generous."

"Excuse me for asking, but why does she sponsor you?" Jenny asked. "I mean, is she a patron of the arts or something?" They couldn't find any link to the Arts Council or anything like that in Dame Constance's history. The only charitable work she did was for her own organ donation foundation. She wasn't particularly interested in classical music, from what they could make out.

Zeke shifted in his chair, clearly uncomfortable. "I guess she just felt sorry for me."

Jenny leaned forward. "Sorry, Zeke, but that's not reason enough to fund someone's education, even someone as talented as you. There must be something in it for her. What connection does she have with your family?"

He sighed. "Okay, I'll tell you, but it was a long time ago. My father saved her life."

They both stared at him.

"She got hit by a car," Zeke explained, "and my dad, who volunteered with St John's Ambulance, managed to keep her alive while the emergency services came. Ever since then, she's been paying for my education. I guess it's her way of saying thank you."

"That's quite a story." Jenny smiled at him, clearly touched. "Thank you for sharing it with us."

Zeke nodded, then took a sip of his herbal tea.

Rob had to admit, it made sense. Dame Constance Blanchard felt like she owed Mr Hamlin, and so had offered to sponsor his musically gifted son. They would confirm that with her when she was back from the Algarve.

"Did you talk to Debby at the party?" Jenny asked, once they'd assimilated the information.

"Of course. Debs got me the gig."

"Oh?" Jenny glanced at Rob.

"She suggested it to Dame Constance, who thought it was a cool idea."

Rob put his cup down. "Did Debby know about your relationship with Dame Constance?"

"Yes, I told Debs when we were at school. She's always known."

"Okay." Rob dismissed the idea he'd been about to run with. If Debby had always known that Dame Constance was funding Zeke, there was no motive there. Not that he thought Zeke or Dame Constance capable of murder, but they had to consider every angle.

"How did Debs seem to you?" Jenny used the name Zeke had called her. "At the party."

Zeke glanced down at the table.

"Was she out of sorts?" Jenny pushed. "Or upset?" Like Rob, she sensed he was holding back.

"She was angry." He looked up, worried now. "I'd never seen her that mad."

"Do you know why?" Jenny kept her voice even.

"I don't." His shoulders hunched over with regret. "I wish I'd listened, but I had to go back to the piano. I told her we'd talk later, but she left early, and I didn't get the chance."

"Did she give any indication about what was bothering her?" Jenny asked. Rob sensed the momentum slipping away.

"No, not really. She came over and said we needed to talk. I asked if she was all right, and she said no, far from it."

"She actually said those words?" Jenny asked.

"Yes. Then Roman Petrovic asked me to start playing, so I said I'd talk to her after my set."

"Except you didn't?"

"When I stopped at midnight, she was gone. I couldn't find her anywhere, so I assumed she'd left."

At midnight, Debby Morris was being attacked in the park. Rob thanked him for his time, and he and Jenny left the café.

“She was upset about something,” Rob said, as they walked back to the car.

“I know, but what?” Jenny scratched her head. “Chloe and the affair?”

“That’s the most obvious answer.” Rob paused, his hand on the car door. “When she arrived at the party, she was fine. Everyone who talked with her at the start of the night said she was in good spirits. By the end of the night, she was furious.” He turned to Jenny. “So, what happened during the course of the evening, and who pissed her off?”

“And was it that person who killed her?” Jenny met his gaze.

“That,” said Rob, getting into the car, “is what we have to find out.”

CHAPTER 25

Felicity, still buzzing from the press conference, decided to take herself out for lunch. The Commissioner had been careful with his praise, but she finally felt like they were heading in the right direction. Hopefully, once this case was concluded, she would have put the department firmly back in his good books.

Cezanne's was an upmarket fish restaurant in Putney, and since she hadn't had breakfast, Felicity was looking forward to tucking into a salmon fillet with a side portion of vegetables. What she didn't expect was to see DCI Miller and two of his team skulking in Caffè Nero as she crossed the street.

Luckily, they didn't see her, and she ducked behind a building as soon as she got to the other side. An innocent break for coffee? Or were they up to something?

She sighed. When had she become so paranoid? It was this bloody job.

Too many secrets.

Miller had said very little on the way home after the press conference, and she got the impression that he wasn't in favour of broadcasting Ian Morris's arrest. That worried her. They had more than enough to charge him. The CPS was happy, so why wasn't he?

The salmon was excellent, and while she ate, Felicity used her phone to catch up on her emails. There was one from her sister, Faith, asking if they could get together for lunch. Obviously, Faith thought the best way to get hold of her was via her work email. How sad was that?

Then again, Felicity barely had any contact with her family. Ever since Mike had left, she'd thrown herself into work. Her career was more important to her than their relationship — his words, not hers — so she might as well make the most of it.

On the way back to the office, Felicity stopped at a small florist and bought herself a bunch of yellow roses. They'd look lovely on the dining room table. She needed to brighten the place up.

In her office, after she put the flowers in water, Felicity sat down at her desk and opened her laptop. A lot of her job was reading. Reading reports, reviews, and legal documents. She had no idea how long she'd been working, when a knock at the door made her look up. DCI Miller's presence filled the doorway. Felicity couldn't explain it, but she instinctively knew her day was about to take a turn for the worse.

"What's up?"

Miller entered but didn't sit down. "We need to talk about Matthew Gray."

She stared at him. "The Assistant Commissioner? Why?"

"He knew Chloe Brooke a lot better than he let on."

She shook her head. "I don't understand."

"Chloe threw a party for him a couple of months back. His fiftieth birthday. The guest list was almost as prestigious as the Lifegiving Foundation Christmas party." Miller placed a piece of paper on the desk in front of her. The top name caught her eye.

Raza Ashraf.

"You're kidding?" She looked up at him. The feeling she'd had earlier intensified. "Raza Ashraf was at Matthew Gray's party, organised by Chloe Brooke?"

"Correct. Gray lied to you, Superintendent. When he mentioned that he knew Chloe Brooke, he didn't say how well."

Felicity gazed at the roses. Suddenly, they didn't look so fresh anymore. Yellow wasn't her colour anyway. She didn't know why she'd bought them.

"Thank you, DCI Miller." She kept her voice level. "I appreciate your giving me the heads-up."

He didn't move. "Excuse me, ma'am, but what are we going to do about it?"

A raised eyebrow. "Does something have to be done?"

"A suspect lied to you, ma'am. No offence, but shouldn't we ask why?"

"We have our killer, DCI Miller. And Gray didn't lie. He simply neglected to mention his birthday party. So what if he threw a bash and invited the Mayor? It's not against the law."

"No, but it is strange that he neglected to mention it was organised by the same woman who arranged the party we're investigating."

It was. She'd give him that much.

Removing her reading glasses, she asked, "Is there any reason to think the Assistant Commissioner is involved in Debbie Morris's or Chloe Brooke's murder?"

Rob hesitated. "Not as yet, ma'am."

"Well, when there is, you let me know. Until then, we're going to keep this under wraps."

Can I count on your discretion?

"But ma'am—"

"That's enough, Miller. If you don't mind, I have work to do. Please close the door on your way out."

She closed her eyes as he left the office, then dropped her head in her hands.

Shit. Shit. Shit.

Why, of all the people to be mixed up in this, did it have to be her boss?

Now what?

She couldn't very well go back to Scotland Yard and demand to know why he'd omitted to mention he knew the second victim. That she'd planned his birthday party.

It wasn't relevant, he'd say. She could hear his words, mocking her. He'd give her that arrogant smile. *Let's focus on what's important.*

Was it relevant? She rubbed her temples, the beginnings of a migraine starting to form. To be fair, Matthew hadn't said he didn't know Chloe Brooke, only that he'd asked her to leave his and his partner's name off the list she'd given the police.

On the other hand, Chloe Brooke had been alive and well when she'd last spoken to Matthew Gray. There'd been no reason to withhold that information. Not unless he had something to hide.

Felicity couldn't think what that could be. He'd already confessed to having an affair. What else was there? Was he embarrassed about the party? If so, she couldn't think why.

Her phone rang. It was her sister. She debated ignoring it, then decided she needed the distraction. "Faith, I'm so glad you called. I got your email."

To her surprise, her sister burst into tears.

"Is everything all right?" Clearly, it wasn't.

A sobbing reply. Jeff was having an affair. After twenty-two years of marriage, he was shagging someone else. Oh God. What was she going to do? What about the children?

"I really need to talk. Can we meet up?"

"Of course we can. How's tomorrow after work? Six-thirty? At that little wine bar at the bottom of Dover House Road. Okay, see you there."

She hung up feeling marginally better. Wasn't it awful that someone else's life falling apart put yours into perspective? At least she didn't have a cheating husband. She gave a bitter laugh. At thirty-seven, she was usually the other woman. Not many single, available men around at her age.

Take Matthew Gray, for example. Successful, respected, married. Yet the stupid arse had taken his mistress to Roman Petrovic's party. Presumably his wife had been at his fiftieth birthday celebration, though.

It was while she was walking home that the thought occurred to her. Chloe Brooke had planned both parties. She'd met both women. The wife and the mistress.

Felicity stopped, ignoring her burning cheeks as the icy wind buffeted them. Had Chloe threatened to tell Mrs Gray about her husband's affair? Had she been blackmailing the Assistant Commissioner?

The thought left her far colder than the weather could.

Maybe she ought to have another chat with Matthew Gray, after all.

But first, she needed proof.

CHAPTER 26

Rob got to work early the next morning. To his surprise, he found Mayhew in her office, hard at it. She looked up as he zigzagged between desks, so he gave her a mock salute.

At the incident room, Rob stopped and entered a code into the pad on the wall. They kept it locked overnight, so no one could go in and tamper with any evidence that was lying around. Currently, the contents of Chloe Brooke's study were spread out all over the boardroom table.

Now where was that print-out? Yesterday, he'd spotted an email from Roman Petrovic to Chloe Brooke outlining his requirements for the party. Chloe had obviously printed it out and kept a copy in her client file. He wondered what other information she had on the Serbian billionaire.

Last night, he and Jo had done some digging. Roman Petrovic had bought the river house in Marlow almost twelve years ago, after moving to the UK from Serbia. According to the estate agent, he'd bought it outright, paying £800,000 in cash.

Trent had been right about Petrovic's wife, though. She'd travelled to the UK with him, but had passed away almost a year after their arrival. End-stage heart failure. She'd been approved for a heart transplant, but had died before she could have the procedure.

Rob scanned the material spread out on the table. Something didn't look right. He couldn't put his finger on it, but something felt out of place. He cast his mind back to the previous afternoon. They'd organised the paperwork into two small piles. Clients and accounts. In the middle was a similar pile containing Chloe's correspondence with the foundation's leader, Dame Constance Blanchard. So, why was there an email from Blanchard on top of the accounts pile?

The door opened and Jenny walked in. "Hiya, guv."

He turned. "Have you been in here this morning?"

"No, I've just arrived. Bloody traffic. What's up?"

"I think someone's been looking through this stuff." He pointed to the two piles. "This isn't how we left things."

Jenny stared at the table, then she turned around in a slow circle, scanning the empty squad room. "But who? There's no one else here. Only you and . . ." They both turned to look at the Superintendent. She was typing furiously on her laptop and didn't seem to notice them staring.

"You don't think . . . ?" Jenny asked.

Rob's eyes narrowed. "I wouldn't put it past her."

* * *

The rest of the team came in, including PC Trent, who Rob had messaged the night before. The young constable put them all to shame in his crisp white shirt and ironed black trousers complete with seam down the middle. His boots were so shiny they reflected the fluorescent lights overhead.

"I've been looking into our host, Roman Petrovic," Rob began. "You were right, Trent, he's a shady character. There isn't much about him online, but Interpol did have him on a watch list at one point, although that was over a decade ago."

"What for?" asked Harry.

"Suspected illegal arms dealing," Rob explained. "But then, all of a sudden, they removed him."

"Maybe he retired," Celeste suggested.

"It does coincide with his move to the UK," Rob said. "So you could be right. Still, he's got a murky history." He turned to Will. "Did you manage to get hold of those phone records?"

"He doesn't have any," Will replied with a grimace.

Rob frowned.

"No contract," Will continued. "He must use a prepaid cell."

"A burner," Rob muttered.

"That's not suspicious at all." Jenny arched an eyebrow.

"Trent, you see him around Marlow. Fill us in on what you know about him." Trent had given him a brief rundown before, but for the benefit of the team, he wanted the young constable to elaborate.

"Petrovic's always been this mysterious figure around Marlow." Trent gathered his thoughts. "Nobody knows him that well. He doesn't appear to have any friends, apart from business acquaintances. I spoke to Lily, the housekeeper, like you asked, and she said he often gets visitors at odd hours."

"Describe 'odd hours'."

"The middle of the night. She has a room at the manor, although she rarely stays there. She says it creeps her out."

Celeste shivered. "It would creep me out too, by the looks of things."

"He also takes a lot of business trips."

"You mean he leaves the country?" asked Rob.

"I don't know, but whenever he goes away, he asks her to make sure his laundry and ironing is done, so he can pack."

Rob rubbed his stubble. "How long does he go away for?"

"Sometimes a few days, other times it's weeks." Trent hesitated. "Also, and I don't know if this is relevant, but he often takes insect repellent with him, and malaria tablets."

"How do you know that?" Harry asked.

"He gets Lily to pick them up from the pharmacy."

"He's going somewhere with a lot of bugs," Harry murmured. "South America?"

"Africa?" suggested Will. "There's malaria in Africa."

"Third-world countries," said Rob, thoughtfully.

"He's definitely still operational," Jenny concluded. Then she snapped her fingers. "What if he's working for the government?"

They all stared at her.

"I know it sounds crazy, but hear me out. Twelve years ago, he's on an Interpol watch list. He moves to the United Kingdom and is suddenly a bona fide citizen. No more watch list. He lives quietly in Marlow, but gets strange visits from nefarious characters in the middle of the night. People who don't want to be seen."

"Could be criminals," Rob said. "Suppliers or even customers."

"Could also be the British government," she added, her eyes gleaming. "Off-the-book operations."

This was beginning to sound like a conspiracy theory, although he was the first to admit the Serb was dodgy as hell.

"I think I know someone who might be able to help us," he said.

Jenny grinned. "How is Jo?" It had been Jenny who'd called the paramedics and saved Jo's life after the attack. Rob shuddered when he thought back to that awful day. It was thanks to her quick thinking that his partner and the mother of his child was still alive.

"She's doing great," he said. "Going back to work in January."

"I'm glad to hear it."

"Can she find out about Petrovic?" asked Will.

"Maybe. She has a couple of contacts at Whitehall. They might be able to shed some light." Jo worked for MI5, the British Security Service, but had taken extended leave to recover from her injuries. They'd supported her with physiotherapy, occupational therapy and trauma counselling once she'd got out of hospital. It had been a long road back to health, but she'd done well, and Rob was immensely proud of her.

Sometimes, when he woke up drenched in sweat, the guilt eating at him like a cancer, he thought she'd fared better than he had. Sure, he'd had therapy too, for a while, but he wasn't good at talking about his feelings. The sessions made him feel worse. Better to bottle them up and forget about them. Move on. That's how he'd always done things, and while he knew it wasn't the recommended approach, it worked for him.

"Okay, let's get back to Debby Morris," Rob said. "We need to find out why she was so upset at the party. Something happened to make her angry. I want to know what."

"Maybe she found out about her husband's affair," suggested Jenny, echoing his thoughts. "Chloe Brooke was there. They could have had a run-in. Chloe could have told her about the relationship, or maybe Debby confronted her."

"Except Chloe didn't kill her, because she was at the party the whole time. And she was a victim herself."

"What about the trustees?" Harry said. "We haven't talked to them yet. I know we ruled them out, but they were all there. One of them might know something."

"Good point." Rob nodded to Trent. "You're going back to Marlow after this. Why don't you pay them each a visit and report back? Harry's right. They may not have been involved, but they might know why Debby was so angry."

He nodded eagerly.

"We'll keep trawling through this stuff." Jenny gestured to the paperwork on the table.

"Okay, and we need to find out more about the foundation's founder, Dame Constance Blanchard. Will and Harry, why don't you guys investigate her? See if she has any skeletons in her closet. Everybody else seems to."

"She's away in the Algarve," Will told him. "I asked one of the trustees."

"When she gets back, then."

Rob ended the meeting shortly after that, and they filed out, all except Jenny and Celeste, who were still sorting through Chloe's items.

Mayhew's office was empty when he left the incident room. They needed a lead quickly, if there was one to find. Ian Morris was appearing in court today, and then it would go to trial. After that, the case would be closed, and his team would be reassigned. It would go down as a win for the department, but if he was going to sleep at night, he wanted to make sure they had the right man.

CHAPTER 27

Trent met Agatha Roundtree at the Lifegiving Foundation offices in Marlow. It was a cold, blustery day, the kind that turned your nose red and made your eyes water. Still, Trent had worn his thermals, and a black fleece beneath his yellow high-vis jacket, and so had a few extra layers of warmth. His hands were bitterly cold, however, despite the gloves, and he was looking forward to getting inside the building.

Agatha Roundtree was a big woman. There was no other way to describe her. She was tall, wide and had large facial features that gave her a masculine appearance.

"Come in, come in," she fussed, as soon as she opened the door.

Trent stepped gratefully into the warm interior. Rubbing his hands, he looked around the office. Situated above a bakery, it was the size of a small studio apartment, carpeted, with a wooden desk in front of the wide bay window. A doughy smell of baked bread made his stomach rumble.

"Would you like a hot drink?" she offered.

He was tempted but shook his head. This wasn't a social call, and DCI Miller would be disappointed if he found out Trent was drinking tea with potential witnesses.

"Thank you for seeing me," he said. "I would like to ask you some questions about the party."

"Such a tragedy." Agatha Roundtree shook her head. Her greying bob didn't move, and Trent suspected it might be a wig. "Please, take a seat."

Trent sat on one of the two cream wingback chairs positioned around a small coffee table. "Do you remember talking to Debby Morris that night?"

"Yes, yes. Lovely girl. Good treasurer, too. Always on top of things, you know? Rare, in this day and age." She eased her robust frame into the other chair. It groaned loudly, and Trent wondered if the little wooden legs would hold her weight.

"Yes, of course." He gathered his thoughts. "Mrs Roundtree, do you remember if Debby was upset or angry the night of the party?"

"Hmm . . . now that you mention it, she was a bit off colour towards the end. The only reason I remember is because I asked her if she needed a lift home and she snapped at me. Said she was going to walk because she wanted to clear her head. I thought it was odd at the time. I mean, it was a frigid night, and it's so unlike Debby to snap like that. But then, she didn't live far away, and I figured something had happened to get her knickers in a twist."

Trent smiled at the old-fashioned phrase. "Do you know what it was?"

"No, but I did see her talking to Roman Petrovic a short while before. Heads together, deep in conversation, they were. I don't know what they were nattering about, but Roman is a man of few words, which is why I was surprised."

"Did she look annoyed with him?"

"Not then, but maybe he said something to set her off. She left soon after that."

"What time was that?" Trent's pulse ticked up a notch. So far, Agatha Roundtree was the only person to notice what time Debby Morris had left the party.

"It was around midnight." She smiled. "Pumpkin hour, as I tell my grandchildren."

He smiled politely, but his brain was working overtime. If she left at midnight, it would make her time of death around twelve thirty. Most guests would still be at the party. "Did you speak to her before she left?"

"Sadly, no. If only we'd known. I blame myself, you know. I should never have let her walk home alone."

* * *

"Roman Petrovic?" Rob held the phone to his ear. "That's who she was talking to?"

"Yes," replied Trent. He was calling DCI Miller from the car outside Agatha Roundtree's house. "It was after that her behaviour changed. She became angry and agitated and told Mrs Roundtree that she wanted to walk home to clear her head."

"What on earth did he say to upset her like that?" It was late afternoon, and Rob had just got off a call with Jo. She'd spoken to a contact at Whitehall who'd hinted — off the record, of course — that Petrovic was working with the armed forces to protect British interests in Africa. The contact hadn't been able to say what, exactly. Only that it was most likely to do with mining.

"Do you want me to ask him?"

Rob hesitated. Marlow was a good hour away by car, and Trent was already there, but Rob didn't feel like this was something the young constable should do alone, and he was the only other member of the team who'd met the shady billionaire. Roman Petrovic would eat Trent alive.

"Wait for me," he said. "I'll meet you at Marlow Police Station in about an hour."

Trent uttered an excited, "Yes, guv!"

Rob sent Jo a message saying he was going to be late, and he'd make it up to her when this case was over, then set off for Marlow. The late-afternoon traffic was terrible, and it took Rob nearly an hour and a half to reach the Buckinghamshire town. The radio presenter had said snow was predicted, and the bookies were giving ten-to-one odds for a white Christmas.

Trent was waiting for him at the police station but came out as soon as Rob hooted. "I called Lily, just in case," Trent said as he got into the car. "Petrovic is at home."

"Good thinking," Rob said.

They drove past the entrance to Higginson Park, where Debby had been murdered, and turned down a narrow lane. At the bottom, he took a right into Petrovic's driveway. The steel gates, like the last time they'd visited, were open, and the car's headlights cut through the gloom as they approached the house. Rob spotted a dark figure patrolling the perimeter. He pointed him out to Trent.

"Roman Petrovic always has a couple of guards lurking around," Trent said. "They act as a deterrent more than anything else, but Lily says they freak her out."

"I'm sure they do." The man in the shadows watched in silent judgement as they drove past.

The manor house was floodlit from below, making the protruding stone balconies and cornices look grey and foreboding. It reminded Rob of a scene from a horror movie. All that was missing was a gargoyle or two.

Roman Petrovic stood silhouetted in the doorway. "Good evening, officers." He gave them a grin that could also have been a sneer. "My housekeeper told me you were coming."

"Thank you for seeing us," Rob said, as Petrovic moved aside to let them enter. "I apologise for the lateness of the visit."

"Not at all. I come alive at night." At Rob's surprised look, he smirked. "Insomniac. Don't sleep very well."

Why wasn't he surprised? Black suit, black shirt, pale skin. Give the guy a cloak, and he could be Dracula.

"Would you like a drink?" Petrovic led them into the same reception room as before. The house was large, but most of the lights were off. Only the living room was warm and cosy.

"No thanks, we're working."

"You don't mind if I do?" Without waiting for a reply, Petrovic poured himself a glass of red. "It's been quite a day. Actually, you're lucky you caught me. I'm leaving on a trip tomorrow."

"Where are you going?" asked Rob.

"South Africa," he replied.

"Business or pleasure?" asked Rob.

"A bit of both."

"What is it you do, Mr Petrovic?" Rob came right out and asked him. Enough with the secrets.

The dark eyes flickered. "I am a consultant."

Could he be any vaguer? "What kind of consultant?"

"Security. I provide security solutions for British organisations based in Africa."

"Like mining companies?"

A slow smile. "Exactly."

"Mr Petrovic." Rob looked around. Lily was nowhere to be seen. "We have a few more questions about Debby Morris."

"I answered all your questions last time."

"Yes, you did, but unfortunately, we have some more. You see, you didn't tell us the whole truth."

A scowl. "What do you mean?"

"You said Debby appeared normal to you, but one of the other guests told us she was angry and upset after speaking to you."

His jaw clamped shut.

"Would you tell us what you said that upset her so?"

He glared at them but said nothing.

"Mr Petrovic, it's important we know what Debby was upset about. It was because she was angry that she decided to walk home instead of getting a cab."

"Are you saying her death was my fault?"

"Is it?"

"No, of course not." He hesitated. "She wasn't angry with me. She was angry at what I told her."

"Which was?" Talk about drip-feeding information. Trent watched the exchange, his gaze switching from Rob to Petrovic and back again like he was watching a tennis match.

"Who her parents really were."

There was a pause as Rob processed this.

"Her parents?" he said eventually.

Petrovic sighed. "I don't know if you know, but her parents were killed in Africa."

"I had heard, yes. They were tea importers or something."

He gave a dry laugh. "That's what she thought too, but it isn't true. They lied to her."

Rob stared at the Serbian, confused. "Why would they lie to their own daughter?"

"I don't know, but I met them once, in Kinshasa, and they weren't tea importers. Her father worked for AngloCore, a British mining company."

"Where's Kinshasa?" Trent spoke for the first time.

"The Democratic Republic of Congo," Rob replied.

"You know your geography, Detective Chief Inspector." Petrovic smirked. "Sadly, tragedy struck. The hotel they were staying in was attacked by rebel militia, and they were killed along with a bunch of other people."

"That part was true, at least," Rob said. "Although I heard it was terrorists."

"Over there, it's the same thing," he shrugged.

"And you told her this at the party?"

"That's right. We got talking about Africa. She said her parents travelled there a lot because of her father's business. When I asked who they were, I was surprised to find that I had met them. I told her this, but she said I must be mistaken. She told me that her father was a tea importer."

"Are you sure you had the right couple?" Rob asked.

"I am sure. I remember them clearly. Peter and Maud Barrett."

"Barrett was Debby's maiden name," Trent whispered.

"You see, Detective Chief Inspector, I am not mistaken. Peter Barrett was a lead negotiator for AngloCore, not a tea importer."

Rob thought about this for a minute. Debby had been in a good mood, enjoying the party, and then Petrovic had dropped his bombshell. Stunned, she'd left the party, saying she needed to clear her head.

"Did you see her leave?" he asked the Serb.

"No, I'm afraid I did not. The last time I saw Debby, she was talking with Sir Ainsworth."

"Leland Ainsworth, the Tory MP?"

"That is correct."

"When was that?"

"Right after I spoke to her." He shook his head. "He came to me afterwards and told me how upset she was. I should never have said anything about her parents. It was a mistake."

"Opened up a can of worms, did it?"

Petrovic looked at him blankly, not getting the reference.

"Never mind." Rob scratched his head. "Did you speak to Sir Ainsworth after that?"

"Yes, for a long time. Mostly about politics. Now, if you'll excuse me, I have an early start."

"Mr Petrovic," Rob said, standing up. "Would you show me where you held the party?"

He looked annoyed. "If you insist."

"It would help to get an idea of the layout of the house."

They followed Petrovic across the main hallway and through a door identical to the one they'd just come out of. It was cold in here, much colder than the other side. The heating was probably off. Rob couldn't blame him. A house this size must cost a fortune to heat.

The Serb flicked on a light and a big chandelier blazed overhead. They were standing in a large reception room with wood panelling, bay windows, and elaborate gold curtains.

"This is where I held the reception." Petrovic nodded to a door on the other side of the room. "Through there is the bar area."

Rob walked through to take a look. "I don't use this wing unless I'm entertaining," Petrovic said.

"Makes sense." He was about to turn around when he saw a door in the far corner, behind the bar. "Where does that go?" he asked.

"My gym," Petrovic replied. "I like to keep in shape. It's important to have good cardiovascular health."

Rob recalled that his wife had died of heart failure. "May we see it?" he asked.

Petrovic sighed, but headed in the direction of the door. "I don't know why you want a tour of my house, Detective Chief Inspector." Trent looked equally perplexed. "Are you thinking of making me an offer?" He smiled at his little joke.

Rob didn't reply.

The Serb pushed open the door and they stepped into a purpose-built studio with a mat laid out on the floor, weights lined up along the side, a stationary bicycle, a rowing machine, and several other pieces of gym equipment positioned around the room.

"Wow." Trent's eyes were out on stalks. "This is a great home gym."

The Serb nodded.

"What's through there?" Rob motioned toward a set of sliding doors at the far end of the studio. Despite being glass, it was too dark to see what lay behind them.

Petrovic pulled open one of the doors and they were hit by a whiff of chlorine. Rob knew what was in the room before the light went on.

A swimming pool.

CHAPTER 28

"Do we think Roman Petrovic killed Chloe Brooke?" Jenny stared at Rob. Caffè Nero had become their new briefing room, out of sight of Mayhew's beady eyes. He'd just filled them in on the events of the night before.

"I don't know." Rob rubbed his eyes. He'd barely slept, turning what he'd learned over and over in his head. Roman Petrovic. African rebels. AngloCore. Leland Ainsworth. Chloe Brooke. Was there a connection?

"Why would Petrovic kill Chloe?" Harry frowned. "He'd known her for years. Four years, to be exact. Why kill her now?"

"We don't know that he did," said Jenny.

"But the pool—" Trent blurted out. After all, he'd seen the suspect escape across the Thames.

"There's no motive." She tapped the lid of her double-shot Americano. "None at all. She was his event planner."

"Unless she found something out about him," suggested Celeste. "Something he didn't want her to know."

Rob pursed his lips.

"And what about Sir Ainsworth?" added Will. "He was the last person to see Debby before she left. He must have been. Why didn't he mention that before?"

"We'll have to talk to him again." Rob was sick to death of people lying to him. Everyone had their own agenda. Roman Petrovic hadn't wanted to tell them the truth because he didn't want to draw attention to his work in Africa. Sir Ainsworth hadn't mentioned, when asked, that he'd spoken to Debby at the end of the night.

"Hang on." Celeste began flicking through her iPad. "I know I saw something on Leland Ainsworth yesterday, when I was doing background checks on the other guests."

Rob waited.

"Here it is!" She smiled triumphantly. "I knew it had something to do with Africa."

"What is it?" Jenny leaned over to look.

"Before he was an MP, Leland Ainsworth worked for the Foreign Office." She glanced up at Rob. "He was Her Majesty's Ambassador to the Democratic Republic of Congo."

There was a brief pause as this sank in.

"What were the dates of his tenure?" asked Rob, quietly.

"From 2013 to 2016."

Rob did the maths. "He would have been there at the time Debby's parents were killed."

Trent checked something on his phone. "Yep, her parents were killed in May 2013."

"What does it mean?" whispered Celeste, her eyes wide.

"I don't know," said Rob. "But we need to speak to Sir Ainsworth. Pronto."

* * *

Felicity was waiting for Rob when he got to the office. She'd seen the rest of his team walk in one by one and go to their desks. Nobody spoke to each other. Something was going on; she just didn't know what.

"DCI Miller, can I have a word?"

"Now?" He threw his coat on the back of his chair.

"Yes, if you don't mind. In my office."

She saw his shoulders slump, but he followed her across the squad room. It was at times like this that he reminded her of a naughty schoolboy who'd been caught skipping class. "How are the trial preparations coming on?"

He wouldn't meet her eye. "Good. We're making progress."

"Ian Morris had his hearing today."

"I heard. He refused to plead."

"It's going to the Crown Court. Trial date is set for the twenty-fourth of June next year." Six months was pretty standard these days, thanks to the court's caseload.

"Did he get bail?" Rob asked.

"He did, and rumour has it he's hired Pearson Willoughby as his criminal defence solicitor."

Rob's eyes widened. "Where'd he get the money for that?"

"It's a high-profile case," Felicity grimaced. "Everybody wants it. I heard Willoughby contacted him."

"Willoughby doesn't take cases he can't win," Rob pointed out.

Felicity felt a frisson of annoyance. "Well, he's not going to win this one. We have an airtight case, right?"

Rob shifted, clearly uncomfortable.

"What?" she barked, then saw his gaze harden and regretted the sharpness of her retort. Rob Miller was the type of person that shut down when pressured. She'd worked with him long enough to know that.

Felicity sighed. "What's going on, Rob?"

His eyebrow arched at the use of his first name.

She leaned forward, increasing the intimacy. "You'd better tell me now, before this goes any further."

He sighed, then gave a resolute nod. "Okay, but you're not going to like it."

Damn it. She'd bloody known there was something going on. Steeling herself, she asked, "What is it?"

"We've uncovered some information that's put a different spin on the case."

She narrowed her gaze. "What information?"

He got comfortable, folding his arms across his body. "Debby Morris discovered something at the charity Christmas party that shocked her. Something about her parents."

"I'm all ears." She listened while DCI Miller told her about Debby's folks being killed in a hotel in Kinshasa, wherever that was.

"I'm sorry, I don't see how this has any bearing on the case."

He held up a hand. "I'm getting there. Bear with me." He took a deep breath. "Debby's parents had told her they were tea importers, which was why they were always travelling to Africa."

Felicity watched him, waiting for the *but* . . .

"When, in fact, her father worked for a British mining company called AngloCore. Roman Petrovic met them in Africa — before they were gunned down in the hotel shooting."

Felicity gave a sharp intake of breath. "That's quite a coincidence."

"It is." Rob fixed his steely gaze on her. "What's even more of a coincidence is that Leland Ainsworth was the British Ambassador to the DRC at that time."

"He was also there?"

Rob nodded. "Roman Petrovic, Leland Ainsworth and Debby's parents were all in Kinshasa at the same time, ten years ago."

Felicity closed her eyes and felt a vague spinning sensation. Shaking her head, she said, "What does this mean? That Debby was killed because of something that happened ten years ago?"

"I honestly don't know, ma'am. I'm just telling you what we discovered. I think it's worth looking into."

"Roman Petrovic is an arms dealer, right?"

"Not officially. He claims he's a security consultant."

"But at the time, he was dealing arms."

"I think it's a safe guess, yes."

"And he told Debby about her parents? She didn't know what they'd done for a living?"

Rob shook his head. "It came as a shock to her. She was angry and upset. Roman said she went to speak to Sir Ainsworth immediately afterwards, so she probably discussed it with him."

"Ainsworth would have had to deal with the hotel shooting," Felicity extrapolated. "If he was ambassador at the time."

"He was responsible for the flow of information," Rob said. "Back in London, Debby was told her parents had died in a terrorist attack on the hotel."

"But you don't think it was random?"

He held out his hands. "Do you?"

She stared at him for a long moment, then blurted, "Jesus, Rob. Why does everything have to be so complicated with you? Why can't the husband be guilty? Go to trial. Get sentenced. End of story."

There was the faintest sparkle in his eye. "I'm sorry, ma'am."

She shook her head. "I take it you're going to talk to Sir Ainsworth again?"

"I have to. He's the last person Debby spoke to before she left the party."

Felicity heaved a great big sigh. "I don't like this, Rob. We're getting into murky water here. Sir Ainsworth has some powerful allies. We can't afford to ruffle any more feathers."

"I'm aware," Rob said coolly. "But if he had something to do with her death, then he deserves to be punished, just like anybody else."

"*If* he had anything to do with it," she pointed out. "Don't assume he's involved until you've spoken to him. Keep it light. I don't want him to feel like he's being interrogated."

"He should be interrogated."

She shot him a dark look. "You know what I mean."

Rob rubbed his hands on his trousers, then got up. "There's one more thing, ma'am."

She was almost afraid to ask. "What?"

"Roman Petrovic is a strong swimmer. He has a pool in his basement in Marlow."

It took her a few seconds to put together what he was saying. "You think he's the man who killed Chloe Brooke?"

"Again, I don't know. All I'm saying is, he fits the description PC Trent gave us of the assailant, and he could easily have swum across the Thames and escaped."

She spread her arms. "But why? Why would he want to kill his party planner?"

Rob shook his head. "I can't tell you that either, ma'am. Yet." He shot her a sympathetic grin, then left her office. Felicity stared after him, not knowing what to think.

She dropped her head into her hands. This case was another bloody disaster.

CHAPTER 29

Sir Ainsworth wasn't answering his phone. When Rob called the MP's office, he got his brisk assistant, who told him the politician was tied up in meetings for the rest of the day. So Rob intercepted him outside the Houses of Parliament when he left to go home to his London townhouse, where he stayed during the week.

"What do you want?" Sir Ainsworth said, much less jolly now.

"I'm just wondering why you lied to us, Sir Ainsworth. You do realise it's a crime to lie to an officer of the law."

Ainsworth stopped and faced him. "I did not lie."

"You told us you spoke to Debby Morris during the evening and that she appeared fine. But she wasn't fine, was she? She was angry, very angry. You should have told us what you were talking about."

Ainsworth's eyes turned to slits. "The topic of conversation is unimportant."

"I beg to differ. She asked you about her parents, didn't she? She wanted to know the truth about what happened to them in Kinshasa."

"How do you know about that?" Before Rob could answer, he gave a stiff nod. "Ah, yes. Roman bloody Petrovic. I knew that Serb couldn't be trusted."

"Trusted with what?" Rob asked.

Ainsworth gave a quick shake of his head. "There's no mystery, Detective Chief Inspector. Debby's parents were shot in an attack on a hotel in Kinshasa, along with many other people. It was a fucking disaster. I was ambassador at the time, as I'm sure you know by now, and I had to clean it up."

"Why did you lie to Debby? Why not tell her the truth, that her parents worked for AngloCore?"

"To protect her," he said simply. "Her parents didn't want her to know, in case she mentioned it to anybody. You see, the situation in Africa was volatile. The mining companies were doing deals with the dictators, who didn't last for very long before there was a bloody coup and a new leader took over. It was a mess. We were constantly trying to stay on top of it, protect the mines from rebels and keep production going."

"What part did Roman Petrovic play in all this?"

"He supplied our security forces with weapons."

"Legally?"

He waved his hand in the air. "It was a grey area. We had men on the ground protecting the mines. They needed arms and ammunition. Petrovic got it for us. We didn't ask where from. That's the way it is over there. You don't ask too many questions."

"When Petrovic told Debby, she was upset."

"Very," Ainsworth added. "Can't say I blame her, to be honest. I tried to calm her down, but I don't think I succeeded. She stormed off, saying she needed some air. That's the last I saw of her."

Rob studied him. In the uneven street lighting, he appeared older than before, wearier. The lines under his eyes were more pronounced, but he seemed to be telling the truth. "Why didn't you mention this before?"

"What would you have made of it?" Ainsworth asked. "Debby left that party in a state after talking to me, and an hour later she was dead. I didn't need the additional headache, and I certainly don't need to rehash what happened in the DRC all those years ago."

Rob stared coldly at him. "Well, I'm sorry to have inconvenienced you." He had one more question before he left. "Did you notice anyone else leave the party that night?"

"No, but I wasn't watching to see who left; I was enjoying myself. In fact, Roman and I got into a long conversation about the future of the Party, and the next thing I knew, it was well after midnight."

Rob gave a stiff nod. "We'll be in touch if we have any more questions. Have a good evening, sir."

* * *

"I couldn't believe the audacity of the man," Rob fumed when he got home. Trigger, alarmed by his master's foul mood, trotted up and down beside him. "To say he didn't need the headache. The woman was murdered, for Christ's sake."

Jo put down the jar of baby food. "You're upsetting Trigger."

Rob stopped pacing and fondled the lab's ears. "I'm sorry, I'm just so frustrated. This case is doing my head in."

"Do you think he had anything to do with her death?"

"I don't think so. He's in his sixties. I can't see him hitting Debby Morris on the head, dragging her unconscious body all the way to the river and then drowning her. He's just a selfish prick who didn't want the whole Africa thing to blow up again. I get the feeling the Foreign Office tried to bury it."

"It does sound messy. He's right about the instability, though. It's one of the reasons why doing business in Africa is so difficult. The power base is always shifting. Support the wrong side, and you're supporting a coup. People die, and it hits the media, and you've got an international incident on your hands. It's no wonder they tried to keep it quiet."

Rob grunted. After he'd spoken to Ainsworth, he'd gone back to the office and told the team he was going home. This case had been all-consuming of late, and he wanted to spend some time with his family. They all needed a break.

Except here he was, still talking about the case. "Ainsworth would have had to have left right after Debby to accost her in the park. She was younger and fitter than him, and it was a freezing-cold night. She would have been walking fast. I don't think he would have caught up with her. Not on foot."

Jo tested the temperature of the milk on the inside of her wrist. "Did anyone see him at the party later?"

Rob sank down on to the bench at the breakfast nook. "I'm not sure, I'll have to ask the team to check tomorrow."

She nodded. "I'll just take this up to Jack."

Rob took it from her. "I'll do that. You sit down, drink your tea." She had an untouched mug on the countertop beside the kettle.

She picked it up and took it to the table. "Thanks."

Jack was waking up, his eyelids heavy, his pale blue eyes slightly bewildered, as if he wasn't sure what was happening. When he saw his daddy, he gave a little smile and Rob's heart melted. This was what was important, not some selfish bastard who was more worried about his reputation than a dead mother of two. Rob exhaled and leaned over to give Jack the bottle.

His son reached up, wrapped his chubby hands around it and popped it straight into his mouth. Rob stroked his head while he drank, marvelling at how soft his hair was. The eyes began to close again.

Leaving Jack to fall asleep, Rob went back downstairs and took Jo in his arms. "I'm sorry I've been in a mood. This case is getting to me."

She smiled. "That's okay. I'm quite envious, to be honest."

He tilted his head back to look at her. "You are?"

"Yeah, it's good to see you back at work. I remember what it felt like, getting stuck into a case. Couldn't leave it alone. I miss that."

"You'll be back in a couple of weeks."

"I know. It's not the same though. MI5 is . . . different."

Rob studied her. Apart from the silver scar across her throat, she'd made a full recovery. He knew she was doing Pilates every morning to build up her strength and was in better shape than she had been before the attack.

"Are you thinking about packing it in and going back to major crimes?" Before she'd joined the Security Services, she'd worked for one of the major investigation teams up north. That's how he'd met her. They'd paired up to work a case. Catching the infamous Surrey Stalker was as much thanks to her as it was to him and his team.

"No . . . yes . . . maybe." She shook her head. "I don't know. I guess I'm just eager to get back to work."

He could understand that. They kissed, and he said, "Now, put me to work. What are we having for supper?"

She laughed. "You should come home early more often."

He put his hand on her face and felt a surge of contentment. Despite everything, he still had this. Jo, Jack, Trigger. The Labrador raised his head as if to say, *I know you're thinking about me.*

He said, "I intend to."

CHAPTER 30

Felicity arrived at the wine bar she and her younger sister used to frequent. It was lit up like a Christmas tree, and there was much laughter and jollity inside as revellers celebrated the end of the working year.

God, she'd forgotten it was the week before Christmas. Would they have an office Christmas party? Maybe they had already, and she hadn't been invited.

She sighed.

When had life become so serious? She and Faith used to come here at least once a month and catch up, but at some point over the last few years, they'd stopped coming. Her work had taken centre stage, and Faith had joined the parents' committee at her daughters' school and seemed to be taken up with sports days, Christmas parties and fundraisers. The sad truth of it was, they didn't have anything in common anymore.

She bought a glass of wine and took a seat by the steamed-up window. Picking up a napkin, she wiped away the moisture so she could see outside. It had been dark for hours, but the cluster of shops along Upper Richmond Road twinkled festively. Felicity had never felt less Christmassy. There weren't any decorations up at the office. Murder was too serious a business for frivolity. It felt wrong to be celebrating when people were dying.

Her little investigation into Matthew Gray had turned out to be a waste of time. On the afternoon Chloe was killed, Matthew Gray had been talking at a police conference on the "urgent reforms" which would lead the country's biggest force out of crisis.

She snorted. That was ironic.

A few minutes later, she watched Faith get out of a cab and hurry into the restaurant, coat and scarf wrapped firmly around her. Unlike Felicity, Faith had a fuller figure, a softer, more nurturing nature, and was very homely. The only thing they had in common was their flaming red hair, inherited from their mother's Irish side of the family.

While Faith took after their mild-mannered father, Felicity was ambitious, driven and fiercely independent. It was hard to believe they were sisters. Sometimes, she wondered what would have happened if she'd met the right man. Would she have settled down too? Had children?

Sighing, she sipped her wine. Doubtful. Anyway, it didn't matter, the opportunity had never presented itself. Things just hadn't worked out that way for her.

"It's because you're too opinionated," Faith used to tease. "No man could handle you." They'd laughed about it then. Now Felicity had a career, and Faith had her family.

Until now.

"I'll just get a drink." Faith rushed over and dumped her handbag on the table. "Be right back."

Felicity smiled. Her sister dashed over to the bar and came back with a bottle and two glasses. At her raised eyebrow, Faith groaned and sank down into the chair opposite. "Yes, it is that bad."

It was time to be the caring older sister. "Tell me what's going on."

"I caught them together, Fee. Oh God, it was awful. I'll never get that image out of my head."

No one had called her *Fee* in a long time. "I'm so sorry. How? What happened?"

"Mike's been acting weird for a while." Her eyes were wild, and flashed red and yellow as they reflected the fairy lights in the tree opposite. "He's a terrible liar. I could always see right through him. He started hiding his phone, keeping it in his pocket, on silent. He never does that, so I knew something was up."

"Did you ask him about it?"

"Of course. At first, I thought I was being paranoid, but then I began to suspect he was having an affair."

"So you followed him?" It's what she would have done.

Faith nodded, tears sliding down her face. "He was working late, so I went to his office. I was going to pretend to surprise him, but there they were . . ." Her voice changed to a hiss. "Going at it on the couch." She shook her head, unable to continue.

Felicity took her hand across the table. "I'm so sorry, Faith. Did you talk?"

"We shouted, if that counts. He was shocked to see me standing there, and I felt like a fool, so I left."

"Did he come after you?"

"He did, but I wasn't in the mood to listen. I drove off without speaking to him, and when he got home, I pretended to be asleep."

"When was this?" Felicity asked.

"Two days ago."

"And you still haven't talked about it?"

"What is there to talk about? He's been shagging his PA. That's not something you can get over."

Felicity looked at her sister and saw the pain in her eyes. Not for the first time, she was grateful she had her life together. Sort of. And didn't have a man to mess it up.

Except for a certain DCI, she thought sourly.

"What are you going to do?"

"I don't know. You tell me."

"I'm not sure I'm the right person to be dishing out relationship advice, Faith."

"You're always so together, Fee. I feel like I'm falling apart. I don't know what to do."

"Where is Mike now?" Felicity asked.

"He's staying in a B&B. I don't want him near me." She recoiled into the seat. This was bad.

"I'm so sorry, sis."

Faith's tears fell into her wine, and she sniffed. "I don't know what to do. I don't feel like I can forgive him, you know?"

"Maybe you just need a bit of time to process what's happened."

Faith gave a sad nod.

"But then, you must talk to him. He might feel terrible about this and want to make amends."

Her expression hardened. "Am I supposed to just forget it happened and take him back? Carry on as if nothing's happened?"

"No," Felicity said diplomatically. "But it would be a starting point. Perhaps you can repair your relationship. I'm not saying it's going to be easy, but what's the alternative?"

"I could leave him." She sniffed, her hand gripping the glass so hard Felicity thought it might shatter. "Get a divorce."

"You could." That was an option, of course. Except Faith wasn't the type of woman to go it alone. She'd always needed support. Her sister was a wonderful mother, but emotionally, she needed a partner. She wasn't independent like Felicity. "But give it some time. You might regret rushing into something as final as a divorce."

Her sister chugged down half the wine in her glass. "What do I tell Mike?"

"That you need time to think. He'll understand. He's hurt you, and you have every right to take the time you need to consider your options. Besides, it'll put the fear of God into him."

Faith snorted. "Serve him bloody right."

Felicity couldn't agree more. She liked Mike, but this was a stupid, idiotic thing to do. He'd risked everything for the office floozy. A meaningless fling.

Or was it?

Perhaps it was more serious than that. Was Mike in love with his PA?

"What do I tell the children?" Faith moaned. Her sister and her husband had two girls, two years apart. Theresa was twelve, and a real little madam. She loved dressing up, was experimenting with make-up and hanging around with her friends. A bright, motivated young lady, she reminded Felicity of herself when she was that age. When the world was her oyster, and anything was possible.

Helena was less confident than her older sister. At ten, she was shy and bookish, and didn't go out much. This would be hard on them, but they were young, and children adapted.

"Tell them their father has to look after a friend's home for a while, just until the owners get back, or something like that. Don't let on you're having problems, not yet." She knew what it was like to have your world rocked. Their own parents had split up when they were in their early teens, and while she and Faith had moved to London with their father, their mother had stayed in Dublin, where she lived to this day.

Faith gave a snivelly nod. "Okay, that's good. Yes, I can tell them that."

"You'll have to talk to Mike at some point, though. Let him know what you've told the girls, so he doesn't give them mixed messages. Try to keep them out of this."

"I will. I still remember . . ." Her eyes welled again.

Felicity squeezed her hand. "I know. So do I." A moment passed, then Felicity said, "This isn't like that, you know. You and Mike are not Mum and Dad."

The hope in her sister's eyes was crushing. "You think there's a chance for us? After this?"

"There's always a chance," she said, more optimistically than she felt.

Her sister managed a weak smile. "I hope so."

* * *

It was ten thirty when Felicity got home. It took her a while to get the key in the door. Consoling her sister meant she'd drunk more than she'd meant to and felt quite tipsy. Strangely, even though Faith was having such a rotten time, the talk had done them both good, and she felt closer to her sister than she had in years.

Kicking off her shoes, Felicity sank down on the bed. God, she was tired. The central heating had come on at some point during the evening, and her apartment was warm and cosy. Outside, the bare branches of the silver birch creaked in front of the streetlight. She stared at the jumble of patterns on the ceiling until her eyes began to close.

A shrill ring made her jump. Her phone. She'd turned the volume up in the wine bar so she would hear it if anyone called. Heart still racing, she rolled over and answered it.

"Hello?"

"Felicity, this is Matthew Gray."

She sat up.

Shit.

"Sir, good evening. How can I help you?"

"You don't need to be so formal, Superintendent. This is a courtesy call. I apologise for the late hour. I didn't wake you, did I?"

"No, sir."

"Please, call me Matthew. You and I know each other well enough now to use first names."

Did they? He'd shared a confidence, and she'd promised to keep his secret, but they were hardly friends. "Yes, sir. I mean, Matthew."

"I'm just giving you a heads-up," he said. "I received a perplexing call from Sir Ainsworth today. I'm not sure what to make of it."

Her heart sank. *Here we go.* "He's a person of interest in the Debby Morris case." She hoped she wasn't slurring her words. *Person of interest* wasn't the easiest thing to say when you'd had a few.

"I see." There was a pause, which went on for too long.

"What did he say?" she asked.

"He's concerned that your questions about Debby Morris's parents' deaths are encroaching on a potentially sensitive subject."

"You mean the shootings in Kinshasa?"

Another pause.

"Yes, and the situation in the DRC at the time."

She cleared her throat and looked around for a glass of water, but there wasn't one. "I can assure you, the Kinshasa incident doesn't have anything to do with the Debby Morris case. It's just that Debby found out about it on the night of the party."

"How?" he asked.

"Roman Petrovic told her. Apparently, he was there, too."

"In Kinshasa?"

"That's right. He knew her parents. That's the reason she left early, sir. She was upset by what he'd told her."

"Matthew, please."

She hesitated. "Matthew."

"Is that why she gave Leland an earful?"

"I expect so. We don't think it's relevant, but we had to look into it, you understand."

Softly: "I understand."

She thought he was going to berate her for rocking the boat. Didn't they already have a suspect? Ian Morris had been charged with his wife's murder. Why were they still investigating? Instead, he said, "Good police work, Felicity."

"Sir?" She blinked, surprised by his docile response.

"You guys are doing a good job there. Keep it up."

"We will, sir. Thank you."

He didn't correct her this time. "Would you like to get dinner sometime, Felicity?"

She froze. Had her boss just asked her out? The same boss who was cheating on his wife? Who'd asked her to cover up his mess?

"Um . . . I'm sorry, sir. I'd like to, but I'm really busy at the moment. This case—"

"I understand. Another time, perhaps?"

"Yes, sure." What else could she say? Turning him down outright would be a bad career move, but then again, she wasn't about to date him either. A serial adulterer, by the looks of things.

Hanging up, she nearly laughed at the irony. The only man to ask her out in the last year was her prick of a boss. Felicity lay back on the bed and closed her eyes. In seconds, she was fast asleep, dreaming disturbing dreams of Matthew Gray.

CHAPTER 31

It was two days before Christmas. "Looks like snow." Rob glanced up at the muted sky as he stepped outside the next morning.

"Bookies are saying five to one." Jo stood in the doorway seeing him off, Trigger by her side.

Rob shot her a grin and he unlocked the car. The odds had decreased. They'd had a good evening, and he felt more grounded than he had in weeks. "See you later."

He was about to get into the car when he noticed the white envelope under the windscreen wiper. Glancing left and right, he checked the street was clear.

"What is it?" asked Jo, sensing something was up.

"There's a note on my car." Pulling on a pair of forensic gloves, he extracted the envelope from underneath the wipers. It felt cold, but not wet, so it hadn't been out here very long. He turned it over.

DCI Miller was written on the front.

"Who's it from?" she asked.

"I don't know." Relocking the car, he went back into the house. "I'll open it and see."

"Should we be worried?" Jo bit her lip nervously. "I mean, it could be anthrax or something."

It wasn't like her to catastrophise, but he got it. After what had happened six months ago, and with a toddler in the house . . . They had a lot more to lose now.

"It could just be a note." He held it down for Trigger to sniff. The dog's tail didn't stop wagging. He thought Rob was coming back to stay.

Jo looked at Trigger and nodded. "Okay, open it."

Rob went into the kitchen and got a knife from the drawer. Then, he carefully sliced the envelope open. No white powder puffed out; no chemical reaction took place. They were safe. He opened it wider and took out an A5 piece of paper. It was lined, like it had been torn off a notepad. His first thought was *journalist,* but you could get those notepads in any stationer. No clues there.

"What does it say?" Jo whispered.

Carefully, Rob unfolded the note. It was typewritten, and said:

Community Grants Programme

"What does it mean?" Jo stared at the note. "I've never heard of the Community Grants Programme."

"Me neither." He thought hard. "It sounds like something a charity would run."

The sound of crying came from upstairs. "I've got to go." Jo leaned over and kissed him. "Have a good day, and for God's sake, be careful."

"I will." He put the note back in the envelope and stuck it into his inside coat pocket. Forensics could take a look at that once he got to work.

Jo went upstairs to see to Jack, and he walked back to the door, Trigger trotting after him.

* * *

"You mean it was just there, under your windscreen?" Jenny stared at the note, which Rob had unfolded and laid out on the incident room table.

"Yeah, and it hadn't been there for long, because it would have fallen apart in this weather."

"Someone was watching the house?" Will asked.

"Or they just took a chance. It was early. I would have left for work shortly afterwards."

"What's the Community Grants Programme?" asked Jenny.

Celeste, who'd been tapping her iPad, read out loud: "A community outreach programme run by the Lifegiving Foundation to empower community, faith or belief organisations to educate ethnic minorities on the importance of blood, organ and stem cell donation." She glanced up. "Apparently, they're underrepresented in that area."

"But why has someone put this on your car?" Harry butted in. "Do they want us to look into it?"

"It's a tip-off." Rob gave a thoughtful nod. "Someone knows something."

"You think the charity is embezzling funds?" Jenny looked around the table at the others.

"I don't know, but we should follow it up." Rob turned to Celeste. "Can you call SOCO? We need to get this analysed. Ask them to put a rush on it. The typewriter has left whoever wrote this wide open."

"Not many typewriters around these days," muttered Will.

"We find the typewriter, we find the author," confirmed Rob. But, of course, that was easier said than done.

"I didn't see a typewriter at Ian Morris's house." Jenny nibbled at her thumbnail.

"It's something an older person would have," said Harry. "My money is on that trustee, Agatha Roundtree, or Dame Constance. They're in the right age group."

"I doubt she'd implicate her own charity." Rob scratched his head, but he had to agree with Harry. "There are probably a few typewriters lying around the Houses of Parliament."

Celeste's eyes widened. "You think this is from Sir Ainsworth?"

"I don't know, but it could be an attempt to distract us from the incident in Africa involving Debby's parents. Light a fire over here, so we don't look over there."

Harry frowned. "I didn't think the African incident had anything to do with Debby Morris's death?"

"We can't rule it out," Rob said. "Unfortunately, the Foreign Office isn't going to give us any information, so if Ainsworth did want to prevent Debby from issuing a complaint, we're going to have to prove it some other way."

"It's not going to be via their mobile phones either." Will grimaced. "Reception in Marlow, particularly along the river, is abysmal. I couldn't do a location lookup on any of the guests who were there. Hollyhock Manor is in one big black spot."

"Bugger," muttered Rob.

"How does Petrovic do business if there's no phone reception?" Jenny asked Will. It was a good question.

The techie shrugged. "He must have a booster, or he's using Wi-Fi and an app, like WhatsApp, that's encrypted."

"He probably planned it that way," growled Rob. "Besides, he'd know all the tricks. That man is used to flying under the radar."

"Do you want me to draw up a search warrant?" Jenny asked.

Rob nodded. "I'll get it signed off. We need access to the Lifegiving Foundation's financials."

"You want us to go over there and execute it?" Harry asked.

Rob shook his head and took out his phone. "Trent can get a couple of officers from Thames Valley to do it."

While he made the call, he glanced at Mayhew's office. She was staring at her computer, a million miles away. He'd probably have to update her at some point, but now wasn't the time. Once they had something definite, he'd take it to her.

Trent arrived that afternoon with boxes of files and one desktop computer. "This was Debby's." He huffed as he placed it on the boardroom table. It had taken him three trips to bring all the material up from his car, but at no point had the computer or any of the boxes been left unattended. He placed a chain of custody form on top of it. This would prove nothing had been tampered with during transit. "The other trustees use their private laptops for work, including Dame Constance, who is back from the Algarve and coming in later today."

"Excellent."

"She's livid about the warrant," Trent warned. "I could barely get a word in."

Rob shrugged. She'd get the same treatment as everybody else, Dame or no Dame. Nobody was above the law.

Trent grimaced. "I did what you said, guv, and told her she could make an official complaint at Putney Police Station. She's meeting you there at four o'clock."

"Good work, Constable." Rob gave a pleased nod. They conducted most of their interrogations at Putney nick, as it had a custody suite, and the proper protocol could be followed. The Major Investigation Team's headquarters was mostly administrative. Plus, it was across the road, so wasn't hard to get to.

Trent took a deep breath. "Oh, there's something else."

Rob was gazing at the three boxes on the table. "Yeah?" Already, Will was plugging in the computer. All Chloe Brooke's items had been repackaged and stood in sealed boxes in the corner. The foundation's paperwork had taken its place.

Rob was surprised Mayhew hadn't been in to see what they were up to. She was usually on them whenever a delivery came in, and no one could miss Trent lugging boxes across the squad room.

"I saw Lily last night." He flushed. "We met at the Two Brewers for a drink."

"Yeah?" Rob had a lot on his mind, so he was only half listening.

"She walked through the park to meet me. When I asked her how she got there, she said there was a gate that led from Petrovic's property into the park."

"What?" Rob spun around.

Trent took a step back. "Um, I thought you'd want to know."

"Why is she only mentioning this now?" Rob threw his hands in the air. "Christ, we should have checked when we were there. The manor house is right next to the park. It makes sense there's a gate leading right to it."

"We're not familiar with the area," interjected Jenny. "It takes a while to get your bearings."

Trent hung his head. "I should have checked, guv. I know the area."

Rob ignored his attempt at an apology and drummed his palm on the boardroom table. "This changes everything. It makes everyone a suspect." He turned to Trent. "How long does it take to get to the park from the manor house?"

"Five minutes. Maybe less, if they were running."

"Jesus." He swiped at his hair. "The killer could have left the party that night, snuck through the side gate and into the park to lie in wait. Debby left via the front entrance, so she would have walked down the driveway and around to the park. That's a ten- or fifteen-minute walk at least."

"Sir Ainsworth could have done it," said Jenny.

"Anyone could have done it," growled Rob.

CHAPTER 32

Dame Constance arrived at Putney Police Station in a cloud of Chanel No. 5. "Putney nick's never smelled so good," Harry quipped, before Rob led her to the interview room.

"I would like to file a complaint," she said loudly, as her heels clacked down the corridor. "It's preposterous the way your people barged into my office and confiscated my files." She didn't mention Debby's desktop computer.

"I apologise for the inconvenience, Dame Constance, but I'm afraid it was necessary." Rob tried his best to be diplomatic. "Your employee was murdered. We're trying to find out who did it." She could draw her own conclusions. Ostracising her further by telling her that they were looking into the Community Grants Programme was probably not a good idea.

She held up a manicured finger. Rob noticed she wore several large rings, almost like costume jewellery. "You don't have to remind me. Such a terrible thing. Poor Debby. I don't know what we're going to do without her."

"Did you know her well?" Rob gestured for her to sit down.

Dame Constance brushed a speck of imaginary dust off the metal chair before easing herself and her faux-fur coat on to it — at least, he assumed it was fake. She'd refused to take it off when she'd arrived.

"Not as well as the other trustees, but she's worked for me for a long time, so you could say I knew her *quite* well." She emphasised the "quite" in a high, clipped tone.

"How did she seem to you, the night of the party?" Rob kept the tone conversational.

"She seemed fine, but we spoke very briefly. The Christmas party is an opportunity for me to thank my largest donors, so I was engaged with them for most of the night, not my staff."

"Roman Petrovic being one of them?"

"Of course. Roman has been a friend of the charity for a long time, ever since his wife . . ." She hung her head. "Well, his wife passed away."

"I heard. Did you know her?"

"Never had the pleasure. When I met Roman, he was reeling from her death, and he needed an outlet. Something to pour his grief into. I suggested helping with the charity, but he said he was no good with people." She gave a smug grin. "Imagine my surprise when, the next day, I got a cheque for a hundred thousand pounds."

"He donated a hundred thousand pounds?"

"That's the type of man he is," she said. "So generous."

Interesting.

So the shady arms dealer had an emotional side — or maybe he'd been looking for a tax break. Who knew? He wasn't kidding when he said he wasn't a people person, though.

Rob gave a quick nod. "I understand your husband was at the party too?"

"Yes, poor Ralph. He doesn't enjoy these events, but he and Roman get on well, and he's fond of Zeke, too."

"He's not involved with the foundation?"

"No, that's my baby." She didn't say what her husband did for a living, but Rob knew from their research that Ralph Blanchard was a retired eye surgeon who spent most of his time at their villa in the Algarve.

"I believe you paid for Zeke Hamlin's education?" Rob glanced down at his notes. He had a lot of questions for Dame Constance.

"I did, and I still do. He's a remarkable young man."

"Why do you feel compelled to do that?" Zeke had said his father saved Dame Constance's life, but he wanted her take on it.

"It's a long story," she said. "Our paths crossed a long time ago, and I could see his potential. Being a singer myself, I recognise musical talent. Zeke had a bright future as a classical pianist, but his parents didn't have the means to support him."

"So he's a charity case?"

"You could say that. I like to think of it as giving a young man a chance in life he wouldn't otherwise have had."

"A noble cause," Rob agreed.

She gave a satisfied nod.

"Zeke mentioned his father saved your life, is that right?"

Her shoulders stiffened. "That was how we met, yes." She sighed. "Do we have to go into that? It was a long time ago, and had I met Zeke after that, I would have still sponsored him."

Rob let it go. The details were not important.

"Okay, fine. Let's move on to your charitable work. Tell me about the Community Grants Programme."

Her eyes widened. "What do you want to know about that for?"

"We found a reference to it in the files we confiscated."

She sighed. "There are several projects we run, Detective Chief Inspector. That is just one of them. It's an outreach programme where we work with local organisations to promote organ donation within their communities. There are several ethnic groups that are underrepresented in that area, and we're trying to raise awareness."

"How's that going?" he asked.

"Not as well as we'd have liked, but we will persevere. Sometimes these initiatives are slow to build momentum.

Our trustees run it. I don't know if you've met Agatha Roundtree, Silvia Peacock and Greg Jamieson? They're the engine that drives the foundation."

"I haven't, but one of my team spoke to Ms Roundtree a few days ago."

"They do a marvellous job." She rested her hand on her heart. A dramatic flair from her operatic days.

"I believe you yourself had a life-saving transplant, is that right?"

Her hands fluttered to the prayer position. "It's no secret, Detective Chief Inspector. That's why I started the charity."

"Kidney, wasn't it?"

A nod. "It was some time ago now, but I'm happy to report I'm doing well." She leaned forward. "That's why the work we do is so important. I want to give other people a second chance at life, like I had."

He respected that. Rob tilted his head to the side. "Who decides which organisations receive the funds for the community outreach programmes?"

She scowled. "Are we back on that? The trustees do the research, of course, and put through recommendations, although I make the final decision. It's a transparent process; everything is documented, as I'm sure you'll see when you go through those files you took." She shot him a sour look.

"How well do you know Sir Ainsworth?" Rob asked, changing tack.

She hesitated, momentarily thrown. "Oh, um . . . we've met once or twice at various dos. He was at the Christmas party."

"Is he involved in the running of the charity at all?"

"No, although he is a supporter. He made us charity of the month in his constituency last October."

Rob noted this in his notebook, then snapped it shut. "Thank you for your time, Dame Constance." That was enough for now. He didn't want to spook her. She wasn't the type to take criticism well. Once they had something more definite, they could question her again. "You've been very helpful."

"Are we done?"

"Yes." His phone beeped as she got to her feet. Glancing down, he saw a message from Jenny. After scanning it, he glanced up. "One more thing."

"Yes?"

"I see you kept Chloe Brooke on a retainer. Was there a reason for that?"

"She was my event planner. As a charity, we have a lot of events."

"What exactly did she do for you?" Rob asked.

"Luncheons, dinners, soirées, flower arrangements, canapés, that sort of thing."

He nodded, glancing up at the camera. Jenny would be taking notes.

"I'd still like to file a complaint." She gripped her coat around her like a security blanket.

"Of course. I'll call one of the police constables. You'll have to fill in the appropriate paperwork, which can take a while, but you're totally within your rights to do so."

Dame Constance hesitated, then glanced at her watch. "Oh, you know what, let's forget it. You'll return everything in due course, won't you?"

"Of course." Unless it was used in evidence, in which case it would go into a police file, but he didn't say that. So far, he hadn't found any reason to suspect the charity of any wrongdoing. Whoever put that note on his windscreen was either mistaken, knew something they didn't — or was trying to divert attention to the charity for their own reasons.

"Thank you for your time." He showed Dame Constance out, then went back across the road to the MIT office.

"She seems on the level to me," he said to the team, who'd been watching on the live stream. "What do you guys think?"

"We'll dig a bit deeper into the Community Grants Programme," Jenny replied. "If there's something funny going on, we'll find it."

"I'll follow the money trail," Will added.

"I'll go and visit the community organisations," Harry volunteered. "Just to make sure they're on the level."

"Okay, good." Rob nodded at them. Between them, they'd covered all the bases. "Okay, let's get on it first thing tomorrow and see what we can find. I hope she's on the level, but you never know."

"Sounds like they do a lot of good work," Celeste said.

"Agreed. Maybe the tip-off was a hoax."

"Designed to point us in the wrong direction?" Harry asked.

"Could be. Still, we can't ignore it." Rob glanced towards Mayhew's office. It was empty. "Ian Morris isn't going anywhere. His trial is in six months. We owe it to him to make sure we've got the right guy, because he's going away for a very long time, otherwise."

Nods all round.

Walking through the underground car park, Rob noticed Mayhew's spot was empty, too. The Superintendent had left for the day. That was unusual. A workaholic, she was normally one of the last to leave the office.

It struck him that he used to be like that, before he met Jo. Dame Constance's words had registered with him. Everyone deserved a second chance. He'd been given one with Jo, and then Jack. His family. It had almost been taken away from him earlier this year but, thankfully, Jo had survived, and his family had remained intact, if a little bruised and battered. He was going to repair that and cling to them for all he was worth.

Nothing was more important.

CHAPTER 33

Saturday had never felt less like a weekend. It was hard to believe it was Christmas Eve. He'd never been big on the festivities, not having celebrated it much as a kid. Now they had Jack, they'd made more of an effort, but he was still too young to truly appreciate it. Jo had hung some decorations around the house, and an out-of-the-box Christmas tree sparkled in the living room. Jack liked to gaze up at the lights, flickering in multicolours, while Trigger gave it a wide berth.

"I think I'll go and have a word with Sir Ainsworth," Rob told Jo over breakfast. Jack had woken up hungry at five o'clock that morning, so they were both a little frazzled. An unsettled Trigger loped around, getting underfoot.

"Won't he be working today?" she asked.

"No, he'll be in Marlow, at his country house."

"Tanya's not in today." He could see the exhaustion in her eyes. "She's spending Christmas with a friend in Bermondsey."

Rob had an idea. "Why don't we all go? Jack will sleep in the car, and we can have lunch somewhere afterwards. It'll make a nice change."

Jo brightened. "Are you sure? We won't get in your way?"

"Of course not." Jo was a seasoned detective. If anything, she'd be an asset, not a hindrance. Besides, the thought of spending Christmas Eve with his family was appealing.

In better spirits, they got ready, said goodbye to a forlorn Trigger and left the house. The hour-long drive from Richmond to Marlow was relatively seamless, although traffic was starting to build by the time they crossed the suspension bridge into the town.

All Saints Church sat quietly at the other end, as it had done for centuries, a reminder to visitors that it was always there, silently judging.

"According to my weather app, there's a sixty per cent chance of snow." Jo studied the battleship-grey sky as they turned into a steep lane that led to Sir Ainsworth's country pile. On either side of the road, stark trees, their naked branches intertwined, seemed to huddle together to ward off the chill.

"Let's hope for the best." If it did snow, the roads would be chaos. He didn't want to get stranded out in the country. They stopped at a set of electric gates, not dissimilar to Roman Petrovic's. Rob pressed the buzzer and waited for someone to open them. A wooden signpost said *Marlow Grange*.

A female voice answered. "It's about time."

"Sorry?" Rob was taken aback.

"Oh, sorry. I thought you were Leland."

"Um, no. This is DCI Rob Miller. I've come to ask Sir Ainsworth some questions."

He glanced across at Jo, who shrugged. Jack was fast asleep in the back, dummy falling to the side of his mouth, lulled by the motion of the car.

"Come in." The intercom clicked off and the big gates jolted as if they too had been dozing, then slowly squeaked open.

Rob drove up the gravel driveway to the triple-storey country house. Sandy-coloured bricks, faded-white window frames, more than a few tiles missing from the roof. Leafless ivy had woven a drunken web all over the front.

"I guess this is what an estate agent would call charming," mused Jo, gazing up at the rather forlorn facade. "We'll stay in the car while you do your thing. I don't want to wake Jack."

"Okay, but by the sounds of things, Sir Ainsworth may not be here." He shot her a wry smile and got out of the car. It was the risk you took when you didn't call ahead; however, he wasn't about to give Sir Ainsworth a chance to scarper. If the MP had left the tip-off note, Rob wanted to know.

The front door opened, and Lady Ainsworth appeared, dressed in jodhpurs and riding boots. The interior was brightly lit compared to the dim winter greyness outside. "Oh, hello." She gave him an apologetic grimace. "Sorry about that. I'm about to put Princess through her paces, and thought Leland would be back from his walk."

"He's not here?" Rob assumed Princess was her horse.

"Well, the dogs are back, but he's not." She shook her head. "He's probably watching the murmurations."

At his blank look, she elaborated, "The starlings are at it again. It's that time of year."

"Oh, right." Rob frowned. "Where would he be doing that?"

"In the grounds somewhere, I expect. Chestnut Mound has the best aspect. Fred and Rupert came back panting, and are now slobbering all over the kitchen floor, so he can't be too far behind."

Lady Ainsworth had an annoying habit of assuming he knew every animal in the household. At least, he *hoped* she was talking about their dogs and not their children. "Do you mind if I go and look for him?"

"Suit yourself. Take the cobbled path past the giant horse chestnut, and you'll see the mound up on your right. When you find him, please tell him I've taken Princess out for a ride."

"Will do." Rob turned and walked back to the car.

Jo was leaning back against the headrest, her eyes shut. They fluttered open when he eased the door ajar. "Everything okay?"

"Apparently, he's watching the starlings in the garden somewhere. You okay to wait here while I go and look for him?"

Jo tilted her head toward Jack. "He's still asleep, so I'm going to do the same. Wake me up when you get back."

"Okay." He closed the door quietly, then strode off in search of Sir Ainsworth.

Fifteen minutes later, he was still looking. The Tory MP wasn't at the horse chestnut tree, or up on the mound. Rob did see some impressive murmurations, however, and watched for almost a full minute, before his feet began to turn numb. Turning away, he continued his search.

"Ainsworth!" He was losing patience. The estate stretched for at least a half a mile in each direction. From his position up on the mound, Rob could see most of it. If he wasn't so cold, he'd appreciate the frosty beauty a lot more.

Squinting toward the north-west, where the countryside gave way to woodland, he spotted a round, stone structure. It looked like a folly or a temple. Was that part of the estate? He wasn't sure, but he suspected so. In the olden days, the landed gentry used to build whimsical structures on their grounds for shelter and to entertain in.

Perhaps Ainsworth was taking a breather there. Rob took off in that direction, gritting his teeth to stop them chattering. The icy wind penetrated the material of his coat and chilled him to the bone. He was looking forward to a warm pub lunch.

"Ainsworth!" he yelled again. Where the hell was he?

As he got closer, he realised the circular structure was supposed to resemble a mini-Grecian temple, complete with pillars and intricate detailing, although it was run down and overgrown with weeds, dead ivy and thistles. The once-vibrant white hue of the stone was muted and ghostly in the pale light.

The wind whistled eerily as it blew through the pillars and twisted around the thick, central column, making the hairs stand up on the back of his neck. It was almost like it was warning him to stay away. Disjointed shadows from the barren trees nearby danced on the ground. Rob shivered. Bloody hell, this place was spooky.

Feeling distinctly uneasy, he walked around the back of the folly. The screech of the wind grew louder, carrying faint echoes of voices long gone. A Grecian statue stared down at him from a pedestal carved into the middle of the folly, making him start. Its face was etched with anguish, frozen in a moment of agony or terror. Frowning, he kept going, but the eyes seemed to follow him, making the hair on his neck stand up.

This was ridiculous. The MP wasn't here. He was wasting his time.

"Ainsworth!" he called one last time. The only response was the wind.

Enough was enough. He'd do a full loop, then head back to the house before hypothermia set in. It was mind-numbingly cold. Rounding the last stone pillar, he froze. Slumped against the back column, a knife sticking out of his chest, was Leland Ainsworth.

CHAPTER 34

Rob stepped away from the body and called Jo on his mobile phone. "He's dead," were the first words to come out of his mouth. "Stabbed through the heart."

"Holy shit," she exclaimed. "Oops, I mean 'shoot'." He gathered Jack was awake. "Do you want me to find Lady Ainsworth?"

"She's out riding her horse. Could you bring me the crime scene pack in the boot? I'm going to have to cordon off the area until we can get SOCO out here."

"Of course. Jack and I will be with you shortly."

A frigid twenty minutes later, at the same time as he heard faint sirens approaching, he spotted Jo's slim figure striding over the mound — Jack, in the baby carrier on her back. She handed him the crime pack. "Is it bad?"

"Not really. It's a knife wound and there's some blood, but it's frozen." The frigid conditions had meant there was little mess, but it would also make time of death hard to pinpoint.

Jo edged around the folly, careful to stay well clear of the small stone steps leading up to it. Jack, bundled up like a little sherpa, beanie hat pulled low, was sucking his dummy contentedly, oblivious to the drama around him. She surveyed the MP's body. "Looks like a standard kitchen knife. You think the wife did him in?"

"When I spoke to her, she didn't strike me as having just killed her husband." Rob thought back to the encounter. She'd been waiting for him, ready to go out on her ride. Could she have been lying? Had she only moments before, knifed her husband at the folly? He took the police tape out of the rucksack and handed the end to Jo. Familiar with the procedure, she secured it to one of the pillars, while he wound it around the folly.

"It's pretty isolated out here." She looked around, her breath misting in front of her as she spoke. "Anyone could have accessed the property through the woodland."

"That's what I thought," agreed Rob. "Trent is on his way, and I've called SOCO, but they'll take a while to get here. It's Christmas Eve, and by now the roads will be crazy."

There was a loud screech as a woman on a shiny black mare hurtled towards them like one of the Horsemen of the Apocalypse. "Get back!" roared Rob, but Jo had seen her approaching and already stepped behind a tree. The horse reared up in an indignant neigh and came to an abrupt halt. Lady Ainsworth slid off and raced toward the folly. Rob only just stopped her.

"Where is he? Oh God. Is it true? Please, let it not be true."

There was another shout, and a red-faced Trent came running up. "Sorry, guv," he gasped, chest heaving from trying to keep up with Princess. "I had to tell her what happened, and she just took off on that beast. I couldn't stop her."

"That's okay, Constable. Calm down. I've got her."

Lady Ainsworth collapsed, sobbing in his arms. "It's true, isn't it? He's dead."

"I'm afraid so, Lady Ainsworth."

She gripped on to him, afraid to let go. He could feel her shaking. There was no way she was putting this on. Her shock was real. "I'm so sorry."

"Where is he? I need to see him."

Rob knew she wouldn't go quietly until she'd seen her husband, so he handed her to Trent. "He's on the other side of the folly. Stay outside the cordon."

The Marlow constable did a double take when he saw Jo standing there with the baby, but didn't say anything. Then, Ainsworth's wife spotted her husband lying against the column, the knife still protruding from his chest, and screamed. "Oh God. Leland!"

Trent shot a desperate look at Rob, who raised a hand as if to say, *just stay with her*. More Thames Valley Police officers arrived, their bright yellow high-vis jackets bobbing over the frosty natural landscape.

Once they reached the folly, Rob instructed them on what to do while they waited for the forensic crew, and then took Jo's arm. "Come on, let's get back to the house. We can talk to Lady Ainsworth there, and I want to get you and Jack out of the cold."

She nodded, although, despite her windswept hair and flushed face, she looked like she was handling it just fine. "You'll get no complaints from me."

"Bring her back," he told Trent who, still holding a sobbing Lady Ainsworth, gave a relieved nod. Princess pranced around nervously, swinging her glossy head back and forth, frothing at the bit. The officers were staying well clear of her. "And will someone see to that horse?"

"She knows," hissed Lady Ainsworth, clutching Trent's arm.

"Who knows?" Rob frowned.

"Princess. She knows something terrible has happened."

Rob met Jo's gaze. He hoped Lady Ainsworth wasn't going to lose the plot.

"Come on," he reiterated. "Let's get inside."

"Shall I make some tea?" Jo suggested, as they walked into the house. She lifted Jack out of the halter and removed his outer layer of clothing. Lady Ainsworth gawked at the toddler, noticing him for the first time.

"This is my partner, Jo," Rob said, more for Trent's benefit than the dumbfounded Lady Ainsworth. He wasn't sure she was taking much in at all. "And my son."

Lady Ainsworth just blinked, her eyes vacant. Trent gave a polite nod.

"Tea would be good." Rob shot Jo a grateful glance. She picked up Jack, swung him on to her hip and wandered off in search of the kitchen.

"Let's sit down." Rob led Lady Ainsworth from the main hall into an expansive reception room adorned with plush velvet-upholstered furniture arranged around a grand fireplace big enough to park his car in. The embers were still glowing, emitting a sustained warmth, and he moved instinctively towards it.

Lady Ainsworth sank into one of the chairs, paler than the cream upholstery. Sweet tea was what she needed to ward off the shock.

"When last did you see your husband?" asked Rob.

It took her a while to register.

"Lady Ainsworth?"

"This morning. We had breakfast together."

"Okay, then what?" He kept his tone gentle, even.

"Then I went to my studio to paint, while he took the dogs out. He likes to walk them whenever he's here, because . . . because he's in London during the week."

"Was he acting normally?"

She blinked, not understanding.

"This morning, did he appear to be his usual self?"

"Yes." A helpless shrug.

"What about these last few days? Was he upset or anxious at all?"

"No, he was perfectly normal. I-I'm sorry. I don't understand why you're asking these questions."

"Somebody murdered your husband, Lady Ainsworth. We're trying to find out who that was."

She sucked in a sob. He regretted his brusque tone, but he had to snap her out of her detachment. It seemed to work. "I'm sorry, it's just such a horrible shock. Poor Leland." A thought struck her, and she gasped. "Oh God, what am I going to tell the girls?"

"We can tell them, if you like?" Rob said.

Trent nodded. "Where are they?"

She sniffed. "Evie is in Durham; she teaches at the university. Lizzie works in the city. We were expecting them on Boxing Day, but now . . ." She shrugged helplessly.

Rob nodded at Trent, who got up and left the room. He'd get family liaison officers in those areas to break the news to them and ask them to come home early. Their mother would need support in the days that followed. Once reality sank in, he feared she'd take a turn for the worse.

"Lady Ainsworth, I have to ask, is there anyone who harbours a grudge against your husband?"

Her eyes widened. "Heavens, no. Leland was a big teddy bear. Everybody loved him."

Not everyone, clearly.

"What about his constituents? Had he had any threats or arguments lately?"

"I-I don't think so." She picked at her thumb.

"And financially, you were in good shape?"

"Huh?"

He was losing her. "Did you have any financial problems, Lady Ainsworth?"

"No, nothing like that."

Trent returned, carrying a tea tray. Jo walked in behind him with Jack and gave him a warm smile. "Thank you, Victor. That's very kind of you."

He set it down on the coffee table. *Victor.* Rob realised he hadn't even known PC Trent's first name. Jo set Jack on the floor, then reached into a bag to hand him a soft toy. He gurgled and played with it while Jo passed Lady Ainsworth a cup of tea. "Get that down you," she said soothingly.

Rob was immensely grateful she was with him, and that Jack was behaving. Lady Ainsworth took it but didn't drink. It was like she was frozen in time. A little shake of her head. "How can this be happening?"

Rob wanted to know the answer to that, too. They'd only come here to ask Sir Ainsworth about the note, and had stumbled on a murder scene. So unexpected. Why had he been targeted? Why now? What had he known that had got him killed? Then he gasped, as a piece of the puzzle fell into place.

"What?" asked Jo, at the same time as Trent said, "Guv?"

"I think I know who killed him," he murmured, under his breath. Lady Ainsworth was still holding her untouched tea, miles away.

"You know who killed Sir Ainsworth?" Trent whispered.

"Yeah, *and* Chloe Brooke."

CHAPTER 35

"Are you sure?" A dishevelled Mayhew stared at Rob. After hearing what had happened to Sir Ainsworth, she'd recalled the entire team back to the office.

Christmas was officially cancelled.

"I'm afraid so, ma'am. Thames Valley Police are arresting her and her accomplice as we speak, and bringing them in. We're going to question them at Putney nick as soon as they've been processed."

"But why? What is their motive? What did Leland Ainsworth ever do to them?" She was aware her hair was still in a high ponytail, and she wore leggings and a breathable gym top under her coat. No prizes for guessing how she'd been spending Christmas Eve. "And what about Debby Morris?"

"I don't think they're responsible for that one," Miller said.

"Even so, Ainsworth . . . I don't get the connection."

"We're still confirming that. I'll let you know as soon as I do. DS Malhotra is following up on a lead, and if it checks out, we'll know for sure."

Mayhew buried her face in her hands. "We're so fucked."

To her surprise, Rob touched her arm. He wasn't really one for physical contact. "We've got the right person this time, Felicity. That must stand for something."

She looked up, feeling vaguely sick. Miller had been right. She'd rushed into the press release when she should have waited. Too eager to show they'd made an arrest, that they'd got the murderer. "How am I going to explain this?"

Rob shrugged. "We can't let an innocent man go to jail."

And that's the way she'd have to spin it.

The first she'd heard about Sir Ainsworth's death was when Matthew Gray had called her demanding to know if it was true. Embarrassingly, she'd had to tell him to hold on, while she frantically rang DCI Miller on her other phone. Thank God he'd picked up.

"Yes, it's true," he'd told her from his vehicle on the M4. "Stabbed while walking the dogs. I found his body at the folly on their Marlow estate."

Terrific. A fucking MP murdered on Christmas Eve. The media would go apeshit; this was every reporter's wet dream. After that, the phone hadn't stopped ringing. Eventually, she'd walked out of her house and driven to the office. They had to regroup, find out what the hell was going on.

At least DCI Miller seemed to have things under control. Sighing, she thanked him and went to get a cup of coffee. She would watch the interviews in the incident room with the rest of the team.

* * *

Across the interview table, Rob faced an indignant Dame Constance Blanchard and her posh, white-haired solicitor, who didn't look happy to have been called away from his mince pies. This time, there was no fur coat, no jewellery, no perfume. She was wearing the regulatory navy-blue police tracksuit and her hands were cuffed in front of her.

"It's Christmas Eve, Detective Chief Inspector," she snapped. "What on earth do you think you're doing? I'm going to have your job for this."

"Questioning you, ma'am. Now, if you'll state your name for the record."

Her chest puffed out. "Dame Constance Blanchard, and I'd like to state that this is complete nonsense. You people have the wrong woman. I haven't done anything wrong."

Her solicitor rested his hand on her arm and gave his head a little shake. She huffed and sat back in her chair.

"And yours?" Rob nodded at the solicitor.

"Edward Champion."

"Dame Constance, you've been arrested for the murder of Chloe Brooke and Leland Ainsworth," he began — again, more for the record than for her benefit. She'd already had the charges explained to her.

Her mouth flattened into a straight line. "I am not guilty."

"It was clever, getting Zeke Hamlin to do your dirty work for you." Rob startled her into looking at him. Her emerald-green eyes overflowed with hostility.

"I don't know what you mean."

"He'll do time for this, you know. That second chance you gave him, you've just taken it away."

She gave a strangled gasp like he'd knocked the air out of her, but there was fear in her eyes now. "You don't know what you're talking about. Zeke had nothing to do with Chloe or Leland's murder. I don't know where you get your information from, but—" Another touch of Champion's hand silenced her.

For once, Rob was grateful for a solicitor's presence. He seemed like a sensible chap, who knew arguing with law enforcement was not going to get her anywhere.

"What makes you so sure my client is guilty?" he asked calmly.

"You know, it's funny the way this case worked out," Rob said, conversationally. "I'd never have guessed it was you who murdered Chloe, until you killed Leland Ainsworth. That's when I put it together."

Both Dame Constance and the solicitor stared at him, uncomprehending. "I think you'll have to be more specific than that, Detective Chief Inspector," Champion said. "If you want to charge my client."

"Bear with me." Rob smiled, but it didn't reach his eyes. He wasn't enjoying this. The answer had come to him in a rush back at Marlow Grange. It *had* to be her. It could *only* be her, and yet, it seemed impossible. Then he'd realised she'd had help. And who better to do her bidding than her protégé. The young man who owed her his life. The one person she could ask to do anything for her, and he would. Including murder.

"Chloe's killer was young and lithe," he went on. "My constable chased him through the meadows to the river, where he escaped by plunging into it and swimming across. Not an easy feat in the middle of winter."

The solicitor's eyes widened, but he didn't comment.

"That narrowed it down to a handful of suspects." He scoffed. "You, Dame Constance, were not one of them."

She snorted, her arms crossed her chest. "Fancy that."

"Indeed. We even arrested someone else who had motive, but who couldn't have done it because he wasn't a strong enough swimmer."

"I'm still waiting for your point, Detective Chief Inspector," Champion said.

"Here it comes, Mr Champion, and you're going to like this." Rob switched his focus from the solicitor to Dame Constance. "Chloe Brooke was blackmailing you, wasn't she?"

Her face fell. "Of course not. Don't be ridiculous. Why would anyone blackmail me?"

"Because you were embezzling funds from the Lifegiving Charity."

"I was not!" Her face turned red. "How dare you insinuate—?"

"Oh, I'm not insinuating. We have proof. You made regular payments into an account owned by an off-the-shelf company called the South London Blood Donation Group."

"What of it? They campaign for blood and stem cell donations from the black and Asian communities," Dame Constance said. "Sickle cell anaemia is a growing concern in those ethnic groups."

"The director is a man called B.F. Pinkerton."

She fell silent.

"Who's B.F. Pinkerton?" asked Champion.

"He's the American lieutenant in *Madam Butterfly*," Rob supplied. "Dame Constance's last appearance in the West End."

"Is this true?" He turned to her.

"Of course not. I have no idea who that person is, and I'm not embezzling funds from my own charity."

The solicitor looked uncertain now. "Is that the only proof you have, Detective Chief Inspector?"

Rob kept his eyes on Dame Constance. "The problem is, the South London Blood Donation Group doesn't exist."

Champion frowned. "What do you mean?"

"I mean, they have no physical address, no office, no staff. There is a PO Box, signed for by the director, B.F. Pinkerton."

Champion shot Dame Constance a questioning look. She ignored him. "You must be mistaken."

"I assure you, I am not. One of my team went to visit them today to find an empty plot in Brixton."

"Well, I wasn't aware they didn't exist," she said. "I've spoken to them on the phone."

"Do you have a record of those conversations?" Rob asked.

"There will be some, somewhere."

"Could this be an elaborate scam?" Champion asked Rob. "My client may not have been aware of the fraud."

"I think she was," Rob said softly. "You see, Debby Morris was the charity treasurer, and she found out, didn't she? But she wasn't the type to accuse anyone without checking it first, so she didn't mention it to you or the trustees, but she did tell her husband. He, in turn, told his mistress, Chloe Brooke. Unlike Debby, Chloe wasn't as scrupulous, and she saw an opportunity to make some money. Her event planning business was going through a tough time, as are a lot of local businesses at the moment, so she blackmailed you."

Dame Constance sat stonily in the chair, watching him.

"I don't know how she did it, but I think that retainer you were paying her was blackmail money. Chloe Brooke didn't do any events for you other than the Christmas party, and for that, she liaised with Roman Petrovic. We checked."

"Constance?" Champion stared at her.

Still, she didn't respond.

"Shall I go on?" Rob asked, when she didn't contradict him. "We'd never have cottoned on to the fraud if it hadn't been for a tip-off that I received yesterday. You won't know about this," he said to Dame Constance, "but a note was left on my windscreen. I suspect it was hand-delivered by one of Sir Ainsworth's lackeys."

"You suspect?" The solicitor's eyes narrowed. He was looking for holes, any way to mount a defence.

"I was on my way to confront Sir Ainsworth about the note, when I found his body in the folly on his estate."

Champion sucked in a breath. "Leland Ainsworth is dead?"

"Oh, yes. Very dead. He was stabbed in the chest this morning around nine thirty."

The solicitor paled.

Rob turned to Dame Constance. "Where were you this morning at that time?"

"I was still in bed," she murmured.

"Except no one can vouch for you because your husband is still in Portugal, and you were home alone."

"Correct. That doesn't mean I did it."

"It doesn't mean you didn't," he countered.

"Detective Chief Inspector, this is all very tragic." Champion had recovered from the shock of hearing the MP was dead. "But you can't hold my client for this."

Rob continued as if he hadn't spoken. "Sir Ainsworth had that note put on my car because he also knew about the fraud. I think he vetted you before making you charity of the month, and he found out what you were doing."

The solicitor shook his head. "This is supposition. Do you have anything definitive, Detective Chief Inspector?"

Rob fixed his gaze on the charity founder. "The thing is, you were the only person I spoke to about Leland Ainsworth. In your interview yesterday, I asked if you knew him, if he was involved with the charity. That must have spooked you. You thought there was a possibility he'd tell us about the fraud, and you couldn't take that chance."

"Again, this is all circumstantial. Do you have any hard evidence?"

His phone buzzed, and he looked down. "A pair of very wet walking shoes have just been recovered from your house."

"That doesn't prove anything," she spat.

"I think you'll find it does. We have teams of forensic experts who will pick up microscopic grains of pollen and dirt from the shoe and match them to the grounds at Marlow Grange, Sir Ainsworth's estate. You didn't have time to hide the shoes, did you? But then, you never thought we'd suspect you."

Dame Constance glared at him, her face a mask of fury. Edward Champion took one look at her and said to Rob, "I'd like a word with my client, please."

Rob nodded and got up. "You've got fifteen minutes."

CHAPTER 36

Mayhew couldn't take her eyes off the screen. While Dame Constance was consulting with her solicitor, DS Jenny Bird was grilling a quivering Zeke Hamilton in the next-door interrogation room. The posh solicitor had offered to represent him, but DCI Miller had not allowed it, saying it was a potential conflict of interest. He was right.

So the kid was allocated an on-call solicitor, a young Muslim woman in a headscarf over a cheap skirt suit, who was picking up work over the festive period. Even with the solicitor present, it took DS Bird less than five minutes to break him.

"We know Dame Constance asked you to murder Chloe Brooke," she said gently, as if she were speaking to a child. "It's okay. You can tell us what happened."

At first, he clammed up. *No commented* his way through her first couple of questions. Then, she said, "You owe your career to Dame Constance, don't you? Everything you've become is because of her."

He nodded, terrified.

"It's understandable you'd want to protect her." Jenny leaned in. "The thing is, Zeke, you're going to go down for Chloe Brooke's murder, and you'll be an old man before you get out of prison. Your whole life, everything you've worked for, everything you've achieved, will be for nothing."

Tears welled in his dark eyes. He was young and impressionable, and Felicity was pretty sure his benefactor had coerced him into committing murder.

"The only hope you have is to make a deal with us. Tell us what she said to you, and we can work with your solicitor to reduce the charges."

Zeke bit his lip but didn't reply.

"Did she threaten you, Zeke?" DS Bird continued. "Did she tell you the money would stop if you didn't do it? That you'd be kicked out of the Royal Academy?"

He stared at his hands for the longest time, then gave a little nod.

Bingo.

She'd done it.

Felicity heaved a sigh of relief. The kid was going to spill his guts.

DS Bird smiled at him. "Tell me what happened."

The solicitor held up a hand. "You mentioned a deal?"

"Let's hear what Zeke has to say, and then we can arrange a deal."

"Before," insisted the solicitor.

DS Bird leaned forward, and Felicity got a good look at her face. Hard eyes, rigid shoulders, grave expression. There was real fire there now.

"Look, you and I both know that your client is going to prison. There's nothing I can do about that. He killed someone. He valued his future, his degree, his education above another human life. No jury is going to look kindly on that, I'm afraid. The best he can hope for is that the judge shaves time off the tariff. The more he helps, the more likely the judge will look favourably on him. So I suggest he starts talking now."

Zeke paled and glanced, panicked, at his solicitor. "Is that true?"

She sighed and gave a little nod. "You should cooperate, Zeke."

His narrow shoulders sagged. "I had one more year to go at the Royal Academy, and then I was going to be free. I'd have my life back."

"Why don't you tell us about it?" DS Bird said quietly.

Zeke dug the nails of one hand into the palm of the other. "For as long as I can remember, I've been beholden to her."

"You mean Dame Constance?"

A hostile nod. "She told me that if I didn't do this, she'd stop paying the fees. I'd have to leave college. My future would be over."

"So you agreed?"

"I had to. My father died to give me this chance. Do you know how that feels? He literally gave his life for me." His eyes welled with tears.

"In what way?" DS Bird asked.

"There was no car accident," Zeke whispered. Felicity leaned forward to hear.

"Could you repeat that?" DS Bird asked.

"Dame Constance was sick. Very sick. She needed a kidney, but she had a rare blood type. It was difficult to find a donor."

Felicity was listening hard.

"My father had appendicitis a couple of months before and had to have an emergency operation, so his blood records were on the hospital database. One of the consultants noticed that he was a match and told Dame Constance. She contacted him and asked for a meeting."

Felicity shook her head. That wasn't ethical. No patient details should have been given out at all, consultant or not.

"At first, my father said no. No way was he giving her one of his kidneys, but then she found out about me, the *child prodigy*." He spat the words.

"She offered to pay for my education at a top independent school. I told him I didn't want to go, that I didn't care. I liked my school."

What a decision to have to make. To give up one of your organs for your child's success in life. Or a shot at it, at any rate. Felicity blew a hair out of her face. Would she have done that, if she'd had a kid? Maybe. Wouldn't any parent?

"My parents still said no. Then one day, she took my whole family to the Royal Opera House. I've never seen such opulence. There was a pianist on the stage, along with a singer. I'll never forget that moment. I longed to be that pianist, and my parents saw what was possible."

Felicity pursed her lips. She must have really wanted that kidney.

"Dame Constance said it wouldn't stop with school. That she'd pay for university too. A music scholarship at the university of my choice." He cringed. "How could my parents say no to that?"

"So you agreed." DS Bird's voice was soft.

"Not at first. My parents talked about it for a long time. I remember, they were up all night. In the morning, they had decided it was worth the risk. They did it for me." He swallowed a sob.

"How old were you?" DS Bird asked.

"I was thirteen at the time."

"What happened next?"

"She flew my father to Switzerland, and they did it there. He was what you call a live donor. It's legal, if you have the person's consent, but she didn't want anyone to know."

Felicity scoffed. What she didn't want people to know was that she'd coerced a family into selling her an organ in exchange for their son's education. That was not legal.

Felicity wrote the offence and a big question mark down on a piece of paper.

"How did you murder Chloe Brooke?" DS Bird's voice was soft, understanding.

Zeke's voice shook. "Dame Constance told me to go to her house and do it. Make it look like a robbery. I was going to smash her on the head with something, but she saw me, and when she realised what I was gonna do, she started screaming."

"How did you get in?"

"Through the kitchen. The back door was open. I think she'd been cooking or something. It was hot inside."

Felicity nodded. That would make sense. Rob had said she'd been about to leave for an event. Perhaps she did some of the cooking herself, to save money on catering.

"Then what did you do?"

"I panicked and grabbed the knife on the counter. I just wanted her to shut up. I said sorry, that I didn't want to hurt her, but I had no choice." Tears slid down his face as he clutched his hands together in his lap.

Felicity stiffened. *There's always a choice.*

"What then?" DS Bird whispered.

"I grabbed her from behind and slit her throat with the knife. I couldn't believe that I'd done it. There was so much blood." He stared forlornly at his hands. "I didn't expect that. I've never . . ." He trailed off.

"Killed anyone before?" DS Bird prompted.

He gave a silent nod. The tears continued to fall.

"Is that when you ran out into the garden?" DS Bird asked.

He nodded. "I heard that copper arrive, so I bolted. I ran down to the river, but he followed me. He was fast."

DS Bird nodded. "What did you do with the knife?"

"I threw it in the river when I swam across. I knew how to swim from school, and with the policeman on the bank, that was my only way of escaping."

Felicity shook her head. Private school kids.

"Zeke, I have to ask, why didn't you tell anyone? Why didn't you just say no?"

It was a good question. Felicity found herself nodding in agreement.

DS Bird continued, "You'd have struggled to pay your university fees, but you wouldn't have had to commit murder. Surely being a murderer is worse than having to leave college?"

"Not where I'm from," he said. "My father was never healthy after they removed his kidney. He had problems.

Lots of problems. Eventually, he needed a transplant himself, but he refused. He didn't want to jeopardise our arrangement. He didn't want anyone to know what he'd done."

"So you did it because of the sacrifice your family made?" DS Bird summed up.

Zeke nodded. "I did it so it wasn't all for nothing."

DS Bird nodded. His solicitor surreptitiously wiped her own cheek with her sleeve.

Even Felicity felt choked up.

"Okay, thank you, Zeke. You've been extremely helpful. We appreciate your honesty, and I'm sorry you had to go through that."

"What will happen to me now?" His dark eyes probed her.

DS Bird's face softened. "You'll be held in custody until a trial date is set. After that . . ." She shrugged. "It depends on your solicitor and the judge. You may be released on bail, but you may be remanded until your trial." She turned to the solicitor. "I'm sure you can explain it to him?"

She nodded, but didn't meet Zeke's gaze.

"You will also be called on to testify," DS Bird said. "But that won't be until next year, most likely."

Felicity gritted her teeth. At Dame Constance's trial.

CHAPTER 37

"My client denies all wrongdoing," Edward Champion told Rob when he returned to the interview room. "She didn't know the South London Blood Donation Group was fake, and she certainly didn't kill anyone."

"I'm afraid it's too late for that," Rob said. "Zeke confessed."

The colour drained from Dame Constance's face. "To what?" she hissed. "If he confessed to murder, you've coerced him into it. That boy has not killed anyone."

"He freely admits it, Dame Constance." "He's told us about how you harassed his family, then paid his father for his kidney. Do you know he suffered as a result? He ended up losing his life prematurely because of it."

"I can't help that," she huffed. "I didn't pay him. He consented. We had an agreement."

"That's not how I understand it," Rob said. "According to Zeke, you pestered their family until they agreed. You offered money, but they said no. Then you discovered they had a gifted child, so you offered to fund his musical education. Private school, then the Royal Academy of Music. You'd open doors for him that most parents could only dream about for their kids."

"What's so wrong about that?"

"It's illegal, is what's wrong with it. It's a transaction. You paid for your organ. You're still paying for it. There was no consent. You bribed that family into helping you."

"Well now, that depends on how you look at it," Dame Constance said. "I kept my end of the bargain. That boy will play with the London Philharmonic because of me. That's something to be proud of."

"I'm not sure a jury is going to see it the same way," he said.

"Are you arresting my client for buying an organ?" Champion asked.

"No, I'm arresting her for murder," he said. "Chloe Brooke's murder and Leland Ainsworth's. We have a confession from Zeke Hamlin for Chloe's murder, and he's going to give us the clothes he wore, as well as point us in the direction of the murder weapon. Divers will be searching the Thames come morning."

"Edward, for Christ's sake," Dame Constance spluttered. "Do something."

"Forensics will soon be able to place you in the grounds at Leland Ainsworth's estate, which along with the wet shoes should be enough to convict you of his murder. We've got officers searching his home and office as we speak. There is every chance they will come up with something that proves he knew about your embezzlement."

She swallowed, at a loss for words. Desperately, she turned to her solicitor, who sighed. "I will do what I can for you, Connie, I promise, but it doesn't look good. Judges are more lenient on suspects who confess. If you are responsible, I would advise you to do so."

Rob opened the door to the interview room and two officers walked in. "You can charge her," he said.

Rob and Jenny left Putney Police Station together. "It's snowing," she exclaimed, holding out her hands. Rob looked up. Soft whispers fell from the slate-grey sky, leaving wet kisses on his skin.

They received a round of applause when they got back to the squad room. Even Superintendent Mayhew was there to congratulate them. "Stellar job, you two."

"Thanks, ma'am," Rob said. Jenny smiled and went back to her desk.

"Has Ian Morris been released?" he asked.

"No, he might not have killed Chloe Brooke, but we still don't know who killed Debby Morris."

Rob ground his jaw. "I'm working on that. I have a theory, but it needs work."

She stared at him. "How much work?"

"Too much to make an arrest now."

"It's Christmas."

"I know. It'll keep."

"You don't think Dame Constance killed Debby, too? She had a motive."

"She didn't know Debby had discovered anything. Not even the trustees knew. Debby didn't say a word to anyone other than her husband."

"How can you be so sure?"

"Because we asked them. No one suspected Dame Constance of being corrupt."

"Okay, fine. Let's take tomorrow off and reconvene on the twenty-seventh. You can run your new theory by me then."

He nodded. "Will do, and thanks, ma'am."

"For what?"

"For bearing with us. I know how you fought our corner before, too. I just want you to know we appreciate it. *I* appreciate it."

To his surprise, she coloured. "It's my career on the line, too."

"Yeah, right." He grinned at her, then turned and went back to his team.

* * *

Rob woke up on Christmas morning and lay in bed, his arm around Jo, staring out at the snow still wafting down outside. "Merry Christmas," she whispered.

"Merry Christmas."

He thought about Ian Morris, waking up in prison. About Dame Constance and Zeke, both in custody, awaiting their arraignment next week. Nothing would happen over the Christmas period.

But he shouldn't be thinking about that. Not today.

Christmas was for his family. For Jo, and his son.

Speaking of . . . a rustling could be heard from Jack's room, and then a thud, followed by a loud wail. They both sprung out of bed and dashed next door. Jack had managed to climb out of his cot and was lying on the floor, crying.

"That's a four-foot drop," Jo said worriedly, picking him up. "Do you think he's hurt?"

"Looks okay to me." Rob felt around his head, but there were no bumps.

Jack stopped crying and smiled. Jo breathed a relieved sigh.

"Looks like he's outgrown the cot," Rob remarked.

"Guess we're going to have to put a mattress on the floor." She hugged Jack. "You mustn't do that, silly boy. You could hurt yourself."

He giggled, thinking they were playing a game.

Rob's phone rang from the bedroom. He left Jo with Jack and went to answer it. A call from Ian Morris's solicitor, Pearson Willoughby.

"He's ready to give you his alibi," Willoughby said.

"Why the change of heart?" Rob was immediately suspicious.

"My client has realised that it's more important he's free to raise his children," the solicitor replied.

"More important than what?"

"I'll leave that for him to tell you."

"That's cryptic," Jo said, when he told her about the phone call. "Are you going to see him?"

"Yeah, if that's okay? I'll try not to be too long. If Ian Morris is innocent, he deserves to be home for Christmas."

In response, she kissed him on the cheek. "We'll be here."

* * *

The drive to Grendon Underwood, Buckinghamshire, took a little over an hour. HMP Grendon was a category B men's prison where several criminals from the wider Buckinghamshire area were on remand as they awaited trial. Rob shivered as he drove through the imposing brick pillars and black wrought iron gates. Once an experimental psychiatric hospital, its past still echoed in the foreboding bricks, sealed windows, and stark concrete exterior.

On arrival, Rob showed his ID to the prison officer, who gave him a hard time for not booking the appointment at least three days in advance, as was their policy. After hearing it was pertaining to the murder investigation, he was grudgingly allowed in.

They met in the visitors' room, under the beady eye of four mounted cameras, one in each corner. Ian Morris looked pale and gaunt, his eyes sunken hollows in his pasty face. There was a bruise under one eye, and he held his arm at an angle that made Rob suspect he'd injured it somehow.

Prison wasn't kind to newbies.

"I believe you're ready to give me your alibi?" Rob cut straight to the chase. He had a family to get home to. It was Christmas morning. The last place he wanted to be was here.

"Y-Yes. I have to get home to my children. That's more important than . . . than losing my job. I see that now?"

Rob frowned. "Your job? Why would you lose your job?"

"Because . . ." he hesitated. "On the night that my wife was killed, I was working."

Rob shook his head. "I don't understand."

"I was working two jobs. We needed the money. Childcare is so expensive, and Debby didn't get much for her job at the charity. The cost-of-living crisis has hit us hard. Our mortgage has gone up over a thousand pounds a month." His faced was pinched with tension.

"What were you doing?" Rob asked.

"Freelancing. I was moonlighting for a client in Oxford."

"I'm sorry, I—" Rob stared at him. "Doing what?"

"Loft extension. That's my speciality. If my firm found out . . ." He shook his head.

Rob finally got it. "You have a 'non-compete' clause in your contract?"

"It's worse than that. I'm freelancing for an existing client. They wanted to jump the queue, and I was desperate."

"And the reason why you didn't tell us was because you didn't want to get fired?"

He nodded, miserably. "Now I'll lose my job and the bank will foreclose on our house. We'll have to downgrade. That's why I didn't tell you."

Rob was silent a moment. He knew the insurance company had refused to pay out since the beneficiary was on trial for murder.

"And your client will back you up on this?"

Another nod.

"Okay, hang tight until we can verify that."

"Please . . . I can't spend another day in this place. I don't belong here." He swallowed a sob.

Rob gave a curt nod. He felt sorry for the guy, he really did. If Ian Morris was innocent of his wife's murder, he didn't belong here with these hardened criminals. Still, that was the justice system for you. Ian could have offered up his alibi a lot sooner and saved everyone the trouble. "I can't promise, but I'll do my best." It was Christmas, after all.

Jenny answered on the first ring. He explained what had transpired.

"You got Ian Morris's alibi! That's great news. What it is?"

He told her.

"I suppose I can see why he kept it secret."

"We need to get someone to verify it," Rob said.

"I'll call Oxford Central. It'll be quicker to send someone from there to get the client's statement. What's his or her name?"

"His." Rob read the details out to her and heard her scribbling on a piece of paper. "Sorry to interrupt your Christmas plans."

"Not a problem. I'm only due at my mother's this evening."

"Okay, thanks, Jenny. Let me know what he says."

"Will do."

Rob was halfway back to London when Jo called. "I'm nearly home," he said, as soon as he answered using his car's Bluetooth speaker.

"That's not why I'm ringing," she said.

"Oh?"

"I just heard from my MI5 contact. He did some more digging on Roman Petrovic."

"Yeah?" Rob glanced in his rear-view mirror and pulled into the fast lane. "Find anything?"

"I'm not sure if it's helpful." He heard Jack gurgling in her arms. "But you know he supplied arms to the British forces in the Democratic Republic of Congo?"

"Yes." He waited for what was coming next.

"Well, he also supplied the rebel militia."

Rob frowned. "At the same time?"

"It seems like it."

Rob felt the thud of dread. "The same rebel militia who attacked the hotel where Debby's parents were staying?"

"From what I can understand, yes."

There was a sharp pause. "How did your contact find out?"

"He heard it from his source in the DRC, an old mercenary who helped protect the mines. This guy told him the guns used in the hotel shooting matched those used by the rebels when they attacked the mines."

Rob hesitated. "Is he certain?"

"They can be traced back to a cache abandoned after the Serbian war. It's in the secret intelligence service's files. Redacted, of course. Strictly off-limits."

Rob narrowed his eyes. "Leland Ainsworth was the British Ambassador at the time. He would have known Roman Petrovic supplied the rebels with those guns, and that he was also supplying the British forces."

"He kept quiet about that," Jo remarked.

That's the way it is out there. You don't ask too many questions.

"Shit, Jo. If Ainsworth knew, and he told Debby . . ."

"It was too big a secret," she whispered.

"I have to get out there." Rob slammed his foot on the brake and swerved across three lanes towards the slip road. "I have to see Petrovic. I'm really sorry."

"Go. Do what you have to do, but come home for Christmas dinner. I'll be waiting."

"Thank you." He meant it. Ending the call, Rob hurtled around a roundabout, siren blaring, and got back on the motorway heading in the opposite direction towards Marlow.

CHAPTER 38

White, powdery snow dusted the verges of the motorway. It was starting to settle, having snowed all night, but not on the road itself. The heat from the cars had turned the M4 into a river of brown slush. Rob called Superintendent Mayhew from his car and asked if she'd meet him at Hollyhock Manor.

"Why there?" she asked.

"Because I'm about to make an arrest, and I thought you might like to be in on the grand finale. Also, this should be a joint effort with Thames Valley," Rob said. "It seems fitting, under the circumstances."

She paused. "Petrovic killed Debby Morris?"

"He was definitely involved."

"Okay, I'll meet you there. Thames Valley can make the arrest. It'll save us having to work through Christmas."

"I'll notify Chief Superintendent Mullins," Rob said. "See you in an hour."

Instead, he called PC Trent, told him what was going on, and asked him to call the Chief Superintendent. That way, the Marlow constable would get the credit for bringing in the Thames Valley team.

It was quite a crowd that appeared at the gates of Hollyhock Manor that Christmas morning. Rob rang the bell, and to his surprise, Lily answered. "Yes?"

"DCI Miller," he said. "Can we speak with your boss?"

"Sure, come in." Her voice was upbeat.

Rob saw her mouth drop open as she watched the cavalcade of vehicles crunch up the drive. "I was about to lock up and go home," she said when he climbed out of the car. "What's this about?"

"Is Petrovic in?"

"Yes, he's in the gym. Shall I get him?"

"If you wouldn't mind. We'll wait in the living room."

She turned to leave, when Trent touched her arm. "I wouldn't mention how many people are here." She gave a nervous nod.

They filed into the large, chandeliered room with its high ceiling and bay windows. The heavy curtains were open and, outside, the snow continued to fall, sparkling as it settled on the gravel driveway. The fire crackling away in the fireplace cast a cosy glow, but other than that, the Serb had very little in the way of Christmas decorations. The other reception room, where he'd held the party, had been adorned with a Christmas tree, bunting and fairy lights, while this room had nothing more than a sad-looking wreath above the fireplace and a smattering of festive cards on the mantlepiece.

A pile of unopened envelopes lay on the coffee table, along with a letter opener. Obviously, Petrovic hadn't got around to putting them all up yet.

While they waited, he took a peek at one of the cards. A brief message in Serbian. The others were the same. Family, perhaps? Business associates? The barest of wishes. Nothing worth more than a line. Petrovic wasn't one for sentimentality.

Ten minutes later, Roman Petrovic strode into the lounge in a tracksuit, a towel hanging around his neck. He halted abruptly when he saw Rob, Trent, Mayhew, Mullins and two detectives from Thames Valley's murder squad all in his living room. "What is this?"

Rob stepped forward. "I'm sorry to interrupt you, today of all days," he said. "But we need to talk to you about Debby Morris."

"What? Again?" The Serb pulled a disgusted face. "No comment. Get out of my house, all of you."

"I'm afraid we can't do that, sir." Chief Superintendent Mullins stepped forward. "Not until you've answered our questions."

Petrovic looked defiant. "What if I refuse?"

"Then we will arrest you and ask them at the police station," Mullins said.

Rob nodded. "What he said."

Roman Petrovic threw his arms in the air. "For God's sake. What do you want to know now?"

"Why you killed her."

Petrovic froze. An angry flicker made his dark eyes appear almost demonic. The words came out slowly. "I. Did. Not. Kill. Her."

Rob was ready for his denial. "You told her how her parents died, didn't you? That they were gunned down in that attack in Kinshasa."

"*I* told *you* that, you moron." He shook his head.

Rob ignored the snigger. He was just warming up. "Yes, but what you didn't expect was for her to confront Sir Ainsworth about it."

Petrovic flinched but said nothing.

"Did you know he was the British Ambassador to the DRC at the time of the shooting?"

A flicker of recognition.

"Oh, you did? Makes sense, your being there at the time, supplying the British forces as well as the opposition."

Petrovic's eyes narrowed. "Be careful what you say."

"Why? Because it could get you into trouble? Does the British government know you also supplied the rebels? That you're still supplying guerrilla armies in Africa?" That was a guess, based on his recent travel patterns. Flights confirmed going in and out of Kinshasa.

"I am not."

"I have a contact in the British government who swears you are. Apparently, he knows a man called Dirk Hougaard. Remember him?"

A shake of his head. "No."

"Well, he remembers you. Says you're very clever at playing both sides."

Petrovic bounced on his toes like boxer warding off jabs. "You can't prove that."

"I don't have to prove it. The Secret Service will do that when they investigate you."

The Serb shifted, uncomfortable.

"When Debby confronted Leland, he had to tell her the truth. She was angry. Angry enough to threaten to report you both. She wanted answers, didn't she? All this time, she'd thought her parents had died in a random attack, when in fact they'd been targeted by rebels, and the government had covered it up. She was going to put both your and Sir Ainsworth's heads on the block."

"That is not true." His hands clenched into fists. Rob could see the veins standing out on his forearms.

"You and Sir Ainsworth spoke, didn't you? That's when you decided to kill her. You'd take care of Debby, while Ainsworth buried the story in Whitehall. Nobody must find out that you supplied both sides, or you'd lose your cushy job with the government and probably be arrested. Sir Ainsworth would have to explain why he didn't report it all those years ago."

Petrovic said nothing, just glared at Rob, but it was the glare of a trapped animal. He was cornered and he knew it.

"Did you use the side entrance?" asked Rob. "Is that how you got to the park ahead of her? Debby took the long way round, while you laid in wait. Then, when she came past, you hit her on the head, knocking her unconscious."

Lily gasped, her hand flying to her mouth. Mayhew, Mullins and the rest looked on grimly.

"I did no such thing," he growled.

"I saw you go out," Lily whispered, pale in the glow of the chandelier. "I was taking the rubbish out, and I saw you in the garden. It was just before midnight." He shot her a look of such hostility that she stumbled backwards.

"Which places you in the garden just before the murder," Rob smirked.

"I didn't kill anyone."

Rob ignored him. "Once she was unconscious, you carried her body to the river and held her under, until she drowned."

Petrovic shot a desperate glance towards the door. The Thames Valley Police detectives took a few steps closer to the suspect, in case he decided to bolt. "I didn't leave the party."

"Leland covered for you, didn't he?" Rob had placed it all together on the drive there. "He said he'd been speaking to you, when in fact, he hadn't. He was providing you with an alibi. Pity you had to kill him for it."

Mayhew gasped. "I thought Dame Constance murdered Leland Ainsworth."

Rob shook his head.

"But, the shoes . . . ?"

"No, ma'am. I was wrong about that. I thought she had too, but when I found out about the arms dealing, I knew it had to be Petrovic. I think you'll find Dame Constance's shoes will come back negative. They'll prove she was nowhere near Marlow Grange yesterday morning. Roman Petrovic's shoes, however . . ." He left it hanging.

Mayhew just shook her head.

Rob took a piece of paper out of his pocket and held it up. "Roman Petrovic, this is a warrant to search your house. These officers are going to help me."

Petrovic moved so fast Rob didn't see it coming. He picked up the letter opener, grabbed Lily and thrust the blade against her throat. "Come near me and she dies."

CHAPTER 39

Trent made to move forward, but Rob grabbed his arm and shook his head. Trent stopped. Lily had paled, and her eyes were filled with terror.

"You can't run, Petrovic," Rob said. "You're surrounded."

"Get out of my way." The Serb dug the point of the blade into Lily's neck until blood trickled down.

She gasped softly, squeezing her eyes shut. "Please."

"Shut up, you stupid bitch. I would have got away with it, if it wasn't for you."

Lily bit her lip, but her gaze hardened.

Trent, who was closest to the door, stepped aside so he could pass. Petrovic backed out, keeping Lily in front of him, the knife digging into her throat. "One move, and she dies."

As he dragged her over the threshold, Trent caught Lily's eye. He looked down and saw she had a small object in her hand. What was it? Keys. She'd been locking up when they'd arrived.

As he watched, she arranged the keys so that one key jutted out between each knuckle like a pointed knuckleduster. He caught his breath. She was going to go for it.

He nudged DCI Miller and glanced at Lily's hand. It took his boss less than a second to realise what she was going to do. Lily fixed her gaze on Trent. He waited until they were just outside the door, and the letter opener at her neck relaxed, just slightly, before he nodded.

Quick as a flash, she raised the keys and scraped Petrovic across the face.

"Urgh!" He tried to protect his eyes, but it was too late. Then Trent was on him, grabbing the arm with the blade so it couldn't do any damage. Rob wrestled him to the ground, while Mayhew grabbed Lily.

"My fucking eyes!" Petrovic screamed. "She's blinded me."

Chief Superintendent Mullins stepped forward. "Roman Petrovic, you are under arrest for the murder of Debby Morris, the murder of Leland Ainsworth and the attempted murder of Lily . . ." He glanced at her.

"McIntyre," she said.

"Are you okay?" Trent asked, once Mullins had finished and his two detectives had led Petrovic to the awaiting police vehicle. Mayhew, Miller and Mullins were having a little chat in the corner of the room by the flickering fire, but he was more concerned with Lily.

"Yes, thanks."

"That was a very brave thing to do," he said.

She smiled shyly. "I knew you'd be there to back me up."

He grinned. "We make a good team."

"We do." DCI Miller came over. He was smiling, which Trent knew was rare.

"I meant me and Lily." He couldn't help himself colouring. It was his pale northern complexion. It let him down all the time.

Rob grinned. "I know, but I meant you and me. PC Victor Trent, I'd like you to join the Major Investigation Team."

Trent's eyes widened. "Really? I mean, that's great. I'd love to."

Lily slipped her hand into his. "Congratulations."

Rob thumped him on the shoulder. "Good news. I'll be expecting you to report for duty in the New Year."

"Thank you, sir. I mean, guv."

"You're welcome. Now go and enjoy your Christmas."

Trent squeezed Lily's hand. "Got any plans?"

She smiled up at him. "I do now."

* * *

Rob made it back home just as Jo was putting Jack to bed. The snow had blanketed the countryside and was piling up on parked cars and rooftops, but luckily the motorway and main roads were just about usable. Tomorrow, that wouldn't be the case. Not if it kept coming down like this. He walked in to find she'd placed the cot in their room, sandwiched between the wall and the bed. "This way, if he climbs out, he'll land on you, not the floor."

Rob chuckled. It was a good interim measure. He took her hand. "Let's go make Christmas dinner." They'd bought a turkey and all the trimmings, but hadn't done anything with it.

"It's not ready." She grimaced. "I didn't know when you'd be back, so I haven't put it in the oven."

"There's still time. It's only six. We can eat at eight."

Jo perked up. "Sounds good. That'll give me a chance to shower and change. Then, I want to hear all about what happened today."

While she went into the bathroom, Rob put the turkey in the oven, peeled potatoes, carrots, and sprouts. By the time she came downstairs, Christmas dinner was well underway.

"You look amazing." He took her into his arms. Her blonde hair was freshly washed and dried, and she smelled great. "I'm punching way above my weight."

She laughed and kissed him on the lips. "Pour me a glass of wine and let's talk about what happened. I'm dying to know. Did you get him? Did Petrovic do it?"

"He did." Rob got the wine and poured them each a glass. "Roman Petrovic conspired with Leland Ainsworth to kill Debby Morris."

She gasped. "They were in it together?"

"Yep."

"All because they didn't want the government to find out Petrovic was still supplying arms to the rebels as well as the British forces?"

"That's right. Petrovic had been on the government watch list before. It wouldn't take much to send him back there."

"And Sir Ainsworth?"

"He covered up the Kinshasa shooting, rather than deal with the political fallout."

"He ought to have known that would come back to bite him."

"That's why Petrovic killed him."

Her eyes widened. "Petrovic killed Sir Ainsworth? I thought it was Dame Constance?"

"So did I, at first, but once I figured out Petrovic and Ainsworth were in it together, I knew Petrovic had stabbed him. He knew too much. Petrovic didn't want any loose ends. He didn't trust Ainsworth to keep his end of the bargain."

"Poor Debby." Jo stared into her wine. "She had no idea what she'd done when she complained to Sir Ainsworth about her parents."

Rob gave a grim nod. "If only she hadn't threatened to make a formal complaint. That was when she signed her death warrant."

"Bastards," Jo whispered. "They killed her to save their own skins."

"That's usually the way it goes."

"So it wasn't Ian Morris after all. You were right about that."

He shrugged. "It never felt right."

"Have they released him?"

Rob grinned. "He should be getting home to his family round about now."

"That's good."

Rob gestured to the table. "Enough talking about the case. Let's talk about us."

They sat down. Jo tilted her head. "Us?"

Rob took her hand across the table. "If these last few months have taught me anything, it's how important family is. How important *you* are, to me."

She smiled.

"I thought I'd lost you," he continued.

She squeezed his hand. "You saved me. You and Jenny. If it wasn't for you both, I'd be dead now."

"If it wasn't for me, *this* wouldn't have happened." He released her hand and traced the silver scar at her throat.

"You aren't responsible, Rob. We've been through this. You have to let go of the guilt."

"I can't," he whispered.

"I don't blame you, so why do you blame yourself?"

"Because I should have seen it."

"No one saw it." She leaned over and kissed him. "Now stop this nonsense. Let's be grateful for what we do have, and enjoy our Christmas dinner. I've been waiting all day for this."

His stomach rumbled. "Me too."

She shot him an impish smile. "I've got something for you."

"You have?" He'd left in such a rush that morning they hadn't got around to the gift-giving. He didn't have a Christmas present for her, but he had something else that was even better. He'd picked it up last month, but hadn't had the guts to give it to her. The timing hadn't been right.

"One sec." She disappeared, then came back a few minutes later with a rectangular gift about the size of a book but much thinner, adorned with a bow and tag. He read the tag.

It's time. All my love, Jo.

He had a sneaky suspicion he knew what it was. Unwrapping it, he discovered she'd given him his very own iPad. Not a grotty police issue, but his own brand-spanking-new one. He laughed. "I guess I have no choice now." Setting it aside, he reached into his pocket. "I got you something, too. I hope you like it."

She gasped, surprised. "When? I didn't think you'd have time."

"I'm a resourceful guy." He grinned and handed her a small, wrapped box. "Actually, to be honest, I've had it while. I was just waiting for the right time to give it to you, and as you said on your note . . ." He held up the tag.

It's time.

Jo undid it, slowly, savouring the moment. He loved the way her eyes sparkled when she was excited. It made him want to keep giving her things. Finally, she prised the lid off the little box and gasped. Her eyes flew to his face.

"Is this what I think it is?"

Rob nodded. When he'd thought about this moment, he'd expected to be nervous, but instead he felt calmer than he had in a long time. This was right. *She* was right.

"You said to be grateful for everything we have, so I'm just going to come right out and say it . . . Jo Maguire, will you marry me?"

THE END

THE JOFFE BOOKS STORY

We began in 2014 when Jasper agreed to publish his mum's much-rejected romance novel and it became a bestseller.

Since then we've grown into the largest independent publisher in the UK. We're extremely proud to publish some of the very best writers in the world, including Joy Ellis, Faith Martin, Caro Ramsay, Helen Forrester, Simon Brett and Robert Goddard. Everyone at Joffe Books loves reading and we never forget that it all begins with the magic of an author telling a story.

We are proud to publish talented first-time authors, as well as established writers whose books we love introducing to a new generation of readers.

We have been shortlisted for Independent Publisher of the Year at the British Book Awards three times, in 2020, 2021 and 2022, and for the Diversity and Inclusivity Award at the Independent Publishing Awards in 2022.

We built this company with your help, and we love to hear from you, so please email us about absolutely anything bookish at: feedback@joffebooks.com.

If you want to receive free books every Friday and hear about all our new releases, join our mailing list: www.joffebooks.com/contact

And when you tell your friends about us, just remember: it's pronounced Joffe as in coffee or toffee!

ALSO BY BIBA PEARCE

DETECTIVE ROB MILLER MYSTERIES
Book 1: THE THAMES PATH KILLER
Book 2: THE WEST LONDON MURDERS
Book 3: THE BISLEY WOOD MURDERS
Book 4: THE BOX HILL KILLER
Book 5: THE SOUTH BANK MURDERS
Book 6: THE SOHO KILLER
Book 7: THE MARLOW MURDERS

Milton Keynes UK
Ingram Content Group UK Ltd.
UKHW011317281123
433421UK00004B/359

9 781835 26187